WISHED

SARAH READY

PRAISE FOR SARAH READY

PRAISE FOR FRENCH HOLIDAY

"Ready (The Fall in Love Checklist) whisks readers to the South of France for a saucy enemies-to-lovers romance...This is a winner."

— *PUBLISHERS WEEKLY* STARRED REVIEW ON *FRENCH HOLIDAY*

"Ready has written a tale that deliciously taps into its French trappings...A charming dramedy featuring a promising sleuthing duo."

— *KIRKUS REVIEWS*

PRAISE FOR JOSH AND GEMMA MAKE A BABY

"Romance author Ready gives Gemma rich and complex motivations for wanting a baby...An unusual and winning read about a little-discussed topic."

— *KIRKUS REVIEWS*

"A lively, entertaining, romantic comedy by an author and novelist with a genuine flair for originality, humor, and narrative driven storytelling..."

— *MIDWEST BOOK REVIEW*

PRAISE FOR JOSH AND GEMMA THE SECOND TIME AROUND

"In this sequel—which stands well enough on its own—the happily-ever-after moment is merely the starting point...Ready effectively leads readers to wonder if she isn't going to upend every single one of the genre's expectations. It's a testament to her exceptional writing skill that even the most romantic-minded readers won't be sure which outcome they prefer. A charming and disarmingly tough story of the many ways that love can adapt to crises."

— *KIRKUS REVIEWS*

PRAISE FOR THE SPACE BETWEEN

"...emotional roller-coaster, but in the end true love prevails. For hopeless romantics, this one's got the goods."

— *PUBLISHERS WEEKLY*

"A touching tale of adult reckonings and reunions with some heart-tugging reversals."

— KIRKUS REVIEWS

"...a compelling novel of longing, betrayal, friendship, as well as the undying belief that love and music can heal the world. An original and deftly crafted novel that will be of special interest to fans of contemporary romance laced with humor, "The Space Between" is especially and unreservedly recommended for community library Contemporary Romance collections."

— MIDWEST BOOK REVIEW

PRAISE FOR GHOSTED

"Ready's twisty plot keeps readers guessing how this couple could possibly reach a happy ending."

— PUBLISHERS WEEKLY

"Ready brings her trademark blend of lively tone, amusing details, heart-tugging romance, and adept plotting to this paranormal tale."

— KIRKUS REVIEWS

ALSO BY SARAH READY

Stand Alone Romances:

The Fall in Love Checklist

Hero Ever After

Once Upon an Island

French Holiday

The Space Between

The Ghosted Series:

Ghosted

Switched

Fated

Wished

Josh and Gemma:

Josh and Gemma Make a Baby

Josh and Gemma the Second Time Around

Soul Mates in Romeo Romance Series:

Chasing Romeo

Love Not at First Sight

Romance by the Book

Love, Artifacts, and You

Married by Sunday

My Better Life

Scrooging Christmas

Dear Christmas

Stand Alone Novella:

Love Letters

Find these books and more by Sarah Ready at:

www.sarahready.com/romance-books

SHE MAKES A WISH

When Anna Benoit wishes she's married to the enigmatic owner of the chateau she cleans, she wakes up in a topsy-turvy world where she's Max Barone's wife.

Anna is a romantic who believes in The One and Love at First Sight. Why? Because it happened to her. The second she saw Max Barone she fell desperately, hopelessly in love.

It didn't matter that they were from completely different worlds—he owned a jewelry empire, she cleaned houses—love had no barriers.

Except one.

Max didn't know Anna's name, much less that she existed.

Then one day Anna made a wish. Suddenly she was in an upside down world where everyone believed she and Max had been happily married for years. It was passion. It was romance. It was love. It was everything she'd ever wished for.

Wasn't it?

Wished

SARAH READY

CROWN

W.W. CROWN BOOKS
An imprint of Swift & Lewis Publishing LLC
www.wwcrown.com

Published by W.W. Crown Books an Imprint of Swift & Lewis Publishing, LLC, Lowell, MI USA
Cover Illustration & Design: Elizabeth Turner Stokes

Library of Congress Control Number: 2024938997
ISBN: 978-1-954007-81-9 (eBook)
ISBN: 978-1-954007-82-6 (pbk)
ISBN: 978-1-954007-83-3 (large print)
ISBN: 978-1-954007-84-0 (hbk)
ISBN: 978-1-954007-85-7 (audiobook)

Wished

PROLOGUE

Max

This has to be a joke. I can't think of any other explanation. Exactly one minute ago my life was perfectly logical, perfectly ordered. Everything made sense.

I knew exactly where I fit, who I was, and what I was doing.

The world made sense.

In fact, for most of my life the world has made sense.

For example, I'm Max Barone, son, brother, and friend. Born in Geneva, Switzerland. Still live in Geneva, Switzerland, in the same drafty chateau generations of Barones have lived in. Boarding school in Britain. University in Paris. Took over the family business after my parents and brother were careless enough to die on me.

I'm often friendly, usually charming, and sometimes cynical—but only about relationships.

I'm single by choice. Well, perhaps not entirely by choice. But when your best friend turns down your proposal and marries another man, you tell yourself it's by choice.

In the world I live in, everyone knows exactly who I am, what I do, and what I want.

Which is why this *has to be a joke.*

What else can I believe when my entirely sane, incredibly competent assistant of ten years calls to say something like this?

But just in case . . . "Say that again?"

I lean forward and watch the red light on the phone's speaker. The black office phone sits unobtrusively on my dark walnut desk—a massive antique piece my father, my grandfather, and my great-grandfather, all the way back to my great-great, too many greats grandfather, sat behind to run the esteemed Barone Jewelry International (as far back to when it wasn't international, it was just a man with a dream).

The desk matches the office. Dark burgundy walls, heavy navy curtains framing the view of Lake Geneva, the Jet D'eau sending up its endless spray of water, and the tour boats gliding past. Even with the late morning sun reflecting off the lake and the cloudless pale blue sky the office is still drafty, cool, and dark. It's always been dark.

Dark navy-and-burgundy rug, dark leather chairs, a wall of shelves full of dark leather-bound books. The decades-old scent of tobacco and cognac sunk into the walls and furnishings. It smells just like my father, and probably just like his father before him.

Sometimes I think about gutting the office, airing it

out and filling it with light. I'd paint it white, put the behemoth furnishings in storage, open the windows to feel the breeze and hear the gulls on the water, the hum of the traffic, and the tour boat announcers as they pass . . .

"On your right you'll see Barone Jewelry, the largest family-owned jeweler in the world. Note the four-foot circumference engagement ring above the door. It's covered in twenty-four-karat gold leaf. And the glittering stone? That's the largest crystal gemstone in the world, a foot and a half in diameter, 315,000 karats, with 124 facets. Ladies, if you're looking for a husband, Maximillian Barone is quite the catch."

I can hear them when they sail by. Their script is always the same. I took a tour boat cruise once with Fiona and her daughter Mila. While two dozen people snapped photos of my building and bet on which one of them would "catch me," Fiona covered her mouth to keep from laughing out loud.

None of them would "catch me." The only woman I'd ever wanted to marry was Fiona. She was perfect for me. We'd been friends for years, we trusted each other, we would never hurt each other. That was all I ever wanted.

No passion. No sparks. A heated love affair is my idea of hell. They're both hot, and they both will torment you to no end.

There isn't anything I want or need from that horrific state called l'amour.

If I ever said to a woman, "Tu es ma joie de vivre—" *(You are the joy of my life.)*

If I ever claimed, "Tu es l'amour de ma vie—" *(You are the love of my life.)*

—something would be deeply, desperately wrong with me.

That may surprise some. Surely a man who makes a living from selling engagement rings and expensive jewelry would be a connoisseur of passion. An aficionado of desire. An arbiter of amour.

Right.

Well, if this office is any indicator, the allure of romantic love doesn't extend beyond the showroom. The glittering light of all those diamonds never quite penetrates this office. Which is fine by me.

I leave the décor of the office the way it is to remind myself exactly why I feel the way I do.

No passion. No heated love. No wife.

Life works better when you aren't carelessly tossing out landmines to step on.

Which is why I ask my assistant to repeat what she said. "Come again?"

She clicks her tongue in annoyance. "Your wife is here to see you. Shall I send her in?"

That's what I thought she said.

Just to be clear, I do not have a wife.

I've never had a wife.

I've never even had a fiancée.

Asking Fiona to marry me was the only time I've ever considered that state of matrimonial bliss everyone is so keen to dive headlong into. Half of them (at least) end up bashing their brains out when they finally hit bottom, but they keep trying, poor fools. I'm not interested.

Which is why I say with complete authority, "I don't have a wife, as you know, although I appreciate the levity." Perhaps Agathe is having a late mid-life crisis and has decided to try her hand at stand-up comedy. "I need the Swiss National Bank report sent—"

"Mr. Barone," Agathe says, and for the first time in

our history together she sounds on edge, "Mrs. Barone is here and she is quite distressed. Shall I send her in?"

I lean back in my chair and raise my eyebrows, looking around the office as if I'll find an answer in the bookshelves or the nineteenth-century oil paintings, or perhaps hiding behind the heavy navy curtains. There's no answer, just a cold draft seeping through the stone walls, and a long, blaring horn from a truck stuck in traffic down below.

"Agathe," I say carefully, twisting my family's signet ring on my fourth finger. "Enough. I'm not married. I have no wife. Let's move on. For the conference call at one, I need the—"

"Your wife. She's here!" Agathe hisses.

I jerk back and then turn to look at the heavy oak door to my office. The hair on the back of my neck stands on end, and suddenly I know something isn't quite right.

Agathe isn't joking.

She's never joked before. I only thought . . . maybe . . . but no, she isn't joking.

Her desk is right outside my door. Which means, there's a woman right outside my door that Agathe believes is my wife.

Fifteen feet away, twenty at most, is a woman claiming to be my wife.

I concentrate on the door as if I can see through it. I can't, but I swear there's something in the air. Not the ever-present tobacco and cognac scent. Not the dark, oppressive chill of my father's legacy. Not even the feeling of loneliness and aloneness that has sat heavy on my chest since Fiona turned down my proposal. It's a different feeling.

It's almost like when someone whispers and you can

almost, but not quite, make out the words; all you have to do is lean a little closer to them and you'll be fine. I can hear that indistinct murmur and I'm compelled to move closer. To hear the words.

In fact, it seems imperative that I hear them.

I lean forward in my chair, placing my hands on my cool desk. I watch the door, certain that any second it will burst open.

Yet that's absurd.

To get to the business offices of Barone Jewelry you have pass security, take the stairs or the elevator, pass reception, and then pass Agathe. There isn't any chance an unknown and uninvited guest would turn up and knock down my door.

Yet that's exactly what seems to be happening.

I shake my head. It doesn't matter. It's time to put a stop to this. "Agathe. If there is a woman claiming to be my wife in my offices, I recommend you remove her. Or I will."

There's a shocked gasped, and my previously unflappable assistant says in a tight voice, "This being your seventh wedding anniversary, I would expect you'd be happy to see her. Or did you forget an anniversary gift?"

Wedding Anniversary?

My *seventh* wedding anniversary?

Something is wrong here. Very, very wrong.

I suspect it's that Agathe has lost her grip on reality.

"This is the anniversary for wool. Or is it wood? Which gift is it?" Agathe asks, and then there's the clatter of typing through the speaker as if she's looking up the answer.

What do you do when someone slips out of reality so

quickly and completely? How did it happen? Is it that I've been working her too hard? I've been pulling sixteen-hour days for the past month and Agathe has been staying late too. Is that it? Does she need a holiday?

"Agathe?"

"What?" she asks, distracted, apparently, by finding a wool hat or a wooden bowl for my "wife." "What? Shall I send your wife in?" She says "your wife" with steely censure.

So, yes. She's lost her mind.

"No. Send her away."

I'll look into booking a spa trip for Agathe. A relaxing two weeks in Chamonix should clear her head.

I've moved on, brushed off the odd exchange and ignored the strange feeling buzzing over me. I've turned my attention back to the upcoming call with our Canadian diamond supplier when Agathe says tetchily, "I wouldn't have come to the wedding if I'd known you'd treat her this shabbily. I have a mind to quit." There's a scrape as she covers the phone and says in a softer voice, "I apologize, Mrs. Barone. He says he won't see you."

A soft, feminine voice murmurs a response, her words indistinguishable through the phone line. Yet, the soft edges of her voice seep through the door, a gentle caress of indistinct words hitting me right in the gut.

I can't make out a single word, but the sound of her voice nearly doubles me over. I recognize it, like someone who's never heard the rush of a waterfall still recognizes the roaring sound when they're finally standing in front of the cascading water, the cool mist abrading their skin.

I'm short of breath, dizzy, feeling almost as if I've swan-dived out of the window and bashed my head into the ground.

I pull myself back from the husky, mellow notes of the woman's voice and cling to what Agathe said.

"My wedding?"

"Excuse me?" she asks.

"You said you came to my wedding?"

Agathe's worse off than I thought if she thinks she was at my wedding.

She gives an angry scoff. "Of course I did. So did all the employees. So did half this city. What of it, if you aren't going to see your own wife on your anniversary? I wouldn't have bought you those fancy silver salt and pepper shakers. I would've bought cheap pewter ones if I'd known you'd turn away your own wife. Shameful."

"Are you feeling all right?" I ask carefully.

I glance out the window, checking to make sure the sky is still blue, the buildings are still rooted to the ground, and the sun is still shining.

"He asked if I'm feeling all right," she says to the mystery woman waiting outside my door.

The woman murmurs again, and at her voice a warmth works its way over me. All I want to do is lean forward—or better yet, walk across the dark confines of my office and press my ear to the solid oak door so I can feel the vibration of her words.

It's bad. I'm nearly as bad off as Agathe.

"I'm feeling better than you will be. I put your anniversary in your calendar, didn't I? Not that I should need to," Agathe says.

She *what*?

I jerk forward and click open my calendar. There it is, two words.

Wedding Anniversary.

My breath is hot and tight in my lungs. I forget about

my afternoon calls, about the aloneness I've felt since Fiona left for her tropical island. I forget about everything except the reminders in my calendar.

I scroll back, marveling, alternating between disbelief and anger. The reminders span seven years.

It's all there. Dates with Mrs. Barone. Opera with Mrs. Barone. Dinners with Mrs. Barone. Flowers for Mrs. Barone. Jewelry design meetings for surprises for Mrs. Barone. Weekend trips to Paris with Mrs. Barone.

When I'm done scrolling through seven years of this fake calendar marriage, I have one question. Who in the hell is Mrs. Barone?

No, two questions.

Who in the hell is Mrs. Barone, and how did she convince my assistant to alter my calendar?

There's nothing to it—I'm going to have to see this woman. I'll confront her, end this farce, and then make sure she never comes around again.

"Send her in," I say curtly, clicking off the call.

I stride around my desk and stand on the old, dark rug in the darkest, most shadowed spot in the room. It's something I learned from my father. Always face an opponent standing up, preferably from the shadows.

I face the door, the chill draft blowing over me. It scrapes against my hot skin and I let out a calming breath. The sound of traffic is still there, an almost imperceptible hum. Although it's not loud enough to smother the sound of my heartbeat in my ears.

This is nonsense.

I don't get nervous. At least not when facing a lone lying woman in my own office. But, there's something more happening. I can feel it.

I'm still compelled to lean forward, to hear that

whispered breath. There's something happening. Something that's about to happen, or something that already has.

The brass door handle turns slowly, and then the thick door swings open, sweeping over the rug. The bright light from reception spills into the dark office and the woman cautiously steps into the room.

Hell.

Hell.

I don't know her.

I've never seen her before in my life.

I would remember if I had.

I'm swept under and carried along, a flash flood crashing over me. I've never experienced anything like this before. I've never wanted to. But even though I've never felt it, I know exactly what it is.

There's a roaring in my ears. The room is fuzzy and watercolor-soft, the woman the only point of vibrancy. My blood pulses, my heart thudding a hard, painful beat, and I clench my jaw against the almost overwhelming urge to walk forward, take this woman in my arms, and kiss her. There's a freckle over her lips that's irresistible. I want to taste it and—

Hell.

It's hot in here. I'm sweating. I know exactly what this is.

The woman is beautiful. Not in the traditional sense, but beautiful like a fallen angel. Her eyes are wide. Dark blue, almost night-sky black. Her hair is wild, black and curly. It falls around her, messy and bed-rumpled, and all I want to do is run my hands through it and pull her close. Her mouth is cherry-red and tempting.

She closes the door behind her, and when she does, a

cool sweep of air brushes over me, bringing with it a familiar scent. She smells just like my freshly laundered bedsheets.

A bolt of lust hits me hard.

Who is this woman?

Strangely, she's barefoot, wearing only a white button-up shirt with a black trench coat thrown over it.

Wait a moment.

That's *my* white button-up shirt. That's *my* black trench coat.

I narrow my eyes.

And that—*that*—is my grandmother's diamond ring on her left ring finger.

A clamp squeezes my rib cage and a fire rages through me. It's an inferno, and I burn.

I don't know if it's a response to the nearness of this woman or the fact that she's wearing my grandmother's ring.

As of this morning, that ring was locked in my safe, hidden behind the painting of Mont Blanc, secure in my library at home. There is no reason, no way, she could have that ring.

Yet she does.

Whoever this woman is, she isn't getting out of this unscathed.

I hate the passion burning through me. I hate the fiery inferno of it all. I especially hate that I want to thrust this woman against the cold wood of my desk—no words, just mouth, hands, teeth—and bend her over the hard surface, capture her beneath me, flip up the tails of the white shirt conveniently covering her bare thighs, and drive into her until she's coming around me.

I can picture it as if it's already happened. I can feel

the tight heat of her wrapped around me, hear her throaty cries, taste the sweet, salty taste of her. I feel her like she's my own personal cataclysm.

I clench my teeth. Mercilessly slice through the image of my fingers digging into her hips, her hands gripping the desk, her desperate, throaty cries as I plunge into her. I thrust aside the image and douse the fire ravaging me with its heat.

I shove it aside.

I don't do passion.

I don't do *this*.

A woman like this is dangerous. She's a liar, and she's a thief, and she's trying to take advantage of me.

When I acknowledge that she's a liar the clamp around my rib cage loosens. I can breathe again.

All I have to do is sort this out, get rid of her, and this feeling will go away.

Get rid of her. Get rid of this feeling.

The woman takes a small, hesitant step forward, her bare feet sinking into the rug. The shirttails whisper against her legs, letting out a soft rustling noise. I can smell her again, the bedsheet scent, and I steel myself against it.

She's cautious, careful, her eyes wide and innocent. I don't buy the act. I've seen enough wolves in sheep's clothing to know not everyone is as innocent as they pretend.

She lifts her hand when she's close and the small bit of sunlight streaming through the window catches and lights the diamond ring.

She watches the stiffening of my shoulders and the hardness in my expression, and then she says in a soft, hesitant voice, "Max?"

What does she expect me to do?

"Who are you?" My voice comes out cold, hard, rough-edged.

Her face loses what little color it had, and I don't exactly blame her. I know what I look like when I'm confronting a thieving liar. Dark, hard, cold. Not someone you want to mess around with.

I won't take my tone back though. No matter how beautiful this woman is, and no matter what sort of fantasies are burning through me, she isn't anyone I'm going to befriend.

"Well?" I ask sharply.

Then the woman surprises me. She lifts her chin, and instead of cautious and pleading, she looks angry. "You don't recognize me? You don't know me?"

She's shocked. Irritated. Angered.

But why should I know her?

"Should I?"

Her face flushes, her cheeks turning bright red. "Max, you've known me for years—"

That gets my attention. "Years? Who the hell are you?"

She gasps, then she clenches her fists and takes a hard step forward. "I'm your wife. You arrogant prick."

She's close, and I fight the urge to kiss her. Instead I say with sardonic emphasis, "My *wife*?"

We both know that isn't true.

It's an irrefutable fact.

We aren't married.

But then something unbelievable happens.

I'm slammed with a sudden cracking, wallop-to-the-head, stunned, room-spinning, dizzy realization. And suddenly, I know—I *know*—the erotic, blood-pumping image I had of bending this woman over my desk and driving into her until I was out of my mind with need wasn't my horny, fevered imagination. It wasn't my imagination at all.

It was a memory.

A *memory*.

I'm . . . married.

And this woman?

She's my wife.

1

———————

Anna

"Now there's a view I will never get tired of," Dorene says in her scratchy early-morning, post-cigarette voice. Her words are laced with a suitable amount of appreciation and awe even though we have the same view every single week, at 6:30 a.m. sharp, Monday morning.

"I agree," I say, not caring that I sound wistful and half-in-love. It's early. I'm tired. I'm allowed to sound wistful and in love.

Besides, it's true. I'll never get tired of this view. There's no place like the Barone Estate right before the sun peeks over the still waters of Lake Geneva. The sky is the pink of an iced raspberry, with golden clouds feathering over calm purple waters. A cool, insubstantial mist drifts off the water and curls over the soft, grassy shore, tangling around my ankles, wet and cold. Swifts swoop and swirl above in acrobatic glee and the breeze they ride on teases my cheeks.

The sweet morning scent of dew-covered grass and summer clover hangs in the air, waiting to be burned away by the sunrise. Far across the lake are the mounded blue hills of deep, cool evergreen forests. They promise pine and loam and quiet. Curving along the shoreline are the still-sleepy stone edifices of Geneva. The streetlights wink out in expectation of day. It's a romantic, beautiful picture. But the best view of all is the chateau towering above us.

The first time I saw it, three years ago, I thought I'd been transported to another time. The chateau is starkly beautiful. Austere in its severity. It's three stories of cold, gray stone, hewn from the surrounding mountains and cut to withstand centuries of bitter winds and unexpected twists of fate.

There are two conical towers with rooflines that sweep sharply like the edge of a dangerously angled mountain slope. The windows are narrow and lead paned. In the sunrise they're limned with gold.

The chateau is notable because of its lack of decoration. No arches. No gables. No finials. No columns or spires. No whimsy or romance. In my mind its beauty is in its bareness.

What's more beautiful? The loud, bright colors and heavy perfumes of the jungle, or the endless silent glide of an arctic glacier, towering and alone in the deep, dark sea?

The Barone Chateau is terrible in its beauty. Beautiful in its aloneness. Not even its proximity to Geneva, its perch at the edge of the jewel-like mountain lake, or the wild, untamed gardens that bloom and blossom around its base, can fool anyone into imagining this home is anything but what it is. A fortress.

A lonely, stark fortress that rejects romance, denies softness, and laughs at love.

All the same. It's beautiful.

On Monday mornings, when we wend down the long, winding gravel driveway, I sometimes feel like the chateau is only waiting. Maybe it's been waiting for years. It's caught in that breath-held moment right before sunrise when the world is at its most magical. You only have to step outside right before the sun crests over the edge of the world to find it.

You can breathe in the pine-needle and wet-grass smell. You can listen for the quiet melody of the wood thrush carried on the gentle breeze. You can let the cold mist rise off the lake and bring a shiver over your skin. The world is whispering, "Just wait and see. This day is going to bring the most wondrous, magical things your way."

It's just like that moment between making a wish and blowing out your birthday candles. There is so much magic and expectation between dragging in that great gust of air and blowing out your wish.

That's how I feel about the Barone Chateau.

It's captured in that moment, waiting for the sun to rise and the wish to be made.

I arch my back and glance up at the sheer wall of the eastern tower. The stones emit a dull gray glow in the early-morning light. The late-spring air is cool, almost brisk, and I rub the goose bumps on my arms.

Dorene knocks her fist against the back of her van and then swings open the doors. They let out a querulous creak, like they're protesting the early-morning wake-up thump. The van should be used to it though—Dorene always gives it a whack before opening the back end. She's superstitious and has specific rituals to make sure her day goes the way she'd like. Whacking the van before opening the doors is one of those rituals. She also plugs and unplugs the vacuum three times before the first use of the day. And she refuses to clean any rooms with books in them. I don't know why. That's just Dorene. I don't mind—I like rooms with books. They're cozier. Homier. Happier.

The astringent scent of bleach and furniture polish greets us as Dorene and I pull free the supplies we'll need to clean. We move in the steady choreography of partners who have been working together for years.

Dorene brought me on seven years ago, after my stepdad left and my mom and I were in a tough spot. She told me, "This may not be the job you dreamed of, but it's a job, and that's more than you have now. What do you say?"

I said yes.

Before that day, I'd only known her as our frizzy-haired, wrinkled neighbor who chain-smoked in a lawn chair on the stoop while watching angsty art films at maximum volume on an ancient portable TV.

I never knew she watched art films because her late husband was a French director in the eighties, or that in her twenties she sang mezzo-soprano in the opera, or that once she drove naked through the streets of Paris in a stolen Bugatti convertible, belting out "La Marseillaise," the French national anthem. The owner of the Bugatti proposed to her after that escapade. She turned him down.

Dorene drops a bucket full of cleaning supplies to the gravel and grunts as I pull out the vacuum.

"It's too bad," she says, giving the chateau a gimlet-eyed appraisal, "that the owner of this chateau is not as appealing."

I think about Maximillian Barone. He's here sometimes, when we're cleaning. It's a full-day job for us, from 6:30 a.m. until 4:30 p.m. There are twelve bedrooms, six bathrooms, a mammoth kitchen, a butler pantry, a staff kitchen, two formal living rooms, a library, two home offices, a gym, a garage full of exotic and vintage sports cars . . . You get the idea. It's a big job.

Usually, he's gone by the time we're punching in our code at the front door, but sometimes he's still here. Or sometimes he works from home.

I have to admit, I like those days. The chateau feels less empty and less cold. All those closed-up rooms echo with too much emptiness when it's just Dorene and me.

We dust them, we vacuum, but the deep cleaning is reserved for the rooms Max uses. His bedroom. His office. The library. The kitchen. The gym.

If he's here and he sees me he gives a quick nod, a polite, "Madame," and that's that.

There's only one time in three years he's said more than that single word to me. It was the first time I saw him, the fourth time we cleaned his home. I felt I already knew him a little. It's hard not to learn things about someone when you clean their house.

I knew he had a sweet tooth and that he loved milk chocolate and hazelnut ice cream. I knew he preferred mint toothpaste and that he used a hand-milled soap that smelled like autumn rain in the mountains. I knew he was meticulously neat and always picked up his laundry and made his bed. I knew he listened to classical music in the library from the playlist left open, and I knew he watched British detective shows while making his dinner from the episodes paused and waiting to resume. I knew he was slowly working his way through the stack of Dickens novels on his nightstand, although I didn't know whether he was reading them because he liked Dickens or because Dickens put him to sleep. I knew he had straight black hair, thick stubble, and from the clothes he owned, he was probably in his early thirties.

I'd never seen him. I hadn't looked him up. But I thought I knew him. A little.

I thought I had him figured out.

Then I walked into his office, pushing the vacuum in front of me, the roaring hum drowning out all ambient noise. I didn't expect him to be home. Dorene was upstairs working her way through the bathrooms. I had a pair of headphones on and I was listening to Motown. My family's from Detroit, and when I was little we always played Motown when we cleaned our house every Saturday.

I was sashaying with the vacuum, doing a sort of half-dance, half-push move. The main office was large, with old, honey-colored wood floors, a massive desk, and a computer that collected dust like a miser hoarding gold coins. There was a large potted plant in the corner that I liked to say hello to while I dusted its leaves. The room always smelled like warm leather, printer toner, and sunshine on wood floors.

I didn't look at the desk. I was watching the vacuum as I thrust it across the wood floor in time with the music and my mostly terrible singing voice. But then a slow tickle swept over my spine until a buzzing tingle, almost like the vibration of the vacuum, infused my whole body.

I was vibrating with a strange awareness I'd never felt before.

The office didn't smell like printer toner. Instead it smelled like coffee, hazelnut croissant, and Max's hand-milled soap.

I paused in a spray of sunlight falling through the lead paned window and slowly turned toward Max's desk.

He was there, watching me as if he'd just asked me a question and he was waiting for my answer.

I couldn't say anything.

I couldn't move.

The blasting chords of Motown disappeared. The roar of the vacuum receded. The familiar, comfortable lines of the office faded.

He was *beautiful*.

He was the most beautiful man I'd ever seen.

Not classically beautiful. Not magazine beautiful. Not movie-star beautiful.

When I say beautiful, I mean he was beautiful like the chateau.

Looking at him was like looking at the desolate sweep of an arctic winter the moment before the sun rises for the first time in months. I was struck, pierced, and flayed by the promise of that sunrise.

I forgot the vacuum roaring in my hands, I forgot the music blasting in my ears, and I stared at Max while I waited for the sun.

He had thick, night-dark hair that was short on the sides and long enough to run your fingers through on the top. His eyes were dark brown and framed with thick lashes. They had a spark of intelligence, drive, but also the closed-off, distant expression you'd expect from the man who called this fortress his home. His features were sharp. Hard cheekbones, a square jaw, deep-set eyes that saw everything and trusted no one. He was thirty, maybe. There was a hint of hardness in the set of his shoulders that spoke of years of hard work or hard living. But there was also a softness lingering at the edges of his lips that promised he smiled sometimes, and when he did, it was glorious.

I'd never been in love before.

I didn't know what it felt like.

But I thought, probably, this was it. This tingle sweeping through me like a shooting star casting across the night sky—this had to be love. My heart thudded wildly in my chest and I felt every beat, like it was pumping out the word, *love, love, love.*

Then Max spoke again.

He spoke to me.

I realized I couldn't hear him. The vacuum was loud; my music was louder. A flush ran over my cheeks and down my neck and chest.

I flipped off the vacuum, yanked my headphones free.

The office was electric in the silence.

"Sorry? What did you say?" I asked, and I was surprised my voice came out sounding normal, as if I was asking my sister to pass the salt.

I didn't realize I'd spoken in English until the words were already out of my mouth.

Max didn't even blink.

By that point in time, I realized that whatever he'd said, it wasn't words of undying love and devotion. It wasn't, "You're an angel fallen from heaven!" or, "This is love at first sight!" or even, "What are you doing tonight?"

No.

Because while Max was the sunrise at the end of my arctic winter, I was . . .

Me.

My messy hair was knotted in a bun and hidden beneath a wrinkled, bleach-stained red bandana. I was wearing very large, very round green tortoiseshell glasses (this was in my era of fashion-forward glasses, which, in hindsight, were very, very ugly). I had on my gray, bleach-stained Detroit Tigers sweatshirt, baggy bleach-stained jeans, and years-old tennis shoes with shoelaces that had disintegrated into stringy, ugly wads of fabric. My hot-pink rubber gloves hung from my pocket, and I had a dirty rag hanging from my other pocket. Beyond that, I was sweaty, breathing hard, and an uncomfortable shade of bright red.

The music from my headphones blasted between us, the Supremes telling us that love can't be hurried.

So there I stood, dumbstruck by love, and Max glanced at me without seeing me and said with careful politeness, "Could you please wait until I've left to clean in here?"

His English had a British accent with only a hint of French. He must've learned British English as a kid or studied in Britain for school. Lots of people do. It's like my French. Since my mom and I didn't move here until I was eleven, my French is forever tinged with the American Midwest.

But his accent wasn't why I didn't answer right away. It was his voice. Before, I'd thought it was love. Once he spoke, I knew it was. And this man, he barely looked at me. In fact, he'd already looked away. His gaze was on his computer screen, scrolling through whatever business I'd interrupted.

I was glued to the floor, disbelieving that I'd finally experienced what my dad always said I'd find—the kind of love that lasts lifetimes—and the man was as indifferent to me as the ocean is to the sky.

I stood for a moment longer, too stunned to move, the Supremes still singing tinnily through my headphones. Max looked up one last time, his eyes moving to the vacuum in my hand, not to me.

"Are you all right?" He finally looked at me. But that was even worse than him not looking at me, because there was nothing in his expression—nothing except a cold, stark, gray stone wall.

He was Maximillian Barone. And I was Anna Benoit. And it was clear from his expression that the two of us weren't destined to be.

Love at first sight had soared like a swan on summer winds for a joyous, wondrous moment, and then it took a tumbling nosedive out of the sky and smacked the stones of the chateau to die a painful, squawking, feathery death.

My insta-love was insta-gone.

That yanked me out of my tingly, love-infused delusion. "Sorry. Yes. Sorry."

I dragged my vacuum across the wood floor and stumbled backward out of his office. Max didn't watch me go.

Since then, for three years, if we ever cross paths, he'll say, "Madame," and I'll say, "Bonjour, monsieur."

And that is the extent of our interactions.

But for Dorene to say he isn't appealing?

"That's not true," I say, not able to deny that even though I squelched any tingly feelings, I still admire the man.

I know him even more than I did the first time I saw him. I've heard him on business calls—direct, fair, intelligent. He's serious on those calls, never smiling, always firm. But then I've heard him on the phone to Fiona Abry, the woman he actually loves, and his voice always has an intimate, happy quality that hints at the warm sunlight he keeps hidden behind tall stone walls.

I even saw, months ago, an engagement ring on his nightstand. It was beautiful, and I knew right away he'd designed it himself. And I suppose it's okay to admit that when I saw it, there was a hollow, empty feeling in my stomach that even a dozen chocolate mocha truffles from my favorite chocolatier didn't fill. Nothing could.

So. I guess that insta-love isn't completely insta-gone.

Dorene smirks at me and slaps my pair of pink rubber gloves into my hands. I scoff and shove them into my pocket.

"Why don't you ask him on a date?" she asks.

According to Dorene, in her day she had thirty-six marriage proposals, most of them after a first date. She never remarried after her first husband, but that didn't mean men didn't try. She says marriage proposals are as easy to get as well-wishes on a Sunday.

She's well aware I've had two boyfriends, no marriage proposals, and no weddings.

"Why would I do that?" I busy myself checking my inventory. I'm cleaning the rugs in the library today.

"Because you're young. Because you'd like to have unforgettable sex before you die. Because he's nice to look at. I don't know. Choose one."

"How about I chose none?" I say, lifting my bucket and grabbing the vacuum with my other hand. I start toward the front door.

I hear the van doors slam behind me and a hard thwack on the door.

Dorene hurries after me, her steps crunching on the gravel. "I'm only saying, I see that glint in your eye every time we pull up. You can't fool me. It's not a craving for coffee. It's a craving for a certain man."

Ugh. She watches too many romantic movies. "I'm confiscating your television."

She snorts, then continues. "You depress me. Twenty-five years old and all you do is work, take care of your sister, read that boring Charles Dickens, and go to bed too early. No drinking. No smoking. No sex. You are tragic."

"And you are the nosiest neighbor I've ever had."

Also, yes. After I saw Max read Dickens, I bought *Nicholas Nickleby.* It's not my fault I was hooked.

"Ask him on a date."

I punch our code into the front door. It's exactly 6:30 a.m. The security system records our arrival, all our entries and exits. The bolt unlocks and I swing the door open.

"No," I say. "Didn't you know he's in love with Fiona Abry?"

"She married someone else."

I stop in the threshold. Turn to look at Dorene. She's fluttering her eyelashes innocently. It's not a look that works for her.

"Didn't you hear?" she asks.

I shake my head. My gut clenches and a funny feeling trips through my insides. "Why? Who?"

Dorene shrugs.

How could Fiona say no? How could *anyone* say no? How could anyone not want to marry Max? He's . . . he's . . .

"I see that look on your face. You're going to ask him, aren't you?"

I grip the door handle, shake my head, then step inside the cold, dark interior of the chateau. "No," I say, "I'm going to clean his house."

And that's all I'm going to do.

Forever and ever and ever.

After Dorene stomps inside, I close the front door, shutting out the golden sun finally rising over the deep, placid lake.

2

—————

I DIDN'T ALWAYS WANT TO CLEAN HOUSES. IT WASN'T WHAT I dreamed of as a kid. I didn't play games with a broom or a mop or a toy vacuum. It wasn't what I wrote in proud cursive on my elementary school career-day proclamation.

Nope.

When I was little I wanted to be a genie. While other kids were dreaming of playing pro basketball, starring in movies, or racing to the rescue in bright red firetrucks, I was planning my life as a grantor of wishes.

It started when I was six and my after-school babysitter, Mrs. Stunkle, watched an old episode of *I Dream of Jeannie*. Before then I hadn't really put much stock in Mrs. Stunkle's opinions. She served carrots and celery instead of cookies for my after-school snack. She played Sudoku instead of Go Fish. All her furniture had plastic covers and her house smelled like cats and canned green beans. I'd count down the ninety minutes I spent in her living room like I was counting down the last days of a prison sentence.

But then I saw that some grown-ups were magic. That they could grant wishes. Because of Mrs. Stunkle I found out genies existed, and they could make dreams come true.

After that I watched *I Dream of Jeannie* every day after school, and I devoured every story, movie, or myth about genies I could find. I was convinced that when I grew up I could be a genie, just like Jeannie.

When adults asked me, "What do you want to be when you grow up?" I'd lift my chin and say, with the pure confidence of a child who doesn't know any better, "A genie!"

They always laughed. I didn't know what was so funny.

If I were a genie I'd have the power to give everyone what they wanted most in life.

When my mom came home exhausted after a long night shift, her feet swollen and her shoulders sagging, and said, "Anna, love, I can't make pancakes. I'm too tired. I wish I could, but I have to go lie down." Well, all I'd have to do was snap my fingers, or blink, or wiggle my nose, and my mom would get her wish and she wouldn't be tired anymore.

Or when my dad was waiting for a kidney and he said, "I wish I'd get that kidney." Well, I'd blink and magically he'd get his kidney, and he'd be healthy again.

Or later, when he said, "My Anna, I wish I could see you grown up." All I'd have to do was wiggle my nose and my dad would be there, for all my childhood, all my teenage years, and all the way into adulthood.

My genie power wouldn't be only for my family though. When Mrs. Stunkle said, "I wish I could figure this Sudoku out." Well, wish granted.

Likewise, when my teacher, Miss Ayaba, said, "I wish you kids would remember what I taught you!" Okay, Miss Ayaba, wish granted!

The list goes on.

"I wish it were sunny today."

"I wish he'd notice me."

"I wish I had a puppy."

If I were a genie, all those things would be in my power to grant.

So that was my goal. I wanted to give people their heart's desire. I wanted to make people happy. I was powerless though, and I knew it. My dad didn't get his kidney. He didn't get to see me grow up. My mom is still worn out. And poor Miss Ayaba, she's still plagued back in Detroit with entire classes of six-year-olds who don't remember what she taught.

My mom always figured I'd grow out of wanting to be a genie. I guess I did. I realized I didn't have the power to grant wishes. Not in the magical kind of way. If I could, I'd grant Dorene's wish to see her husband one more time. I'd grant my little sister's wish to spend the summer on the French Riviera. I'd grant my mom's wish to finally have enough money to buy our very own house: a little stone cottage in the country with bright blue shutters and a flower garden.

That's what it means to be a genie. You grant other people's wishes. I never thought about the fact that genies don't have their own wishes come true. I don't know if genies even have wishes.

I drag the carpet cleaner over the thick wool rug in

Max's library. The white soap churns and froths, pulling up stains and dirt. I started off by cleaning the windows and blinds, moved to dusting, transitioned to vacuuming, and now I'm finishing with the rugs.

The rumble of the carpet cleaner is overwhelmingly loud. It echoes around the wide expanse of the library, bouncing off the white plaster walls, the stone columns, and the stacks and stacks of books. The machine is heavier than a vacuum, and my arms ache from slowly shoving the behemoth across half a dozen rugs. The library smells of wet wool, frothy soap, and furniture polish.

The room is expansive, wide enough to need six large rugs, with walls of bookshelves and a wooden ladder to reach the tallest shelves. There are cozy leather chairs spaced around the room, a little sitting area centered around a small fireplace, and a large cushioned chair by a tall window with a pile of Dickens novels next to it. Sometimes the side table next to that cushy chair has a half-empty cup of coffee on it too. And sometimes, if I can't help it, I wonder if Max is lonely when he sits in this huge library, alone, reading a book with a cup of coffee.

But usually, I just clean. I dust the books, I dust the desk, I dust the oil painting on the wall behind his desk. Cleaning people's homes is a bit like being a genie. When they get home from work, their house is clean, tidy, and smells like fresh linens and lemons, and that *is* a bit like magic. And I think it makes them happy too.

I finish with the carpet cleaner and flick off the machine. It groans and rumbles, then the room descends into a soft afternoon quiet. Outside the windows the sun is falling toward the west, and a light golden stream of color branches across the grass.

Now that I've stopped the flurry of cleaning, I notice the tranquil, quiet, muted quality of the air surrounding me. My arms have that blood-pumping ache they get after nearly ten hours of scrubbing and sweeping, and my skin tingles as the cool air lights on the sweat running down the back of my neck. My heart is loud in my ears, and I drag in a breath.

There's a strange sensation vibrating around me. I run my gaze over the room. It feels as if someone is watching me, or as if someone is there, waiting for me to notice them. Sometimes people claim the Barone Estate is haunted. I've never believed that. It's not haunted; it's just lonely. Waiting.

That's what it feels like now. As if the library is waiting.

I glance toward the desk at the far end of the room. It's dark wood with curling legs and carved, decorative edges. I've never known Max to use it. The surface is always empty, with a fine layer of dust that accumulates between my cleanings. But today, when I cleaned it, there was a small golden box on top of the desk, with an old, yellowed piece of paper beneath it. I didn't look at either. I gently pushed them aside while I dusted, then I put them back when I was done.

But now the box draws my eye.

Sunlight lies across the desk and blankets the box, burnishing it in gleaming gold. It's as if the box is glowing. I can almost hear it humming. I stare at it for a moment longer, and then I swear the gold flares like a flickering flame . . . almost like the gold of a genie's lamp.

The silence of the library rises around me and enfolds me in a breath-held quiet. I can't help it, I step across the thick rugs, the plush fabric whispering under my shoes. The soapy scent rises around me as I pace toward the desk.

I'm sweaty, I'm bleach-stained, I'm dust-covered and tired, but all the same, when I draw to the edge of the desk, all I want to do is reach out and open the delicate gold box.

I shouldn't.

I couldn't.

I won't.

I don't snoop. I don't touch things that don't belong to me. I don't . . .

I look down in shock. I've already opened the box. I don't remember opening it, but there it is, open before me.

"My word."

Inside the box is the most beautiful necklace I've ever seen. The box was pretty. It was flat and the size of a leather bound book, covered in elegant gold filigree. Inside there's white satin and black velvet cushioning a necklace.

The necklace.

I've never seen anything like it.

It's a circlet of brilliant pebble-size sapphires. They're deep, alluring blue; dusky, sky-blue; longing, broken-hearted blue; desirous, seductive blue. The necklace is a chain of blue, spilling in a gradient of color like a river of light.

There are twenty-six sapphires, all linked together with delicate gold collets, set with tiny shimmering diamonds. And then there's a pendant of gold and sapphire in the timeless shape of a lover's knot. It's the promise of forever.

This necklace was made for a woman who was very, very loved.

I wonder what that would be like. To be loved so much.

The glow of sunlight gleams over the blue and winks off the stones like light reflecting off the waves of the lake. The cool air of the room pinches my cheeks, and I resist the urge to reach out and run my fingers over the gleaming sapphires.

After I first met Max I obsessively researched jewelry. I thought if I learned a lot about what he did I might be able to strike up a conversation. Like, "What do you prefer—the cushion cut or the princess cut?" or, "What is your position on lab-grown diamonds?" or, "What do you think of reproduction jewelry? I prefer the Georgian Era."

I thought if I could talk with Max about something besides which room I was vacuuming, he might *see* me.

But I never struck up a conversation. I never wowed Max with my newfound knowledge. In fact, after a few short, frenzied months of research, I realized my time was better spent helping my little sister, Emme with her math homework, helping Dorene file her taxes, and helping my mom by cooking dinner.

All the same, I'll never forget the mad amount of research I conducted and all the random knowledge I accrued.

The necklace nestled in velvet in front of me is either more than two hundred years old or a stellar reproduction. This type of necklace is called a rivière necklace. They were often made from diamonds, and back in the late 1700s they were all the rage. They glimmered in evening candlelight and dazzled the world with their allure.

The Georgian lover's knot is tied in the shape of the infinity symbol. A man gives it to his wife, a promise to love in this life and the next.

I wonder what kind of man commissioned this necklace. I wonder what kind of woman he loved.

I pull the aged, yellowed paper out from under the box. It's crinkly dry, like a leaf in autumn, and the ink is faded to a barely perceptible blue. The handwriting is spidery thin and barely legible. It's in French, an old style—so much so that I have a hard time deciphering the language.

But as I scan the page, my feet aching, my cheeks burning, sweaty and tired, I see one phrase I recognize.

This necklace will grant your dearest wish.

A chill rides over me, raising the goose bumps on my arms. The library stays silent, the afternoon quiet, the cool air soft and still. I'm bathed in the golden light from the window, and the light from the necklace dances across the room and reflects white ripples and rainbows in my vision.

The necklace lies still, winking, waiting.

For what?

For me to make a wish?

I look back at the spidery handwriting on the page, not certain I read the words right. But yes. I did. It says it right there. This necklace grants wishes.

Make a wish. It will come true.

I stare at the necklace. Then my mouth twitches. The sensation of being watched grows.

I smile and a small laugh rushes out of me, like the whoosh of a door flying open in a gust of wind. I look around the library, my eyes crinkled, expecting to see someone there laughing at me. Or with me.

Max, maybe. Although that isn't likely.

It's more likely to be Dorene. She probably planted this reproduction necklace here with this note. I bet she dipped the paper in tea. All in an effort to get me to live a little.

The tension that was holding me releases with the sound of my laughter. It's ridiculous. I was standing here believing a necklace could grant wishes. Like a genie.

Riiiight.

"Dorene?"

My voice echoes then fades as it hits the stacks of books lining the walls.

"Dorene? I found your necklace. Ha-ha. Funny."

I tap my foot against the plush rug, waiting for her to pop her head around the door.

She doesn't.

"Dorene?" My lips are dry. I lick them and swallow. The sensation of being watched is still there.

I spin slowly in a circle, my footsteps rustling in the quiet. No one is here. I'm completely alone in the expansive library. It's just me, a few hundred books, a slew of expensive furniture, and half a dozen freshly shampooed rugs.

"Max?"

Not that Max would be here. Now that I think about it, he isn't the type to play a joke on someone he barely knows, and he would never pull a prank.

So that means . . .

I turn back to the necklace. It glimmers in the softly spilling sunlight, the gradient of blues as varied and vivid as Lake Geneva on a midsummer day.

It means . . .

Whoever wrote this letter truly believed this necklace

could grant wishes. And that anticipation humming through the air—the anticipation that feels like a shooting star waiting to be wished upon . . .?

Maybe it's this necklace.

Maybe it does grant wishes.

"What would be the harm in wishing?" I ask the necklace quietly.

It winks at me like there'd be no harm at all.

I nod.

Exactly.

There's no harm.

I could wish for a holiday to the French Riviera for my sister and Mom. I might wish for a little stone cottage with blue shutters outside the city. I could wish for my mom to get the raise she's spent the past five years hoping for.

Or . . .

I could do what a genie never does, and I could wish for something for myself.

Ever since Dorene told me Fiona turned Max down, there's been a niggling in my chest, a twisting in my stomach, a warmth in my blood.

What if Max finally noticed me? What if, just for a moment, he saw me? And if he saw me, maybe he'd find that he liked what he saw.

I don't know if he's the love of my life. I don't know if I'm the love of his. But for three years I've been cleaning his empty home, hearing the echoes of his past, and wishing I could help fill the emptiness that's always lingering in the closed-up rooms and the cold, barren halls.

I stupidly fell in love with him at first sight. I've always thought that maybe if he saw me— really *saw me*—then he'd fall in love at first sight too.

"I wish . . ." I whisper, feeling wild and daring. "I wish that Max loved me. I wish that we were married."

I stare at the necklace, my mouth dry, my heart stuttering. A cold sweat lines my forehead. I wait, breath held, for a violent lightning strike to carve out of the sky and smack me for daring to make such a pronouncement.

My lungs ache as I stand there, muscles tight, eyes unblinking. Waiting.

Then, slowly, my heart settles into an even rhythm, my muscles loosen, and I let out a long, slow, ragged breath.

Nothing happened.

I laugh. Of course nothing happened. What did I expect?

Besides . . .

"What were you thinking?" I ask myself.

I lean down, stare at the necklace.

"I take it back," I tell it, speaking as firmly as possible. "I don't actually want that. I take it back."

How awful would it be, really, to blink and find yourself married to a man who barely knew you existed a second ago? No, thank you.

And to magic someone into loving you? That's even worse.

I wag my finger at the necklace. "No, thank you, magic necklace. No, thank you. I take back my wish."

With that, I reach forward and snap the lid shut. It gives a sharp click as I reset the clasp.

I sigh and press my pointer finger to the gold filigree —a pretty pattern of gold violets and a twisting vine. Time to head home. I'll find Dorene. She's probably finishing the kitchen. Tonight I'll help Emme with her science project and make a pot of onion soup for dinner. Life goes on, wishes or not.

"Excuse me. *What* are you doing?"

I jerk my hand away from the gold box and grasp it to my chest as if I've been burned. The tips of my ears burn as I slowly turn around.

Max stands a few feet away, his presence filling the space and consuming all the air between us. He's the flame, and all the oxygen in the room has been sucked up by him.

How does he get away with being so beautiful? How is it possible that every time I see him I want to curl up against his side and kiss the stubble lining his jaw? Even now. It's ridiculous.

A wash of heat falls over me and my skin prickles with embarrassment. I wonder, did he hear me?

Yes. I think he did.

I've never seen him look so cold. He's in a dark gray suit and a white shirt. He's devoid of color, and his expression is devoid of warmth. His face is stark and . . . yes, that's anger. Ice-cold anger. It radiates from him in sharp lines, and I shake my head, unsure of what to do with the hostility pointed at me.

"I asked you a question, *madame*."

The way he says "madame" makes it clear he doesn't think I'm worth the title at all.

I swallow and clench my hand, digging my nails into my palm.

I never thought anyone could be so angry at someone wishing to marry them. It's absurd really.

Granted, he's pristine in his suit and I'm sweaty, with frizzy hair tucked under my handkerchief, my old T-shirt damp with soap suds. Still. He doesn't have to look quite so furious. I get it. He doesn't want me.

"It was just a stupid joke. I didn't mean it." My voice comes out as a half-whisper.

A muscle in Max's jaw clenches and his eyes flare. He takes a threatening step forward, cutting across the rug, and I resist the urge to step back. I almost throw out my hands as if I'm warding off a wolf intent on lunging at my throat.

What is his deal?

"You think stealing a million-franc heirloom is a joke? Perhaps we'll let the police—"

"Stealing!" He thinks I stole his necklace! *That's* why he's angry? "I didn't! How could—?"

I swipe my hand through the air, canceling out his accusation, and lightning-fast, he reaches out, grabs my wrist, and holds me still.

"Don't lie."

I'm caught by the cold heat in his eyes, a burning ice that stings. His hand spans my wrist, his fingers pressing into my skin, a hard shackle. I stare into his eyes, lift my chin, and battle against the anger pulsing between us. His gaze has captured mine, or maybe I've captured his. I refuse to look away. Suddenly the pulsing anger twists and shifts into something else. A sharp, violent need.

Something shifts in Max's eyes, a shadow lurking in the dark brown of his irises, and his gaze dips to my mouth. If this were any other time and any other man, I would swear I'm about to be kissed. Roughly. With teeth and tongue and punishing intent.

And I would like it.

But this isn't another time. And this isn't another man.

This is Max, accusing me of stealing.

And staring at my mouth.

My heart rate kicks up.

"Let me go," I hiss, yanking at my arm.

His gaze breaks away from my lips and flashes back to my eyes. He keeps ahold of me, tightening his grip. His cheeks have two bright red spots of color and he's breathing fast. "Turn out your pockets."

"No."

He's gone Dickens on me. Assumed the worst. Jumped to conclusions. He thinks I'm a thief and a liar. I've been cleaning this man's house for three years. I've washed his laundry, scrubbed his toilet, left him soups that I cooked while scouring his grout. I have never, ever, *ever* taken anything of his.

"I'm not a thief."

He looks at my mouth again, seems to get angry with himself. "Liar."

He gives my wrist a shake to emphasize his point.

"I'm not a liar. Let. Me. Go."

He's moved closer. I can feel the heat licking off him, the anger fueling him. There's an awareness dancing over my skin at his nearness, prickly and hot. It's inconvenient since this isn't a seduction. It's not even foreplay.

"Let go!"

"Turn out your pockets and I will." He says this with a low, dark growl.

I shake my head and the hair coming loose from my bun scrapes the back of my neck. "No. I won't. I'm not your Artful Dodger." How dare he accuse me of stealing? I'm not some pickpocket from his bedtime stories.

I glare at him and his eyes widen with a quick flash of surprise.

"The Artful Dodger? You read?"

I want to kick him. Hard. "Yes. Amazing, isn't it? I've been doing it since I was four."

He narrows his eyes, unamused. "Madame, turn out your pockets, or I will for you."

Apparently, he's done with the small talk.

I close my eyes and suppress the urge to twist my wrist free and knock him over the head with a book—one that I've *read*. Perhaps *The Tale of Two Cities* since it's huge and it'd hurt more.

Maybe it'd knock some sense into him.

If I could take my wish back, I would. Instead I'd wish that I never fell in love with Max Barone. Or maybe I'd wish that I never met him.

It wouldn't make a difference to him. He wouldn't miss me. He wouldn't feel a hole in his chest at the thought that I wasn't there.

In fact, I doubt he even knows my name.

"Do you know my name?" I ask him, opening my eyes.

"Excuse me?"

"My name."

He shakes his head, then abruptly stops and says, "Dorene."

"No." My lips turn down. "Not Dorene."

"No then," he says curtly. "I do not know your name. I only know you take what isn't yours."

My shoulders sag, and that empty feeling I had in my gut when I saw the engagement ring Max made for Fiona Abry returns a thousand fold. How stupid is it that I'm in love with a man who doesn't even know my name? After three years of seeing me in his house. After three years of sleeping on the bedsheets that I wash. *After three years.*

He clearly doesn't know me at all if he believes I would steal from him.

I don't know what's worse, him not knowing my name or him thinking so little of me.

"All right," I say, dropping my chin and staring at the perfectly cleaned rug. "But I expect an apology when you realize you were wrong."

Max scoffs. "I never apologize."

Oh gosh. Maybe if I'd talked to Max for more than fifteen seconds, I would've realized he was a jerk. I wouldn't have been swayed by Dickens on the nightstand, hazelnut ice cream in the freezer, and British detective dramas in the kitchen. That would've saved me a few years of wishing for the impossible.

I take my wish back, I mentally project to the necklace. *I take it back. I never, ever want to be married to this man.*

I reach down to my left pocket and flip out the white cotton material. "See? Nothing."

"The other." Max nods to my right pocket.

It's then, as he does, that I notice an unusual weight in that pocket. An unusual bulk.

A strange sensation creeps over me. Whatever is in my pocket is hard like stone, round like coins, heavy like a pocketful of rocks.

I blink at Max as my mind goes blank.

It's not possible.

I closed the box.

I shut the necklace away.

I never even touched it.

Slowly, as if I'm moving through thick mud, I quest my fingers into my pocket. They hit the cold, faceted surface of a stone. As if I'm in a trance, I loop my fingers around the stone and pull the chain from my pocket.

The sapphires catch the sunlight, gleaming like a stream of raindrops falling from the sky. They tinkle and clink and—*holy crap*—I hold the necklace between me and Max, my heart thundering.

There's arrogant satisfaction, angry acceptance, and cold dismissal wrapped in the curl of his lip. His expression fills with disgust. For me.

He looks at me as if he's never seen anyone so low, so beneath him, in his entire life.

I'm the scum of his universe. I'm the dirt he can't wait to wipe off his shoes. I'm the lowest of his low.

But . . .

"I didn't—" I cut myself off. Clearly, I did. But I don't remember doing it. I don't . . . "I didn't take it. I wouldn't—"

He scoffs. "You did. You would."

He pries the necklace loose from my hand and forcefully drops my wrist. I stumble back and my thighs hit the decorative edge of the wooden desk.

A short while ago, the library was bathed in golden solitude and soft, muted quiet. It was breath-held expectation and teasing magic. Now it's stark and barren, and the reality is ugly.

Max narrows his eyes as if I'm one of the mangy rats that slinks through the gutters at night in search of rotting food to nibble and diseases to spread.

"It's all a misunderstanding. If only I can explain—"

"No." He cuts his hand through the air, silencing me. I grow cold at the expression on his face. "I'd like you to leave. I don't think I need to say that you aren't welcome in this house ever again. In fact, I would very much like it if you made certain that I never see you again. Ever. If I do, the police will be involved. Do you understand me?"

I stare at him. At the sharp line of his jaw, at the glint of sunlight in his black hair, at the dark brown eyes I've spent years daydreaming about. I never really believed Max would see me. But I never believed I wouldn't be able to see him.

"Do you understand me?" he asks.

I nod, pushing the words past the pain in my throat. "I understand."

3

THE BEST THING ABOUT CHOPPING ONIONS IS THAT NO ONE asks why you're crying. You can stand in the middle of a busy kitchen with tears streaming down your cheeks and no one thinks there's anything to worry about.

My knife slices through onion number twelve, seesawing on the cutting board as it slides through the crisp flesh. The spray of onion juice mists the air and its pungent scent sets off another stream of stinging tears. My eyes burn, and the sharp tang of onion bites at my sore throat. There's a salty taste on my lips and my cheeks are wet.

I chop the onion with a quick motion of my wrist, creating perfect slender slices. The reassuring *thunk, thunk, thunk* of the knife hitting the wood sets a soothing rhythm. When I'm done I swipe the slices off the cutting board and into a large bowl.

The tiny kitchen of our two-bedroom apartment is overly warm. There's fresh bread baking in the oven, kicking out heat, and a pot of homemade stock is simmering on the stove, sending warm steam into the air, scented with thyme, oregano, and summer savory.

This kitchen is barely big enough for one person, but somehow we always manage to cram at least three people into its tiny confines.

Our apartment was built in the 1950s, post-war, when efficiency and utility were more important than beauty. There was an architectural style called brutalism that influenced the development of many, many hideously hollow-eyed, soulless buildings, where rooms were tiny, often without windows, and without light.

I think architecture reflects the state of a nation's soul and its ideals. If a country aspires to beauty and elevation of the human soul, you can see it in its monuments, its churches, its government buildings, and its schools. But if a country seeks to debase, to discourage, and to suppress; if the nation has lost the belief that humanity should always seek beauty and love, that we can aspire to more —well, you can see that in the architecture too. If you want to know the state of a country, look at what they're building.

I think Geneva has some of the most romantic architecture in the world. Just look at the beauty of the Barone Estate. The elegant stone buildings. The spires of churches. The stone chateaus lining the lake.

Ignore the post-war concrete boxes.

My mom moved us into our apartment after Emme's dad left. They had an explosive marriage. They met in Detroit at a car show, married after one week, and we'd packed up and moved to Geneva a day after the wedding. My mom claims she married Emmanuel because she was still gripped by the grief of my dad dying. She wasn't thinking straight; she only wanted to feel something besides the yawning pain of my dad's absence.

She succeeded.

My mom's marriage to Emmanuel lasted six years. It consisted of mortars and shells lobbed over a crumbling brick wall of passion. Yelling, throwing dishes, pounding against locked doors—they were all part of the great marriage war. Emme was born six months before he left, and thankfully, she doesn't remember any of it. I remember too much of it. If I'd been a genie then, I would've wished Emmanuel away.

However, when I was seventeen, he finally left in a blitzkrieg of red-faced shouting to go and raise shrimp in Vietnam, where another woman waited with open arms.

We moved to our apartment. It was dirt cheap. It was safe. It was quiet.

It was also ugly, boxy, and post-war. However, my mom had just come out of a war, so it matched her mindset. Regardless, we've been here eight years, and now the tiny square rooms, the tiny kitchen, and the windowless bedrooms aren't so dismal anymore.

The walls are painted creamy yellow to capture the slivers of light that fall through the narrow living-room windows. I sewed bright red couch and chair covers to hide the old, lumpy gray fabric Emmanuel preferred. We have tie-dye throw pillows, colorful pillar candles, and Emme's watercolors, which hang on a clothesline in the living room, are taped over the kitchen sink, and are tacked to our plywood cupboards.

It's a home.

And someday, if my mom gets her wish, we'll leave our post-war apartment and find ourselves a stone cottage in the countryside to better match the hope my mom has for our futures.

"All right," my mom says, gripping my chin in her hand and tilting my face up to the kitchen's fluorescent light. "I can't take it anymore. Why are you crying?"

I can't deny that I'm crying since tears are, at this very moment, running down my cheeks. But I can make an excuse.

"Onions." I gesture to the bowl full of the chopped remains of at least fifteen onions.

My mom huffs. It's one of her superpowers. She can load an entire conversation into a single exhale.

She shakes her head, and I realize that I was wrong. Onion tears don't disguise real tears. Or it's that you can't fool your own mother. My mom's eyes are sharp, and even when she's exhausted from pulling a double shift she's not fooled.

"Fine. It's not just the onions."

"That's what I thought." My mom nods. She looks a lot like me, except she's cut her dark, curly hair in a short bob and she has more stress lines on her forehead than any fifty-year-old deserves.

Emme looks up from the watercolor she's painting. She's at the kitchen table, a paintbrush in her hand, a purply brown glass of paint water at her elbow, and a large sheet of paper with a watercolor lake and sailboat in process. She's only eight, but she's already a better artist than me. The kid has skills. It's one of her dreams to go to the French Riviera, set up an easel, and paint to her heart's content.

It's probably spurred by my mom's ardent love of Saint-Tropez—a place she's never been, but dreams of visiting. Some day.

A glop of gray paint drips from Emme's paintbrush and splats on the sky. She ignores it. I'm sure she'll turn it into a seagull or something.

"Anna? Are you sad?" she asks, her eyes wide and worried.

Aww. My heart melts a bit and the stupid, stinging onion tears fall faster. I love my little sister too much.

"No," I say, sniffing and wiping my cheeks with the back of my hand.

When Emme wrinkles her nose and my mom huffs, I say, "Maybe a little."

"Why?" Emme asks.

That's the question, isn't it?

"Well . . ." I glance at my mom, then I decide to avoid answering by dropping a large pat of butter into a thick-bottomed pan. I rotate the pan over the blue flame of the stove, watching the butter slide across the metal. The smell of the melting butter mixes with the stock and the onions. It's buttery sweet and soothing.

My mom and sister are still waiting for my answer.

What should I tell them? The man I fell in love with at first sight three years ago hates me? No. The man whose house I clean thinks I'm a thief? No. Dorene fired me? Yeah. I'll find a new job, don't worry, we'll all be okay? Sure.

"Well, you see—"

I'm cut off by a loud knock at the front door, then the creak of its opening. We never lock our door at mealtime. Any neighbor who is hungry—be they kid, adult, or grandparent—can drop in for a plate of whatever we're cooking. Our herby stocks and caramelizing onions are famous for drawing in all sorts of interesting people.

Dorene blows into the kitchen, two bottles of burgundy in her hands. She's changed into a frilly skirt, a long top, and her long, gray-streaked hair is loose around her shoulders. She swings the bottles and then clinks them together.

"Did you tell them I fired you yet?" she asks.

"Fired!" My mom sends me a stunned look.

In response I drop the fifteen desiccated onions into the sizzling butter. They pop and crack loudly and set off a pungent sweet-onion odor.

"What's fired?" Emme asks, dipping her paintbrush into the blue paint and swirling it around.

"It means Anna doesn't work for me anymore. I canned her. Sacked her. Discharged her. Terminated! Axed! Fired!"

"Anna, why didn't you say anything?" My mom reaches across the sizzling onion pan and squeezes my shoulder. "I had no idea. You should've told me."

"Wine?" Dorene asks, holding out the bottles.

A hot flush works its way across my wet cheeks. "You know, you don't have to be so cheeky about it."

Dorene lifts her eyebrows as she takes in my onion-tear-streaked cheeks and red flush. "Well. I thought I'd shuffle us past the embarrassment and resentment phase and move us into the 'wasn't that time I sacked you so funny?' stage."

"It happened twenty minutes ago. You'd think you'd give me a minute."

"I did. I gave you twenty." She holds out the bottles again. "Take the wine."

"You literally just fired me."

"Well." She shrugs. "It had to be done."

My mom lets out a loud huff and crosses her arms

over her chest. Even though she's short, petite, and soft-faced, she's always been able to look intimidating.

"Dorene. Why did you fire my daughter?"

I grab a corkscrew from a drawer and sink it into the first bottle. Wine sounds good.

My mom glares at the corkscrew. I have to give it to her, she looks ready to take a meat cleaver to the bottle.

"Well, Janice." Dorene says, addressing my mom. "That's what you do when your employee attempts to steal a million-franc necklace from a client." She lowers her voice to a stage whisper. "Stealing is poor form."

My mom swings toward me, and I wince as I pull the cork free. The wine opens with a loud pop.

I refuse to look at my mom.

"I already told you," I say. "I didn't steal it."

"Yes. You were just holding it in your pocket for a moment. I understand," Dorene says.

The silence is a bit too awkward, so I take a moment to splash a large glug of wine into the sizzling onions. They steam and hiss as the wine soaks in. A fragrant cherry and pepper perfume rises in a cloud as I shake the pan.

"What are you making?" Dorene asks. She leans over the pan and sniffs.

"Onion soup."

"Mmm." Dorene reaches into the cupboard above her and pulls out four bowls.

My mom watches her with wide, disbelieving eyes.

"You—" My mom cuts herself off, shakes her head. "You—"

"Got fired." I nod.

My mom smacks her palm against the counter. "Anna. You couldn't have stolen that necklace!"

"I know. I didn't," I say, wanting to make it clear. My little sister is listening, her head tilted, her body still. She's painting the sail of the sailboat in a soft orange. She's pretending to concentrate, but I know she's listening to every nuance, every breath, every word.

I never want her to think less of me. Sure, Max thinks I'm a criminal. Dorene thinks I made a regrettable, stupid mistake and I'm too embarrassed to admit it. I don't know what Emme would think.

"I didn't," I say again, stirring a ladleful of stock into the caramelized onions. "I closed the box. I didn't touch it. But when Max came into the library, somehow it was in my pocket. I don't know how it got there. But I swear I never touched it."

"Of course you didn't," my mom says almost angrily. She takes the bottle of wine and fills three glasses. "Last week you took the bus back to the grocery when you realized they undercharged by two francs. Last month you called the electric company and told them they forgot to include the service fee in our bill. When you were in fifth grade and you saw your teacher marked a problem right that was wrong, you told him to reduce your grade. You don't have it in you to steal or lie! In fact, I've always found your adherence to honesty somewhat inconvenient."

"Inconvenient?" I ask, stunned.

"Sometimes it'd be nice to accept the extra two francs as a mistake gift."

"But it's not. There's no such thing as a mistake gift. It's not right—"

"See?" My mom shrugs. "You're just like your father. I won't believe it." She turns to Dorene. "You shouldn't believe it either. You shouldn't have fired her."

Dorene takes a glass of wine and swallows half in one gulp. "Sorry. It was in her pocket. Doesn't matter if she's as pure as Mother Theresa. The girl tried to steal from a client."

I dump the sizzling onions into the stock and the herby liquid bubbles at the addition. Then I turn back to my mom and Dorene squaring off in the kitchen.

I'm about to say something when Emme waves her paintbrush in the air. A few drops of blue water fling across the kitchen and land on the cracked white tiles.

"I know," she says, waving her paintbrush. "Anna, I know!"

"What?" I ask, smiling at her, because both of her dimples are in full effect and she's bouncing in her chair.

"You didn't put it in your pocket—"

"I know. I didn't," I agree. "Stealing is wrong."

She nods. She waves her paintbrush like a wand and more water drops rain onto her sheet of paper. "It got in your pocket 'cause of magic."

She smiles at me and gives one last wave of her paintbrush.

My mom and Dorene, who were engaging in a hissed back-and-forth argument, stop and stare at Emme.

My sister looks at me expectantly, waiting for me to confirm her theory. I think about the golden, breath-held feeling in the library. The strange allure of the necklace. The wish.

"Maybe it was," I say. "Maybe that's all it was. Mischievous magic."

I say this to make Emme feel better. For me, though, I don't want it to be magic. Not any kind. I took my wish back.

"When I told you to ask Max Barone on a date, I

didn't expect you to go to such lengths to catch his attention," Dorene says, taking another sip of her wine. "It reminds me of when I stole that French politician's Bugatti. I did it while he was watching. Completely naked. Now, *that* is the proper way to steal from a man. It'll get you a proposal every time."

My mom sighs.

"The man was naked?" Emme asks.

"No. I was!" Dorene lifts her glass in a toast. When she sees it's empty she frowns and pours herself another.

"Soup's ready," I say. I glance at the clock. "Bread too."

"Have I successfully ushered us into the post-awkward phase of your firing?" Dorene asks brightly.

"No," my mom says. "I oughtta light your movie collection on fire and toss it out the window."

"Yes," I say, sending my mom a quelling glance. "It's all right, Dorene. I understand. I would've done the same if I were you."

"Good. What will you do now?" Dorene asks, setting the bowls on the table.

Emme has finished her watercolor. I take it and look at the shifting blues of the water and the vivid yellow sun shining on the orange sailboat. The paper is soggy, but the picture is lovely.

"I like it," I tell her. I set it on the little makeshift drying rack at the end of the counter. Then I turn to Dorene. "I don't know what I'll do. I guess I'll eat soup, then I'll help do the dishes, then Emme and I will finish her science project, and then I'll go to bed."

Dorene lets out a disgruntled humph. "You forgot 'drink all this wine and get drunk, casting slurs at the heartless boss who fired you.'"

"Sounds good to me," my mom says, putting the

round, golden artisan loaf on the table. The bread steams and lets out the perfect fresh-baked scent.

"Or we could cuss out that nasty Maximillian Barone," Dorene says. "Did you know he threatened to call the police if I didn't remove my overinflated ego from his residence immediately? He asked if I needed him to call a tow truck to help."

I let out a snort and set my elbows on the table. Grinning, I ask, "Did you stand up for me?"

"Maybe," she says. "Still fired you though."

"What did you say?" I ask, trying to picture Max and Dorene going toe to toe.

She looks toward the ceiling, then a wide smile rolls over her face. "I said, 'You probably put the necklace in her pocket so you could play poke the piggy.'"

"You didn't," my mom says, then she gets a considering look on her face. "Maybe he did. I heard he's a womanizer."

"He is not," I say, pressing my hand to the center of my forehead.

Dorene winks, relishing her retelling. "*Then* I told him I'd cleaned his place for ten years, and if he didn't realize what a good thing he had—meaning me, naturally—he was an idiot."

"Then what?" my mom asks.

Dorene takes another sip of wine. "He said, 'Leave.' I said, 'Stop playing games and tell me you love me.' He said, 'You're deluded.' I said, 'Stop flirting.' He said, 'You're worse than the other one.' I said, 'So you *do* want to take her on a date.' That's when he offered to call the tow truck."

I let out a pained moan.

My mom pats my back. "They're hiring for the night shift at work. The stockroom. I could put in a word?"

I nod. "Sure."

"Can we talk about my science project now?" Emme asks, clearly done with the conversation.

"Of course," I say. "Did you finish your poster? And did you find the perfect potato for your battery?"

My mom's hand rubs a slow circle over my back.

"It'll be okay," she says quietly, and I know she's thinking about how tight things are for us. How tight they always are. Fourteen years after he died, my mom's still paying my dad's medical bills. Eight years after he left, she's still paying for Emmanuel's bad decisions.

I pay my part of the rent, help with utilities and groceries. If my mom didn't have my help, she and Emme wouldn't even be able to afford our little post-war box.

In the morning I'll find a new job. For all that Dorene jokes and makes light of the situation, I know she won't bring me back on. Her trust is gone. She can't afford to employ someone who might be a liability.

On the bright side, I'll be so busy scrambling I won't have a moment to think about the way Max looked at me when he told me he never wanted to see me again. I won't even have to think about what it felt like when a dream smashed into the pavement and a wish came crashing down in flames.

For years I thought I had put that hope behind me. I didn't know how painful it'd be to feel that final glimmer wink out.

After the dishes are done and Emme's science project is finished and she's sent to bed, my mom, Dorene, and I finish both bottles of wine. Then Dorene brings out the cognac and I get gloriously, wonderfully, stupidly drunk.

I decide my life is better without Max Barone. My world is better without wishes. Everything is better without the pain and hope of love.

At midnight I stumble to my tiny, windowless bedroom and fall flat on my mattress. I'm sprawled on my stomach, my arms spread wide. I'm floating, the room is spinning, and when I close my eyes, all I can see is Max looking like he wants to kiss me with rough, punishing, urgent need.

"I wish . . ." I whisper, my voice a soft slur. "I wish I never loved you. I wish I didn't know what it felt like to hurt. To want you so much."

I bury my face in my soft quilt—the one my mom made from my old T-shirts. I close my eyes again, falling into the spinning, swirling darkness of the night.

"I take it back," I say. "I take it back."

I'm not exactly sure what I'm taking back. My wish that I never loved Max, or my wish that he loved me and was my husband.

Either way. I take it back.

I fall asleep floating up to the stars on a vibrant blue river of light.

4

THE SUN STRETCHES OVER ME, LONG, GOLDEN FINGERS tugging at my eyelids and urging me to wake up. I'm pulled out of my dream in tiny increments. I'm cozy-warm, wrapped beneath a soft blanket, and settled in a feathery mattress.

Somehow, overnight, my floor-hard mattress became a soft, springy cloud. It probably has something to do with the second bottle of wine, or maybe the third glass of cognac.

Or more likely, it has to do with the dream. I have this glowy, comfortable feeling that only comes after experiencing a dream you don't want to end.

In my dream, I was in a wedding gown with a long lace train, standing at the front of an old stone cathedral. Max—a younger, happier version of him I've never met—held my hands and promised to honor me and cherish me. While rainbow light shimmered through tall stained-glass windows, and the scent of roses laced around us, we were married.

I can still smell the perfume of the white rose petals trailing down the aisle and the gardenias braided through my hair. It's light and teasing and sweet. I take a deep breath, stretch my arms and legs, and wiggle my toes. I was certain I'd have a hangover this morning, but I feel great.

A little hungry. Waffles would be nice. But overall, I'm great.

In fact, I'm feeling decidedly optimistic.

It's a new day. It's the first day of the rest of my life. It's ... a beautiful day.

A gorgeous day, in this cloudlike bed, with the subtle scent of roses and the soft cooing sound of a mourning dove, and ... everything's great.

Not even the sunlight feathering across my eyelids causes a stitch of discomfort.

Not a twinge.

Not a twitch.

Wait.

I don't have sunlight in my bedroom. I don't have a window in my bedroom. I don't have rose-scented perfume or floral-scented laundry detergent. I don't have mourning doves cooing prettily outside my nonexistent window. I definitely don't have a cloudlike bed.

I open my eyes and bolt upright.

I'm not in my bedroom.

I'm not in my bed.

I'm not in the ratty Motor City T-shirt I was wearing when I finally collapsed face-first into my mattress last night.

No. I'm in a red lace thong and a matching red lace bra. I've never seen this underwear before. In fact, it's so decidedly sexual and provocative that my nipples bead just looking down at the see-through lace. Or perhaps that's the cold air running over me now that I've flung back the thick down comforter.

I scramble back, kicking the sheets and the comforter away, and hit the wooden headboard of the large four-poster bed.

I make a squeaky, whimpery noise and frantically scan the bedroom. It's huge. The bedroom has to be larger than our entire apartment.

The room has tall ceilings with decorative plaster in the gorgeous designs you see in grand palaces and the great houses of Europe. The walls are covered in golden satin and the floor is laid with thick, creamy white rugs. On the far wall is a trio of tall, lead paned windows letting in the soft morning sunlight, with a perfect view of Geneva and the vivid blue of the lake glittering in the morning light. On the windowsill the downy gray mourning dove lets out another coo.

I grip the soft sheet—it feels like Egyptian cotton—and yank it up to cover my puckering breasts. I glance around the room, expecting someone to hop out and yell, "Boo!"

There are plenty of places to hide. The furniture in the room is all of a set. I've cleaned enough chateaus, mansions, and luxury apartments to recognize quality antiques. These are in the style of Louise XIV, made from walnut, elegantly carved with thin scrolled legs and brilliant gilding. There's the four-poster bed with a gold satin canopy, two matching chests of drawers with ornate scrollwork, a spindly-legged desk near the window, and a tall wardrobe on the wall opposite the bed. There's also a gilded mirror on the wall, large enough and angled perfectly to capture the entire bed.

My cheeks flame red as I stare at myself in that mirror. My hair is loose around my shoulders, post-sex curly and bed-messy. My skin has a rosy-pink glow and my lips are pouty full.

I drop the sheet and lift a hand to my cheek.

Is that whisker burn?

And that . . . My heart slams against my ribs...*Is that a hickey?* There's a love bite, a little purple-blue love bite, on my neck, and another on my collarbone.

"Oh no. Oh no, oh no, oh no."

My voice bounces around the room. The only response is another *coo, coo* from the mourning dove.

A slow, needlelike prickle works its way over my skin until every goose bump on my body is standing at attention.

Apparently, I got so drunk last night that I stumbled into the street, picked up a man—probably one driving a Bugatti, in honor of Dorene—and landed in his ornate Louis XIV four-poster bed.

Meanwhile, I traded my old T-shirt for sexy lingerie, got down and dirty, and then . . .

I have no idea.

I literally have no idea.

I bury my face in my hands.

Okay. There's another explanation. I also may have been kidnapped and taken to a luxurious boudoir to play out all my long-repressed sexual fantasies. That's a possibility.

I glance around the bedroom, searching for my clothes. There's nothing. The bedroom is pristine. There isn't a speck of dust, not a bit of dirt, not even a dirty sock tossed on the floor or a half-empty glass of water to be found.

The only thing out of place is a worn book on the nightstand. I glance at the hunter-green hardback and wrinkle my brow when I see the title. *David Copperfield.*

That's weird. How many people keep Dickens on their nightstand?

Suddenly my dream flashes in my mind. Max holding my hands in the stone cathedral. Me saying, "I do."

I shake my head.

Except . . .

Well. This isn't his bedroom. It's not even close.

But the view from the windows? That's oddly familiar.

I kick back the sheets and slide down the bed to the floor. The carpet sinks beneath my bare feet as I hurriedly stride across the room. I stop when I step into the bright glow of the sun falling across the carpet. It's sun-warm beneath the soles of my feet. When I look down over the expansive lawn my heart gives a slow, throbbing thud.

It can't be.

I know that lush green lawn. I know that cool, fern-lined forest that rings the edges of the grounds. I know that sloping, shaggy grass that tumbles into the smooth fall of the lake. I know every inch of this barren, austere, gray-stoned estate.

Yesterday I was told to never set foot here again.

"Oh no," I say, and this time I really mean it.

I have to get out of here. I have to leave before Max sees me. I don't know how the heck I got here, but I'm not waiting around for him to call the police.

I do not need to be arrested.

No.

No, I don't.

That won't help my future job applications *at all.*

I rush across the room and fling open the door of the wardrobe. Thank goodness—inside is a row of suits and a line of white shirts. I grab an Oxford and stuff my arms through the sleeves.

My fingers shake as I struggle to shove the buttons through the holes.

Hurry, hurry, hurry.

I can't let Max find me here.

There's no way it was him who gave me this whisker burn and that love bite, which means I brought a random man to a bedroom I've never seen before and had sexual relations with him in Max's home.

"Oh nooooo."

I take one last look around the room. My clothes aren't here. My phone isn't here. My purse? Not here. Which means I'll be walking across town barefoot unless I can convince a stranger to buy me a bus ticket.

I clench my fists and give myself a quick pep talk. All I have to do is sneak out of this bedroom, make my way downstairs without being seen, and hurry out the front door. That's all.

No problem.

There's a knock at the bedroom door. I jump then look around for a place to hide.

In the wardrobe? Under the bed? Behind the curtains?

"Madame?" a woman calls through the door.

Is she talking to me?

I stare wide-eyed at the door.

Does she already know I'm here? Did she see me come in last night?

"Madame, are you awake? I have breakfast."

I can't move. Instead I stand as still as a stone as the bedroom door slowly swings open.

I take a step back. A small, gray-haired woman dressed in a navy sheath dress, carrying a silver tray, steps into the room.

The tray holds a small silver coffee pot, a delicate china cup and saucer, a plate of fresh strawberries sprinkled with sugar, and a thick golden waffle topped with a dollop of cream. There's silverware, a creamy linen napkin, and a small silver vase with baby's breath crowding around a miniature white rose.

The scent of coffee, waffle, and strawberries and cream knocks into me.

How does this woman know I was craving waffles? How does she know this is my favorite breakfast ever?

"Who . . . who . . . ?" I've lost the ability to speak.

She doesn't even look at me. Instead she strides to the bed and slides the tray onto the nightstand.

Clearly, she thinks I'm someone else. Max's sister. Wait—he doesn't have a sister. His new girlfriend. His cousin. Or . . .

The woman looks over at me. Raises her eyebrows expectantly. "Madame?"

"I . . ." I clear my throat. Look around. She's waiting for something.

Why isn't she asking who I am? Or telling me to leave? Or threatening to call the police?

Her sensible sheath dress, her blocky black shoes, and her placid expression are making me squirm.

"I didn't mean to be here," I say, my voice scratchy and uncomfortably loud. "Please don't mention that I was here."

I nod at her, keeping my eyes wide. Slowly, I inch toward the bedroom door.

The woman—she's probably in her early sixties—gives me a concerned frown. She lifts the silver pot of coffee.

"Wouldn't you like your coffee first?" she asks. Then, before I can answer, she pours a long, steaming stream of black liquid into the delicate china cup.

I've almost made it to the door when she holds the cup out.

Maybe she's involved in how I arrived here. Maybe she drugs unsuspecting women by looking like a sweet grandmother and offering them butterscotch sweets from her purse. When they take the sweet, she drags them back to the Barone Estate so that ... um ... she can serve them a delicious breakfast.

Okay. Scratch that.

"I'm going to go," I tell her. "Thank you, though, for the breakfast. Thanks."

I give a little half-curtsy, holding the tails of the Oxford and dipping my knees. I don't know why. It feels right.

Apparently, it looks crazy, though, because the woman's frown deepens.

"Thanks," I say again. "Thank you." I keep inching toward the door.

As soon as I hit the threshold I'm going to sprint for the front door.

Almost there.

Alllllmost there.

"Didn't you sleep well, Mrs. Barone?"

I stop. Frozen at the threshold, my foot hanging in the air. I look back at the woman.

"What did you say?"

She's still holding the coffee. Still looking sensible and competent and unruffled. "Didn't you sleep well?"

I shake my head, a chill roving over my spine. "No. I mean, what did you call me?"

She frowns and sets the china cup back on the tray. It hits the saucer with a sharp clink. "Mrs. Barone, aren't you feeling well?"

That's what I thought she said.

But just to be sure, I ask, "Did you just call me Mrs. Barone?"

She takes three quick steps forward and then presses her hand to my forehead, checking my temperature. Her fingers are dry and cool against my flushed skin.

She tsks. "Over-warm. I knew it. I warned Mr. Barone —she's coming down with a chill. Do not take her out to dinner and the opera. Do not keep her out all night. But he didn't listen, did he? No, he did not. And now you don't even want your breakfast."

She humphs, and the amount of meaning in that humph nearly trumps my mom's abilities.

There's a lot to unpack in what she just said, but the most important thing is, "When you say 'Mr. Barone,' do you mean Max?"

She turns back to the tray and unfolds the napkin, snapping it in the air and then refolding it. She's grumbling something under her breath that I can't quite make out. I catch snatches of "up all night," "works too hard," and "wear themselves out."

I have a horrible suspicion. A nasty premonition. I've never seen this woman before, but she seems to know me.

I think last night I got blackout drunk and somehow I convinced Max to take me out for dinner and the opera.

I don't even like opera.

Why would I do that?

Yet here I am.

And worse, I think after that, we came back here and convinced this poor lady that we were married. Maybe she's his new housekeeper and he hired her as soon as Dorene and I were out the door. I don't know. He works fast.

Regardless. "I'm sorry for the misunderstanding. But I'm not Mrs. Barone."

She sniffs. Her lips are pinched and there's disapproval in her stern eyes. "Of course, Mrs. Barone. Whatever you say. Shall I let Mr. Barone know he should cancel the holiday he booked for your anniversary?"

Anniversary?

What, our one-day anniversary?

What the heck is she talking about?

I hold up my hands. "No. That's okay. I'm just going to . . ."—I glance at the door—"go."

I don't wait for her response. Instead I hurry into the hall. I was right. The bedroom is in one of the wings that's usually closed up and empty. The hallway is long, with wood floors and closed doors lining the long white plaster walls.

I would run.

I swear, I would sprinted down the hall, down the stairs, and out the door. But I don't.

Instead I stand stock-still, completely dazed.

Because hanging on the wall is a giant oil painting. It's one of those commissioned works people hang in their ancestral homes for generations. It's a beautiful painting.

The oil paint is glossy and rich, and an art light shines over it, illuminating every detail.

It's a painting of me.

And Max.

I'm in a wedding dress with a long lace train. Max is in a tuxedo. My hand rests in his, and on my left ring finger is a giant diamond ring.

I hold up my left hand and find something I failed to notice before.

The giant diamond wedding ring in the painting?

I'm wearing it.

5

———

Okay, there's no need to panic.

Panicking never did anyone any good.

There has to be a reasonable explanation for all this. In fact, I'm sure it's a practical joke or some twisted prank the ultra-wealthy like to play on poor, unsuspecting—

"Bonjour, Madame Barone."

I give a quick shriek and flatten myself against the cold plaster wall.

A man I've never seen before ambles down the hall, a rolling bounce in his step. He gives a quick, rusty chuckle at my reaction as I try to wrap my head around the fact that *another* person just called me Mrs. Barone.

I don't know what's going on, but I do know I'm never drinking with Dorene again. Not ever.

The man is in his mid-fifties, and has curly salt-and-pepper hair and reddened, sun-weathered cheeks. He spins a screwdriver in his hand, flipping it between his fingers.

"Too much wine, no?" he asks, laughing at me.

He reminds me of the handyman who changes the lightbulbs, unclogs the sink, and sets mouse traps in our apartment. Rough, jovial, and entirely happy to spend his day chatting while fixing all the little things that fall apart in daily life. I usually offer cookies, or a drink, or dinner, and we exchange funny stories about life.

The man tilts his ear toward me, waiting for my answer, and at the same time he sets to unscrewing the tiny brass screws in the sconce next to the wedding painting.

I stand plastered against the wall, my bare thighs pressed against the cold surface. A draft drifts down the hall and a chill works its way up my thighs and across all the bits my thong doesn't cover. Suddenly I wish I'd thrown on a pair of Max's wool trousers. If I'm going to make a run for it, I should at least have pants on.

My hands tremble as I dart my gaze first left, then right.

The handyman whistles a tuneless melody as he jiggles the brass fixture.

"Madame Barone," the woman calls from the bedroom, "will you eat breakfast?"

The man's whistle cuts off. He looks back at me, his eyes laughing.

I don't answer the woman. Instead I flee.

The man calls something after me, but I don't respond.

I sprint down the hallway, my bare feet slapping the wood floors, my shirttails flapping behind me. The hall is long, with a dozen closed doors and narrow Louis XIV tables that hold antique brass sculptures, bronze vases with fragrant roses and lilies, and gilt-framed photographs of me. And Max.

I speed past, not stopping to look. There's a quick flash of me and Max in front of the Eiffel Tower. Me and Max sipping frothy pink drinks with paper umbrellas on a beach. Me and Max hugging with full, ecstatic smiles, on the waterfront in front of the Jet D'eau.

There are more photos. Plenty more. There's a whole life in this hallway—one that *never* happened.

I hit the wide, curved stairs, grab the wood railing, and fly down them. Before me is the grand entry hall that for centuries introduced the Barones as a family of consequence. There's the massive gold and crystal chandelier, the golden sun in the towering hall of marble and stone. The furniture is different from yesterday, ornate and gilded rather than austere and unadorned. The wall color is different, light yellow instead of stark white. There are tall vases full of exotic flowers and ceramic pots with flowering trees.

Instead of an estate as empty and echoing as an ice cave in the arctic, where Max lives alone, occupying only a few rooms, this place is full of vibrant color, the perfume of flowers, and the cheer of a house that is a home.

I run across the cool marble floor toward the front door. As I pass the hall leading to the kitchen the aroma of waffles and coffee wafts toward me. A woman in a blue apron pops out of the kitchen and calls, "Madame Barone!"

I don't stop to say hello. I hit the front door, grab the handle, and yank it open.

The lake-scented summer wind hits my face and the bright sun plays white gossamer light across my eyes. I blink, shake my head, and then slam the door behind me.

There's a gardener kneeling in the dirt, a trowel in his

hand. "Madame. A question for your husband, if you would—"

"Sorry," I say, hurrying down the steps. "Sorry!"

I run.

And run.

And as I run, the dew-studded grass wet under my feet, the smell of clover rising around me, the wind ballooning Max's Oxford shirt, I admit there is a very, very strong likelihood this isn't a joke. This isn't a prank. Instead it's a wish . . .

Come true.

6

I BANG THE SIDE OF MY FIST AGAINST MY APARTMENT DOOR. I'm sweaty and exhausted from running miles around the lake and back to my neighborhood. My feet are torn up and stinging, and I'm dreading looking at the damage. For the last mile I sort of hobble-limped down the sidewalk, dragging in great gulps of air. A few people honked, two whistled, and a man offered me his coupon to a steak restaurant on the water. I imagine I look like I'm coming off a massive bender.

There's a stitch in my side that feels like the handyman shoved his screwdriver into my appendix and is still twisting the blade.

I'd double over if I thought it'd help, but I'm pretty sure that would only make the pain worse. My heart rampages around my chest like a wild animal throwing itself against the bars of its cage, and I draw in a great, gulping lungful of air.

Come on, Mom. Answer the door.

She doesn't start her shift until the afternoon. She

might be in bed still, sleeping off the wine, but the volume of my knocking should wake her.

"Mom!" I call, knocking harder.

The door swings open and I stumble forward, caught off-balance by the force of my knocking. A tall woman in a purple sweat suit catches me. She's the size of a professional bodybuilder, with muscular legs, biceps as big as my thighs, and a thick, muscular neck.

I have no idea who she is or what she's doing in my apartment.

She shoves me and I trip backward like a pinball, ricocheting from one point to another. I wince as the cuts on my feet scrape against the tile floor.

"Ow, ouch." I catch myself on the doorframe and give the woman a smile, just to show I'm not upset she shoved me like a rugby player and now she's blocking my door. "You know," I say, "I've had a rough morning. I bet you can tell. Can you please"—I wave my hand, gesturing for her to move—"let me in?"

Instead of stepping aside, the woman crosses her arms over her chest, making her muscles even more prominent. She widens her stance, blocking the door.

Okay.

Fine.

I straighten up and give her the look my mom perfected years ago. "Excuse me, I need to get into my home."

The woman is not impressed. She's not going to move. I might as well try picking up and moving the Jura Mountains.

"Your home?" she asks.

Oh. She must only know my mom. I tap my chest. "I'm Janice's daughter."

I wait, expecting the woman to move aside. She doesn't.

Instead she stares at me as the fluorescent light hums overhead and the air conditioning clicks and moans, sending out a wheezy, anemic breeze.

As she takes in my appearance—my sweat-streaked forehead, my wind-combed hair, my bare feet, and the shirt that hits above midthigh—I get the impression she's about to slam the door.

So I lift onto my tiptoes and shout, "Mom! Wake up!"

But once I'm looking over the woman's shoulder, I notice something I didn't see before. The walls of my apartment aren't bright yellow, the furniture isn't cheery red, and there aren't watercolors tacked to the walls. In fact, the apartment is gray-walled and full of barbells, free weights, and workout benches.

As I'm staring at a barbell loaded with 150 pounds of weights, the woman slams the door. The sound echoes through the hall.

I drop to the flats of my feet and stare at the block numbers painted on the door.

302. That's my apartment.

302. That's where I live.

302. That's my home.

Not anymore, a small voice whispers.

I shake my head. Then I hurry to Dorene's.

She answers right away.

"What?" she asks.

She's in a long pink terrycloth bathrobe and there's a hot mug of coffee in her hands. Her eyes are bloodshot and she looks as if she had as rough a night as I apparently did.

Still, a bit of happiness blooms in my chest at her

familiar cranky morning attitude. Dorene's never happy until she's had three cups of coffee and half a pack of cigarettes.

"Dorene," I say, taking a breath. I press a hand to my side. The stitch has lessened to a mere throb. "You wouldn't believe how happy I am to see you. I could hug you. It's crazy. When I woke up this morning—"

"Excuse me, who are you?" She gives me a disgusted once-over.

All the tumbling, happy relief slides off a cliff edge and hits the ground.

"I . . ." I blink at her. "It's me. Anna."

She lets out a long sigh as her eyes skim my torn-up feet, my bare legs, and my shirt "dress."

"Right. Well, Anna, just like I told the last solicitor, I only donate to the Society for the Better Treatment of Truffle Pigs and the Human Rights Foundation for Human-Mouse Hybrids. Are you with those groups?"

She taps her foot, glaring at me. This is the spiel she always gives people asking for donations. She makes up random charities and claims that's who she's already given all her money to. I can't believe she's using the Truffle Pig and the Human-Mouse charities on me.

"Dorene. It's me," I say slowly. Maybe she doesn't recognize me because I look like crap, or maybe she's hungover and her crankiness is impairing her vision. "It's me, Anna."

"Yeah?" she asks, her eyes brightening. "Anna?"

"Yes!" *Thank goodness.* "It's me. I think something crazy—"

She slams the door.

I hit my fist against the wood. You have to be kidding me. Dorene has no idea who I am. We've lived in this building for eight years. I've worked for her nearly every day for most of them.

If she doesn't know me, then that means . . . we never lived here? We never met?

I shake my head. I need to talk to my mom.

I knock again.

Dorene thrusts open the door. "What? I already told you—"

"Do you know Janice Benoit, in 302?"

"The wrestler?"

I shake my head. "Before her. Did Janice Benoit live in 302?"

"How should I know?" She takes a long sip of her coffee, eyeing me over the rim.

Okay. The situation is desperate. There are two options.

One: The world is suffering from a mass delusion. It happens. There are plenty of instances in history where a whole group of people firmly believed something was the truth and no number of facts, logic, or evidence could convince them otherwise. It's a scary thought. It can lead to all sorts of trouble. I've worried about this in the past. The only way I've found to combat humanity's susceptibility to this is to filter every thought through your own conscience, otherwise you're just an echo chamber for someone else's delusions.

Sadly, if the world is suffering from a mass delusion, there isn't anything I can do about it. Especially because I'm clearly hip-deep in it with them.

I'm not a fan of this option. So, moving on.

Two: That harmless little wish I made on Max's sapphire necklace came true. We're married, he loves me, and all my history for the past seven (eight?) years has been wiped out. Gone. Erased like chalk from a blackboard.

My mom, Emme, and I never moved to this apartment building. I never worked for Dorene. Maybe . . . Is my mom still married to Emmanuel?

My chest tightens at the thought. "You're sure you don't recognize me?"

Dorene takes another sip of her coffee. "Are you looking for a job? How are you at cleaning houses?"

Ha. Funny.

"It wouldn't work out," I tell her. "You'd end up firing me."

She shrugs. "You never know. It's better work than door-to-door solicitation."

"No, thank you." As much as I'd like my job back, now isn't the time. "I hate to ask this, but can I please use your phone? I have to call my mom."

Dorene taps her finger against the rim of her mug and considers my pleading expression. I know her well enough to realize she's leaning toward no. She has the same forehead wrinkle she gets right before I ask her if she'd like to watch a movie made after 2000.

"Please?" I clasp my hands in front of me, giving her my most pitiful expression. "Just a quick call. To my mom."

She slams the door.

But then, before I can turn around, she opens the door again and holds up her phone.

"On speaker," she says. "I'm not letting this phone out of my hands."

I nod. "Thank you. Thank you."

I tap in my mom's number and hit speaker. I let out a relieved breath when she answers.

"Hello?"

I lean close to the phone, ignoring Dorene's critical gaze.

"Mom. It's Anna. Where are you? Are you okay? Where's Emme?"

My mom lets out a laugh. "Good morning to you too. Nothing's changed since last night. Emme and I are still in Saint-Tropez. It's tomorrow that we're taking the day trip to Monaco. Did you forget? This afternoon she's painting the boats—"

"Wait. You're in Saint-Tropez?"

My mom and Emme are in the French Riviera? Emme's wish came true?

"Well, you and Max sent us here, didn't you? What a gift! Three months in our very own villa on the water."

Dorene snorts and then gives me a longer, more considering look.

Suddenly my limbs feel floaty and my skin has a strange, buzzy tingle. My mouth is dry when I ask my mom, "Me and Max?"

"Mm-hmm. How is my favorite son-in-law?"

"Son-in-law?" I mouth silently. *Son-in-law.*

Oh gosh.

The breakfast lady, the handyman, the gardener, the woman in the kitchen, and now . . . my mom.

It's done. I did it. There's no refuting it. Somehow I wished Max and I married.

"Anna?" my mom asks.

I shake my head. "I don't know. I don't . . ." I swallow. "How long have we been married?"

"Oh, don't worry, I haven't forgotten your anniversary. Seven years, isn't it? I know I told you I thought you were getting married too young, but you proved me wrong."

There's the sound of my sister then, calling for my mom to come help her reach a glass in the cupboard.

"I have to go," my mom says. "Give Max a hug for me."

And then she's gone.

I stare at the glowing phone screen, held aloft in Dorene's hand.

My mom and my sister are living in a villa in the French Riviera. Max married me seven years ago today. Somehow I made a wish that shifted reality. Somehow I'm married to Max Barone.

I ... I ...

I erased my past? I rewrote the world?

"You look like you just got hit by a bus," Dorene says. "Is your husband cheating on you?"

I shake my head. I don't know. I don't know anything about our marriage.

She scoffs and drops the phone into her bathrobe pocket. She looks me up and down. "Or perhaps you're cheating on him. Is that your boyfriend's shirt?"

I stare at her.

She takes another long sip of coffee, considering me. "If you want to keep a man, you should always sleep naked. If that fails, steal his car. Naked."

And there's the Dorene I know. I knew she was in there somewhere. At least that part of reality hasn't shifted.

I give her a wobbly smile and take a step back. "Thank you. I have to go. But thanks for everything you've done for me. I really mean it."

Her frown lines deepen. "It was only a phone call."

I nod and then hurry outside.

There's only one place I can go now. There's only one person left to see.

7

———

THE BARONE SHOWROOM IS IN A CLASSICALLY ELEGANT SIX-story sandstone building on the water. The French influence is obvious. The building could easily be transported to old Paris and no one would question its right to sit near the Seine.

It captures the understated elegance of the 1800s, where beauty was found in symmetry, smooth stone, and softly capped rooflines. The sandstone has a soft-buffed glow that sparkles in the late morning sunlight when the rays catch on the glittering quartz. It has the unique effect of making every person on the street turn toward it as they pass. I imagine the light urges them to wander inside the showroom to see more sparkly, beautiful things.

Or maybe that's the giant gold and crystal engagement ring above the door, or the elegantly scripted six-foot-tall gold "Barone" prominent on the façade, and glistening in the sunlight.

Either way, when people walk past, they don't turn

toward the water, where white swans swim past curving their slender necks. The people don't pause and lean over the railing to squint at the Jet D'eau spraying mist high into the air. They don't turn toward the bridges spanning the Rhone, point to the flowering gardens, or marvel at the panorama of stone city, smooth water, and low-slung mountains. No. They turn, like flowers to the sun, toward the Barone building.

It's in the jewel-cluster of showrooms situated near the Jardin Anglais, overlooking the bridges, the Jet D'eau, and the regal stone buildings on the opposite bank. Every jeweler worth its diamonds is within spitting distance of this congregation. I've never been inside Max's building, but that doesn't mean I don't know where it is.

Everyone knows.

The crystal and gold engagement ring on the building is practically a city icon. No matter the hour of the day, you can bet someone will be taking a selfie in front of the ring. Usually, it's an ecstatic couple, newly engaged. Although once I saw two chihuahuas having their doggie wedding photos taken in front of the building.

On a windless day you can hear the carrying notes of the tour guides on the boats pointing out the Barone building to all the tourists snapping photos as they glide past.

Once, years ago, when Emme was still a baby, my mom and I went for a picnic with her in the Jardin Anglais. Afterward we wandered along the bank pointing out the swans to Emme. They swam after us as we meandered along, hoping for a crumbled handful of our leftover baguette. We were about to toss a few crumbs into the sunlit water when Emme saw the giant shining ring. Her arm shot out, her chubby finger pointed at the glittering facets, and she squealed with pure baby delight. She was mesmerized by that giant ring.

I'd seen it a thousand times before, but that day I saw it differently. My mom grabbed a man in a leather jacket and sunglasses passing by, shoved her camera in his hands, and asked him to take our picture. We stood under that giant ring and the gold Barone logo, grinning like fools.

Three years later, I met Max for the first time.

But that day, when a stranger took our picture under his building, I didn't know who Max was. I only knew there was a large, beautiful jewelry store on the bank of the river, and when I stood under the ring I felt happy.

Six years ago I didn't have the money to buy the diamond, sapphire, and ruby creations displayed in the windows. Three years ago, after I met Max, it didn't feel right to wander through his store.

So today is the first time in my life that I've marched into this glamorous showroom. It's entirely the same, and infinitely different than I imagined it would be.

The best word to describe it is . . . light. Walking inside the showroom feels almost the same as walking into a diamond lit from within. Everything is full of light. The windows span the entire front wall. They're tall, beautifully arched, and fill the space with abundant light. The ceilings are a high, beautifully carved plaster, with opulent crystal chandeliers throwing strands of light through the showroom. The marble floors are pure snowflake-white and reflect light off their pristine surface.

The entire effect of the windows, the chandeliers, the tall ceilings, the white walls, and the white marble floors is that when you step into the showroom, you're in a great glittering ball of light.

It reminds me of the absence of light in my bedroom, and then the vast amount of sunlight that rained over me in Max's bed.

The air is cool, with the brisk, clean scent you'd find at the top of a snowy mountain. Classical piano music tinkles softly through the showroom, lending an aura of sophistication and elegance. There are beautifully dressed staff waiting to help. Three women who are all so neatly tucked and ironed I can't tell them apart. Two men in precisely ironed suits, both formal and wearing gold-rimmed glasses. There are plenty of customers, all being helped. Yet everyone speaks in quiet murmurs, with smoothly choreographed movements. It's as if I've entered another world where people all speak softly, drink champagne while browsing, and no one ever has a single hair out of place.

One of the neatly tucked women sails toward me when I come in. I'm certain she's about to politely ask me to leave, or forcibly shove me out the door, but instead she says, "Madame Barone, what has happened? You must see your husband, yes?" And then she ushers me through the showroom, past security, and toward the winding spiral stairs at the back.

As the cool marble soothes my raw feet, half a dozen people nod to me, lift a hand in greeting, or murmur a quick, sympathetic hello.

I may never have entered this building before today, but apparently, in this reality, I'm a frequent flier.

Max's assistant—an older woman who looks like she drinks acid for breakfast and tortures biker gangs for giggles—melts as soon as I step into his outer office.

"You poor dear," she says, thrusting Max's black overcoat at me.

"You're quite distraught!" she cries, pushing a cup of tea into my hands.

"What has happened?" she asks, holding out tissues.

"I'm here to see Max," I say hesitantly, watching the closed door of his office.

"But of course!" she says.

And that is how I find myself about to come face-to-face with the man I've been married to for seven years.

I wonder what kind of memories he has of our time together. I wonder what sort of things we've done. I wonder if he'll try to kiss me when he sees me.

I flush, then I grip the fabric of his black overcoat, pulling it tight around my dress shirt. The coat is an expensive trench that smells just like the sheets on the bed this morning—clean, with an exhilarating hint of fresh air and the subtle scent of the soap Max uses.

"Just a moment, Mrs. Barone," Max's assistant says. She punches numbers into the black desk phone and clamps the receiver to her ear. "Your wife is here to see you," she says into the phone.

I watch the door, waiting for it to swing wide-open. Waiting to see what Max will do.

Her voice lowers, then she hisses something into the phone. I glance back. A red flush is slowly crawling over her cheeks.

I can hear Max's clipped response through the door. His deep voice is brisk and impatient, and although I can't make out his words, I gather their meaning.

He doesn't want to see me.

I glance back at his assistant. Her nostrils flare and

she looks as though she's about to knock some heads together.

"Your *wife*," she says to another of Max's objections.

I frown at the gleaming walnut door barring the way to his office.

Standing on the other side of his door, only feet away from him, I wonder, *why* is he objecting?

Does he have a rule that his wife shouldn't visit him at work?

Did we fight last night?

Do we dislike each other in this life? Not married and in love, but married and in hate?

Did all the photographs in the house lie? Were our smiling faces hiding the reality that our marriage is in tatters?

Is that why he doesn't want to see me?

Along with these thoughts comes another more important thought. We aren't married! Not really! Why am I worrying about the state of a nonexistent marriage and whether or not my husband likes me?

I want to see Max—need to see Max—to figure out what is going on. I need to see him so I can ask to see the necklace again. So I can reverse what has happened.

Whether or not he likes me, loves me, or hates me, none of that makes a difference.

Yes, I know I wished that he loved me. But I took it back.

While the marriage end came through, I'm not sure the love bit did. Especially when I hear Max's grim-faced assistant hiss, "I wouldn't have come to the wedding if I'd known you'd treat her this shabbily. I have a mind to quit."

She covers the receiver with her hand, leans toward

me, and gives me a woman-to-woman "men are idiots" look. "I apologize, Mrs. Barone. He says he won't see you."

I can tell by her expression *exactly* what she thinks about that.

I give her a reassuring smile. I don't know why Max said he won't see me. It doesn't matter. I have to see him. "Please tell him it's urgent."

She nods, then her brow wrinkles as Max says something more.

"Excuse me?" she asks, and then, "Of course I did. So did all the employees. So did half this city. What of it, if you aren't going to see your own wife on your anniversary? I wouldn't have bought you those fancy silver salt and pepper shakers. I would've bought cheap pewter ones if I'd known you'd turn away your own wife. Shameful."

I bite the side of my cheek. I love how this woman is taking Max Barone to task over some salt and pepper shakers.

"He asked if I'm feeling all right," she says, rolling her eyes toward the ceiling.

"Maybe I'll just go in," I say, nodding toward the door, "since it's our anniversary."

"I'm feeling better than you will be. I put your anniversary in your calendar, didn't I? Not that I should need to," she says to Max.

She gives another snort, rolls her eyes heavenward for patience, then bangs the phone down. "He said to send you in." She casts a censorious gaze toward the tall wooden doors. "I worked for his father. Never once have I thought he's anything like the senior Barone. Not once. Until now."

"Umm . . ." I look between the door and the gray-haired woman. "Well. Thank you."

She waves and then pats down her hair, plops a pair of bifocals back on her nose, and turns back to her computer. The keys click under her punching at the keys.

I take a deep breath, step toward the doors, and slowly turn the brass handle.

8

I step carefully into Max's office, closing the heavy door behind me. The wood whispers shut over the thick burgundy-and-navy rugs. The wool is soft under my abused feet, and I nearly sigh with relief. The office isn't at all what I expect. Unlike the light-strewn showroom, Max's office is dimly lit and bathed in the dark shades of rich wood, gilt molding, and leather club chairs. It has an oppressive, intimidating vibe, overlaid with the scent of tobacco and liquor.

Never in my life would I have pictured the man who eats hazelnut ice cream by the pint, binges on British crime dramas featuring sweet granny sleuths, and falls asleep to Dickens, having such a dark and forbidding office.

Well, maybe the Dickens bit was a clue. And his estate too. The closed-up, cloth-draped rooms have the same feel as this office. But the rooms Max uses, they always have a light, soothing, happy feel. Which is why I expected his office to be the same.

A reflection of him. At least the him I always thought he was.

But let's face it, watching someone from the outside for three years doesn't exactly let you know them from the inside out. You just know them from the outside out, which isn't really knowing them at all.

I pull to a stop just on the other side of the wooden door, my feet sinking into the soft wool. A cold draft drifts over my skin and I pull the overcoat tighter. The tobacco smell percolates the air. Max doesn't smoke, but maybe in this reality he does.

While before I knew his outside, in this reality I don't know him at all.

Case in point, he's standing in the center of his office, hands clasped behind his back, shoulders stiff, muscles tight, as if he's a ferocious, hungry wolf about to lunge for the kill.

He's cast in the shadows of the room, his black hair darker than night, his expression calculating and cold, and his mouth a hard line. When I see him a shiver runs through me. This isn't the stance of a man greeting his beloved wife. This isn't the expression of a married man in love. This definitely isn't the look you give your wife on your seventh anniversary.

In fact, this is the look I expected to receive if he found me back in his house, shoving that sapphire necklace in my pocket after he warned me off. Not that I ever would have gone back. Not that I ever wanted that necklace.

Still, the fact remains. This is not a man in love. This isn't even a man in like.

Everything is dark and cold—except his eyes.

At first his expression is as forbidding as the rest of

him, but then, as he takes in my bare feet, his white shirt hitting my thighs, and his trench coat cinched around my waist, his gaze turns less icy and more . . . heated.

It's a quick change, like a block of ice unexpectedly bursting into flames. For a moment I stop breathing. It's too difficult to pull in a breath with Max watching me as if he's imagining stripping me out of his shirt, pushing me down to the thick wool carpet, and thrusting inside of me, quick and hard.

His cheeks turn red, his pupils dilate, the black swallowing the brown, and his chest expands in a rapid rise and fall. A prickly, electric awareness trips over my nerves and I'm caught in the dark deeds flashing through his eyes.

Max may dislike me in this reality, but he also wants me. He sees me and he wants me. His lips part. There's a faraway look in his eyes and a needy tension in his shoulders that makes a long, delicious clench roll through me.

The awareness—the overwhelming, burning heat— nearly scorches my lungs as I draw in a slow, shaky breath. I think I have about a fifty-fifty chance of Max and I making love in the next fifteen seconds.

I take another look at his expression. Make that ninety-ten.

I have to admit, my body sways toward him. My skin is electrified from the inside out, and all I want to do is step forward and press my lips to his.

Would he mind it?

Would he welcome it?

That's what my body is scrambling for, rushing over itself in a gurgling stream. But my heart? That's telling me none of this is real, and even if it appears that Max wants me and loves me, he doesn't really.

Still, he's the only person in this world who can help me. And by helping me, he'll help himself. In no time at all he can go back to who he was. A man who thought I was a thief and a liar. And who never, ever looked at me like he wanted to bend me over and make love to me like his life depended on it.

And that's what I want, isn't it? Max the way he was. My mom and sister back in Geneva. Dorene remembering me.

Right?

So I slowly step forward, lifting my hand toward him. I ignore the tingles running over my skin and the full ache rising in my core, and I say, "Max?"

What does he think of me? What will he say?

His attention snaps to my face and his eyes lose that soft-focus, burning heat.

Then he asks the one thing I didn't anticipate.

"Who are you?"

His voice is cold and hard-edged. I flinch and drop my hand.

Who am I?

All that tingly warmth and glowy heat vanishes in a flash of cold. I snap back to the dark interior of the office, the cold draft running over my bare skin, and the oppressive smell of tobacco.

Max doesn't recognize me?

He doesn't know me?

Every single person in this world recognizes me as Mrs. Barone.

Does that mean he's the only one who wasn't affected by this wish?

I narrow my eyes on his hard, accusing gaze. Even if he wasn't affected, he's seen me cleaning his house for the past three years. He kicked me out of his home and threatened me with the police less than twenty-four hours ago.

Who am I?

"Well?" he asks.

Yes, all that soft, spreading warmth is definitely gone. I take another step forward and tilt my chin, lifting my face to the one dim stream of sunlight that found its way through the heavily curtained window. Perhaps he can't see me well because this room is oppressively dark. Or maybe in this reality he's terribly near-sighted and he forgot his glasses today.

"You don't recognize me? You don't know me?" I ask, giving him a clear view of my face.

"Should I?"

He sounds so condescending, drawing out the word as if I'm beneath even the slightest bit of notice, that I can't help it, I lash out. "Max. You've known me for years—"

"Years? Who the hell are you?" He looms over me, trying to intimidate me with his height.

I take another step forward, clench my fists, and say what everyone else in this ridiculous reality already knows. "I'm your wife. You arrogant prick."

"My wife?"

He's derisive at first, but then just as quickly he looks as if I've knocked him over the head with one of those heavy glass paperweights on his bookshelf. He sways and glances at his desk, back to me, then back at his desk.

I don't know what's important about that wooden

monstrosity, but for some reason, on his third look, Max's face drains of color. When he turns back to look at me, he says in a ragged, shocked voice, "You're my wife."

9

———————

Max's words strike like a lightning bolt, electrifying the dark office. Energy crackles between us, a snap and a pull that flicks as vividly as the crack of static electricity.

You're my wife.

The shock of the words snaps around the office like leaves tossing in a storm. It's not a question. It's an unequivocal statement.

The look on Max's face, though, isn't one of calm acceptance. It's the exact opposite.

Sometimes when Dorene describes an angry client, she says they were "so furious their face was thunder and lightning."

I've never understood. How can someone have a face of thunder and lightning?

Well. From now on, all I need to do is picture Max in this moment.

The clenched jaw, the hard eyes, the intensity of his emotions. His hands are balled in tight fists, and he takes a swift step forward. All my instincts scream at me, to *run, run, run.*

My pulse skitters in my neck, and I stumble back.

Max reaches out, lightning-quick, and catches my wrist in his grip.

When he touches me, his eyes narrow further and his lips flatten.

"I remember now." He looks down at his fingers shackling me. "You're the woman who tried to steal my necklace."

His gaze drags over my features, catching on my mouth.

I tug at my wrist. He holds me firm. "You know, you have a bad habit of holding my wrist when I don't want you to."

At my words he blinks, shakes his head, and then his eyes widen.

"Why is it," he asks, "that suddenly I have a slew of memories telling me you *always* like it when I hold your wrists?"

Jeez.

By his gaze, I know exactly the types of moments he's talking about. A picture flashes in my mind. Me lying naked on the curving marble stairs in Max's home, the cool steps digging into my thighs and my bare back. Max holding my wrists above my head as he drives into me.

Me against the warm wood paneling of this office, my legs wrapped around Max's middle. Max gripping my wrists as he thrusts into me, the books on the bookshelf shaking as he pounds away. Me in the cushy bed I woke up in this morning. Max holding my wrists tight against the soft sheets as he kisses my clit.

He sees it too.

I'm sure he does.

The temperature of the office just went up about five thousand degrees.

He watches me, taking in my appearance. His pupils nearly swallow the dark brown of his eyes.

Apparently, our marriage is full of conjugal bliss.

When I tug at my wrist again his expression cools, and he says in a quiet voice, "Do you promise not to run?"

I lift my chin. "I came to you. What do you think?"

He considers this for a moment, sorting through whatever he knows of me and whatever he sees in his memories. After ten long seconds he drops my wrist. When he does, I take a big step back.

Outside the office the phone rings, and I hear Max's assistant speaking quietly. Inside the office the only noise is Max's measured inhale and exhale and the quiet hum of his electronics.

"All right," he says, rubbing a hand over his face. "I've figured it out. No need to worry. This is a dream." He looks back at me and flicks his hand in the air as if he's shooing me away. "I've fallen asleep at my desk and I'll wake up any minute. When that happens, I'll go back to work and you'll go back to . . ."—he waves his hand again —"stealing. Lying. Hoovering. Whatever."

I glance to the ceiling and send up a prayer for patience. And forgiveness. "It's not a dream."

"It is. Case in point, you don't look like this in real life."

I glance down at myself. There was a mirror in the bedroom this morning. I look just the same as ever. "Yes, I do. I look just like I always do."

Max shakes his head. "No. You wear thick glasses. You cover your hair with a handkerchief. I don't even know what color it is in real life. I thought it was blonde. In real life you dress in dirty jumpers and ugly jeans. You're shorter. Older. Not this alluring or—"

"Okay." I hold up my hand. "Stop."

"Why?"

"This isn't a dream. I look exactly the same as ever. You just never noticed me before."

He shakes his head. He doesn't believe me. "Not possible."

Of course it's possible. I lived it for three years.

"Look," I say, "this can't be a dream. People don't share dreams." I step forward and pinch his arm. Hard.

"Ouch!" He yanks his arm away from me.

"Exactly," I say. "This being a dream is as likely as time travel or switching bodies. Those things don't happen."

Max taps his temple with his pointer finger and says, "Then how are you in here? How do I remember you as my wife? I have years of memories that I know aren't real. They're floating in my mind, parallel to reality. It's like I have two pasts. How do you explain that?"

I shake my head. "I can't."

I don't know why everyone else only remembers me as Max's wife. I don't know why I don't remember us married. I don't know why Max remembers both. I can't explain it.

But, "I know why it happened."

Max tilts his head, leaning closer. "What do you mean, you know why this happened?"

I glance around the oppressive office, at the thin stream of light filtering through the heavy curtains, at the thick wood desk, at the dark colors and weighted atmosphere.

"I wished it."

Max gives me a flat stare. "You wished it."

I nod slowly. "The sapphire necklace—"

"The necklace you tried to steal."

"—had a letter," I say, ignoring his interruption. "Which explained that if you make a wish, the necklace will make it come true."

"That's just a *story*," Max says. "A story my ancestor came up with to explain why his wife didn't get her head chopped off in the French Revolution. She wished it to stay on her shoulders. It's not real."

"Then how do you explain this?" I gesture between us. "And that?" I gesture at his closed office door, where outside I can hear his assistant on the telephone.

Max turns and stalks to the window. He shoves aside the curtain and stares over the water. A tour boat glides past, its reflection blurry in the water.

I walk across the thick carpet until I'm standing in the sunlight next to Max. The tour boat gives me an idea.

"What if," I ask, "the necklace doesn't so much create a new reality? What if when you make a wish, it flips you into your reflection?" I point out the window. "One reality is the boat, the other is its reflection. Right now, we're in the reflection."

"You're deluded," he says. "You. Me. Agathe. It's a pandemic of delusion."

I hold up my hand. "Plus all your staff downstairs, your housekeeper, your handyman, your cook, your gardener—"

"Handyman? Cook?" Max frowns. "What housekeeper?"

"You don't know her?"

Max pinches the bridge of his nose. "Madame . . .

Blinken . . . and Gerard . . ." He glares at me. "Wait a minute. You said you made a wish."

I nod. I guess I didn't think ahead when I admitted that. Of course he'll want to know what my wish was.

"What exactly did you wish?" His eyelashes lower again, and he's suffused with a look of deep concentration. When he looks at me again he says, "What did you wish . . . Anna?"

I stare at Max. "You know my name."

"Anna Madeleine Benoit Barone." My name rolls off his tongue, rough and melodic. "Tell me what you wished."

He knows. He already knows. He has to.

The way he's watching me makes me feel as if his hand has encircled my wrist again and he's pulled me close against him. I can feel the heat of him, his inhales and exhales, the steady beat of his pulse.

I turn my face to the sun, stare at the wavy, distorted reflection of the tour boat rippling in the blue waves, and say, "I wished we were married."

10

———————

MAX SHIFTS HIS VANQUISH INTO FOURTH GEAR, SLINGING us down the road, speeding us along the lake toward his estate. We're low to the road, hugging the curves, drifting in an "S" as the road winds through the countryside.

The purring roar of the V12 fills the interior as thickly as the tension riding off Max. The interior is close, tight, intimate. The leather seat is impossibly soft and it vibrates warmly beneath my bare legs. I'm held tight against the seat as Max shifts, maneuvering the curves of the lake. The car feels as if it's being pulled by a locomotive engine. Its power rumbles through the interior, and I can't help but watch Max grip the shifter as he guides the car through traffic and into the wide-open country.

The air conditioning fans the scents of fresh cut grass and newly leafed spring forests. The flickering of shade and leaves flashes over the windshield in sparks of sun and dark. It paints my bare legs, and I watch Max's hand on the shifter. His grip is firm and reminds me of the way he holds my wrist, both in real life and in my imagination.

"Why married?" he asks, looking over at me.

I glance back at him, but he's staring straight ahead, guiding the car through a series of curves following the sinuous shore of Lake Geneva.

When I admitted my wish back at the office he didn't say anything. Instead he grabbed my hand and dragged me out of there. His assistant called after us, but he only said, "I'm taking the day off." He covered his surprise when several people greeted me as Mrs. Barone on our way to his car. The only way I knew it disturbed him was in the way his hand tightened on mine.

But still he didn't ask questions, he just tugged me to his car, opened the door, said, "Get in," and then sped out of the parking garage.

He flicks on his turn signal and pulls onto his estate's long drive. The house looms ahead, a tall, barren, shadowed behemoth.

"Anna?" He finally glances over at me. When he tilts his head his dark hair falls over his eye, hiding his gaze.

I sigh and stare out the window at the estate drawing closer. I didn't notice it when I ran out this morning, but there are quite a few things different about the exterior. The stone has been scrubbed clean, and now, instead of a dull, somber appearance, the façade glistens in the sun. Before the windows seemed to cast a lonely gaze over the water; now they sparkle merrily, reflecting the sky.

Yesterday the grounds were varying shades of green— thick ivy, lush grass, nodding ferns at the edge of the evergreen forest—but now islands of bright color are strung around the house like pearls on a string. A bed of pink flax. An island of sunny orange marigolds. A river of purple and red tulips stretching toward the sun. An ocean of daffodils waving beneath the front walls. It's a rainbow of flowers, capturing every color God made.

"Wow," I whisper.

Max looks forward again, back at the road and the estate. He lets out a surprised exhale. The car slows as he lifts his foot, and the engine noise settles into a soft purr.

"It almost looks like a home," he says, his mouth twisting.

"It is a home. You live there," I say, although I know what he means. A house isn't always a home. Sometimes it's just the place you stay until you're strong enough to leave.

Max gives me a wry look. "Yes. I live there." Then he asks, "Why marriage, Anna?"

The limestone gravel crunches under the tires and I squirm in my seat. My skin is warm. There's a cavernous emptiness in my center and an embarrassed niggling in my chest begging me not to admit the truth.

I can't tell him.

Hi, Max. I fell in love with you three years ago. You probably don't remember it, but it was life-changing for me. I made the wish because I'm an idiot and for some reason I thought we were meant to be together.

I know what his reaction would be. Disbelief. Disgust. Anger. Antipathy. Take your pick. One or all of the above. The reaction that won't occur is "I love you too."

So, instead of telling the truth, I give a reflection of the truth. "I wanted to know what it was like."

He looks over at me quickly. "What *what* was like?"

In his question is the answer.

As he pulls the car to a stop, parking it in front of the door, I say, "This." I gesture at the glittering estate, at the interior of the car, at Max. "I've been cleaning your house for three years. I've been looking from the outside in. I wanted to know what being married to you was like."

The words beat their wings against the walls of my chest. A partial truth. A distortion of what's real.

He cuts the engine and the car descends into a heavy silence. Max stares straight ahead, taking in the new shine on the gray stone and the patchwork of colorful flowers dotting the lawn.

"You made a wish on a necklace to see what it was like to live in my house instead of clean it? You saw me, thought I had a nice place, and decided you wanted it? And what the hell, while you were at it, you'd take me too?" His jaw clenches and his hands tighten on the steering wheel.

My stomach drops at his accusation. It doesn't feel right, having him think that of me. But what's worse: Max thinking I wanted a Cinderella moment, or Max knowing I fell in love with him years ago and never quite got over it?

The first, he'll think I'm greedy and perhaps dislike me.

The second, he'll think I'm naïve and he'll pity me.

So instead of denying his accusation, I lift a shoulder in a careful shrug.

"Well," he says, "I'm sorry to be the one to disillusion you, but the saying is true. Not all that glitters is gold."

At that he swings open his door and says, "Let's go."

11

THE DOOR TO THE SAFE IS WIDE-OPEN, THE OIL PAINTING ON the wall swung aside. The library is quiet, with the scent of books and leather shifting between us. Nothing in the library has changed. It's the same as it was yesterday, and likely the same as it was decades ago.

Max and I stand facing each other behind the wooden desk. The metal safe is built into the wall and its mouth gapes wide. There are other items inside. Documents. Jewelry. A few stacks of crisp bills in multiple denominations and currencies.

Max holds the sapphire necklace in his hand. The mid-morning sunlight stretches across the library and hits the stones so they shine like a cascading waterfall.

"Do it," Max says. "Reverse your wish."

I tilt my head, stare up into his eyes. I wonder what he remembers about the past seven years. I wonder if he'll remember any of it when we go back to the way we were.

It doesn't matter. It's not real.

I lift my hand and press my fingers into the cool

surface of the sapphires. "I wish," I say, my voice shaking, "Max and I weren't married."

I stare at Max, and he stares back at me. We look into each other's eyes, breath held, waiting.

After ten seconds of nothing, Max lets out a long exhale. "Try again."

Okay. I bounce on my toes. I roll my shoulders. I drag in a breath and—

"What are you doing?"

"Getting into the moment. Building up to it. Letting the emotion rise."

He gives me a flat look. "No buildup is necessary. Just do it."

I raise my eyebrows. "I pity any women who goes to bed with you. *Just do it. No build up necessary.*"

Max's shoulders stiffen. "I've never had any complaints."

Ha.

"Just because no one complains doesn't mean you're doing it right. Maybe they felt sorry for you. Or maybe you were too arrogant to notice no buildup left all the ladies unsatisfied."

Max leans toward me. The air crackles and his lips nearly touch mine. "Do you remember our fake marriage?"

I swallow, disconcerted by the rough edge to his voice. "No, but—"

"I remember it. There were *no* complaints."

My mouth tingles as I lean closer. I can feel the heat of him on my lips. I can almost taste him. "There's only one problem with your claim."

"What?" he asks.

I lean back, pulling my mouth away. "It was all fake.

Your legendary prowess is all in your head." I thrust my hand onto the necklace. "I wish that everything was back to normal. I wish I never married Max. I wish Max never married me. I wish Max never saw me. I wish . . ." I pause, then I add, just to be sure, "I wish Max didn't love me."

I close my eyes and will the wish to work. *Come on. Come on.*

When I open my eyes again Max is staring at me, a strange look on his face.

"What? Did it work? Are we unmarried?"

He shakes his head. "I don't love you."

Oh.

"Good," I say, my voice stupidly high-pitched. "I was just being careful. You never know. I'm very lovable."

He shakes his head. "No."

"I am though. My mom loves me."

"Poor judgment."

"My sister."

"Poor judgment runs in the family."

I scoff. "Dorene loves me."

Max shoots me an incredulous glance. "The woman who fired you in my foyer? She loves you?"

"Yes?"

Okay, I can see how I'm not making a very good case. But at least he's distracted from my wish. I wave my hand. "It doesn't matter. Regardless, last time I made a wish, reality didn't flip until the next morning."

Max nods. "Fine." He holds the necklace up to the light, letting the sunlight stream through the gems. "Just in case, I'm going to wish too."

He glances at me and I give an encouraging smile.

"Good idea."

He closes his eyes. His shoulders relax and he lets out a long breath.

I study the line of his jaw, the little bump on the bridge of his nose, the deep richness of his skin, the sweeping of his eyelashes against his cheeks. His face is just as hard and austere as it was years ago, but it's more familiar now. I have the strongest urge to reach out and brush my fingers along his jaw and smooth my hands over his cheeks. I'd like to touch his lower lip and see if his mouth is as hard as it looks, or if it's actually soft and gentle.

He grips the necklace tightly, and as he's backlit by sunlight, standing with his eyes closed, surrounded by hundreds of books, in the library I've cleaned for years, he says with fervent conviction, "I wish I didn't forget this necklace on my desk yesterday morning. I wish Anna and I never spoke. I wish we never married. I wish we never met."

His words drop from his lips and fall like boulders from a great height, crashing to the floor of the canyon where I'm lying, crushed, beneath his wish.

12

I SIT ACROSS FROM MAX AT THE LONG, FORMAL DINING-
room table. The candlelight casts a warm yellow glow over
the room, glinting off the gleaming wood and reflecting off
the burgundy walls. The chandelier throws sparks of light
off the fine china, the silver, and the crystal wineglasses.
The antique cut of the crystal glasses throws prisms of
light around the room. It's as if we're inside a jewelry box
surrounded by diamonds and rubies and flickering gold.

This room didn't exist yesterday. Well, it did, but
yesterday the walls were a dirty beige and the table and
chairs were covered by a long canvas cloth. It had the air
of a dusty, closed-up attic even though I swept away the
dust every week. But now the room glitters and shines
and romances.

Which is entirely the point.

It's our anniversary dinner. A night of *romance*.

Max closed himself in his office for the day while I
wandered the library, explored the vastly altered interior

of the chateau, and spent entirely too long in the biggest walk-in closet I've ever seen.

When Max came out, hungry, growly, with a hunted expression in his eyes, he was accosted by Madame Blinken. She informed him dinner would be ready in thirty minutes, per his request.

"I don't want dinner," he'd snapped.

"You don't want to celebrate your beloved wife? You don't want the dinner we have spent weeks preparing?" she'd asked, puffing out her chest like a general preparing for battle.

I'd glided around the corner in my new silver silk dress. It hit mid-thigh and was cut simply, with narrow spaghetti straps. I'd settled on it because most of the other clothes in my closet were elaborate, brightly colored, or drew way too much attention to my assets. In fact, I never knew my breasts were so round until I tried on some of the dresses with their built-in bustiers. I never knew my legs were so long until I pulled on a few of the short skirts. It was a revelation. But in the end, instead of pulling on one of the alluring, low-cut dresses, I settled on the simple, classic, unadorned silk.

When Max saw me, his eyelids drooped and his mouth softened. A small puff of air left him as if my appearance had kicked him in the gut. Then his hunted look returned even stronger. I ignored it.

"It's just dinner. You have to eat," I'd whispered.

I'm not hungry, his expression said.

I raised my eyebrows. *I didn't say you were hungry.*

He pointedly avoided looking below my neck.

"Fine," he'd said.

So now we're seated in a jewelry box with candlelight,

wine, and the soft sounds of classic French jazz drifting across the dining room.

It's a seduction scene if I've ever seen one.

The table is set with the most delicious dishes.

Terrine de Foie Gras, marinated in sweet sauternes and freshly grated black truffle. The savory, meaty scent is overlaid with the earthy, mouthwatering allure found in every bite of truffle.

Grilled stuffed oysters, full of lemon and fennel, of course—because there can't be seduction without the flesh of oysters coyly winking from their shells.

Filet Mignon, tender and luxurious, perfectly cooked so that it melts on your tongue.

Souffle Au Fromage, a cheese soufflé so light and airy that when you wrap your lips around the fork, you can't help but smile at the blend of parmesan and gruyere dancing with nutmeg.

There are also platters of honey-glazed carrots, potatoes dauphinoise thick with cream, gruyere, and a hint of thyme, and a loaf of herby bread with pats of hand-churned herb butter shaped like hearts.

I get a lick of satisfaction when I smear the butter across my crusty piece of bread, obliterating the heart.

I glance at Max, feeling mellow from the food and the wine. We haven't spoken for the past fifteen minutes. The chef and Madame Blinken set the table, delivered the dishes, and then disappeared back toward the kitchen. Since they left, the only noises have been our silverware scraping against the plates, an awkwardly cleared throat, and the soft crooning of the jazz music.

"Do you mind if I ask you a question?" I ask.

"Yes," Max says, spearing a cut of filet mignon with his fork.

I take a bite of the bread, savoring the rosemary and thyme flavor of the butter. "I have to get it off my chest."

The candlelight glints off his fork as he takes another bite of his steak. "You don't, actually. You could leave it there." He looks up at me. "I've left things on my chest for years."

I drop my bread to my plate and wipe my hands on my cloth napkin. "Doesn't it get heavy?"

"Not really." He reaches for his wineglass and runs his hand over the stem.

I stare at his long fingers, at the half-moons of his fingernails and the gold signet ring on his right hand. I find I'm becoming oddly obsessed with his hands. Or, more likely, I can't stop replaying the scenes I saw in my mind, when his hands were tracing over my bare skin or gripping my thighs or holding my wrists above my head. His hands did all sorts of wonderfully creative things.

I have to ask.

"I'm going to ask."

"I wish you wouldn't."

"How much do you remember of our marriage? How well do you like me? Do we get along? How did we meet?"

He lifts his wineglass, casually holding it in front of him. The ruby liquid sloshes around the glass as he slowly circles the stem in his hands. "You don't want to know."

I lean forward. "I really do."

He sets his wineglass back on the table without taking a sip. "I called my best friend today."

I lean back, settling onto the cushioned red velvet. My dress slips over my thighs as I shift, the silk fabric cool. It feels similar to a soft exhale rushing over my skin, and I shiver in response.

"Do you know what she said?" Max asks, watching me.

"No."

"She said, 'Max who?'" He gives me a hard-eyed look. "A few months ago I asked her to marry me. I've loved her for years. Today she had no idea who I was. I apologized for calling. Told her I'd made a mistake. Your wish did that."

He's talking about Fiona Abry. There's a pinching in my chest and a pressure at the backs of my eyes. I suppose I didn't realize how badly Max was still hung up on Fiona.

"You still love her? Even though she married someone else?" I ask, looking down at the remnants of my filet and the dark, peppery wine reduction.

"I'll always love her," he says. "That isn't a question. Even if I live in this . . . world." He gestures around the room set for seduction. It seems garish now instead of romantic.

"Even if she doesn't love you?" I ask, curious and surprised he's actually talking to me. But more, I want to know, is Max like me? Loving someone who doesn't love him back.

"She does love me," he says. Then, considering the plate of oysters resting on slowly melting ice, he adds, "Or she did."

Apparently, he's not like me at all. He loves Fiona, and she loves him.

I frown. "If she loved you, why did she turn you down? Why would anyone turn you down?"

He grins at me—a smile tinged with irony. "Because we didn't have that magic spark. Or, I suppose, a magic necklace."

"It would've been handy," I tell him, wishing I hadn't revealed I didn't think anyone could turn him down. "Just think, you had the means all along. Where your charm failed, the necklace would've been your ace in the hole."

He scoffs and then finally lifts his glass and takes a long sip of wine. I follow suit, lifting my glass in a toast and then drinking in the sweet cherry notes and the peppery spice that blends so well with the rich anniversary meal.

"We met at the art museum," he says, studying my expression.

I sit straight. "We did?"

He nods, his eyes cutting over my face and along the line of my shoulders. "You were there to see a photography exhibit. I don't know which one—you didn't make it past the front door. I saw you and . . ." He shakes his head, and a smile touches the edge of his lips. "I asked you to come to Paris with me to tour all the art museums there."

I widen my eyes. "And I said yes?"

He shrugs. "I was very convincing."

Oh my gosh. Max fell in love with me at first sight. In this world, the first time Max saw me, he fell in love. I wonder if I felt the same.

"And then what?"

"And then we saw exactly zero museums," he says, his gaze daring me to contradict.

I laugh, and Max gives me a surprised look. "You're different from the woman I have in here." He taps his forehead meaningfully. "I don't like having two realities floating in my head. I especially don't like having feelings that aren't mine."

From the expression on his face, I know he means the

tight, luminescent pull arching between us. He's never felt that before, and now that he does, he doesn't like it.

"Don't worry," I tell him, pulling a small ramekin of crème brulée from the center of the table. "It'll all be gone tomorrow. You can go back to disliking me—or better yet, never having to see me again."

Then I take my dessert spoon and crack the caramelized sugar coating the crème brulée, breaking the perfect shell.

13

———

Well, there's a word for optimistic naivety, and that word is tomorrow.

Tomorrow everything will be better.

Tomorrow the sun will come out.

Tomorrow everything will be back to rights.

Tomorrow didn't come. Tomorrow never comes.

"You're still here," Max says, standing at the foot of the four-poster bed.

I squint up at him. My eyes are gritty, my head is muzzy, and the weak gray light of dawn is barely seeping through the curtains. I was half-in, half-out of a dream about eating chocolate mousse in bed while Max teasingly kissed his way up my bare legs when his voice pulled me fully awake.

I blink at him, bringing him into focus. He's outlined by the morning light and backlit with a muted silver glow.

I push up on my elbows and the warm sheets slide

free, letting the cool air hit my bare shoulders. I pull myself into wakefulness.

"We're still married?" I ask, my voice raspy and low.

Max quirks an eyebrow at the husky sound, a slight smile slipping free.

He looks oddly refreshed and well-rested. He has an almost eager, happy-to-greet-the-day expression on his face. It's a stark contrast to his mood last night when he said a curt "good night" and left me alone with my crème brulée.

"Still married." The corner of his mouth lifts in a half-smile. He puts his hands in his pockets, rocking back on his heels.

"Why are you so happy then?" I ask, sitting up in bed. The sheets fall to my thighs as I scoot back against the wooden headboard. I'm in a light pink silk nightie. It had the most coverage of all my pajamas, but it still drops in a low vee at my breasts.

It's embarrassing. While Max is in jeans and a navy shirt, freshly shaved and showered, I'm in a tiny nightie, with bed hair and probably a pillow wrinkle on my cheek.

He smiles when I reach up and quickly braid my curls into submission.

"You look well-rested," I say, smoothing a stray curl behind my ear.

He nods. "It's because I haven't gone to bed."

When he says "bed" in his deep, gravelly voice, my stomach gives a little fluttery jump and I taste the lingering smoothness of chocolate mousse.

"Do you mind?" he asks, gesturing to the mattress.

Do I mind? What? If he joins me in bed?

"If I sit," he says, waiting for my answer.

"Oh. No. Of course." I scoot over, tugging the warm sheets with me.

Max sits on the edge of the mattress, leaning toward me with an enthusiastic light in his eyes. "I spent the night thinking."

"Okay?"

Max is a thinker. He's always thinking. I already know this about him. It's why he leaves stacks of books in nearly every room. He reads at least a dozen books at once—classics, nonfiction, economics, history. It's why he works all hours and then watches crime dramas to puzzle through. It's why he has a dozen projects spread across his desk, all going at once. His mind never rests. He's a thinker.

"It was driving me mad, one of part of me disliking you and the other part liking you too much. One part wanting you gone and the other part wanting you to never leave. One part knowing everything about you and the other knowing nothing at all. Do you understand?"

He studies my face, and I feel almost naked with the way he's gazing at me. The lace at the edge of my silk nightgown scratches my skin, and I tug at the material, lifting it higher on my breast.

He's so close, only two feet away, and I can smell the cool, clean scent of the soap he used in the shower. His black hair is still damp and the ends curl at the nape of his neck.

"You're conflicted," I say, and he nods.

"Exactly. I was conflicted. *Exactly*. The part of me that remembers the past seven years with you was angry at how shabbily I was treating you. And the part of me that knows it wasn't real was angry at myself for feeling how I feel. But I've never been one to stay angry for long, because it never does any good. Anger isn't logical and it's rarely useful unless it spurs action. But once you've acted, then you have to dismiss it. So,"—he runs a hand through his hair, brushing it back from his forehead—"I have all these feelings, all these memories, and I want to know how much is real."

"How much of your memories are real?"

He traces his finger over the tiny stitches on the fold of the cream-colored sheet. "I mean, I know the woman in my mind. I want to know how much of her is real."

He glances back at me, and a low heat curls around me and then pulses at the intimacy in his eyes. The sky has transitioned from pale gray to soft gold, and the light catches the small gold flecks in the dark brown of his irises.

"For instance," he asks, "do you really like to cook? And when you cook, do you always listen to the Supremes? And do you always sing off-key?"

I grin at his unexpected question, my bright smile clashing with the pulsing heat pooling in my middle. "I love to cook," I say, "and I love to listen to Motown. The Supremes are my favorite. But I also love the Temptations and the Four Tops and lots more." I pause and then lift my chin. "But trust me, I never sing out of key."

An excited energy crackles around him. "I don't believe you. Sing for me."

"No! You'll have to trust me. I have a perfect ear."

He shakes his head but doesn't press further. "What's your favorite meal to cook? I'm asking because . . ." He taps his temple with his pointer finger.

I think about all the dishes I love to make and all the things I love to eat.

"I cook lots," I say. "I love French onion soup with

freshly made bread and gruyere. Sometimes I use wine in the stock, and sometimes I use whiskey."

He nods. It's clear he remembers tasting both. "Go on. What else?"

I smile, a warmth building in me. "Sometimes I make Coq au Vin because I love the smell of chicken braised in wine sauce and bacon and those beautiful pearl onions. It's so decadent, yet homey and cozy-warm. It's perfect for a fall day."

"Yes," Max says, his eyes becoming more intent on my face. "You always cook it on the first day of autumn because you say its mood matches the yellows and golds of the trees reflecting on the lake."

I smile at Max. "How did you know that?"

"Because you told me. It's real then?"

I nod. "My dad made the tradition back when I was a kid. His was a simple roast chicken guy. I modified it and kept it going."

Max stills, tilting his head. A lock of hair falls over his brow. "Your dad died when you were a kid."

I clutch the edge of the sheet in my hand. "Yes. When I was eleven."

Max watches me, a somber expression on his face. "You miss him."

"Sometimes. Other times I miss the future I thought could've happened. Does that make sense?"

"It makes perfect sense." Max scoots closer on the bed and leans against the headboard, folding one knee up. His hand rests on the comforter between us.

I look down at his open palm and the soft curve of his fingers.

We're separated by six inches. The warm bubble of the bed, the soft sheets and the cushy down comforter, folds around us. Outside the sun has peaked over the lake and the wood thrush are calling out their morning song. Their notes fill the silence.

"You're from Detroit," Max says, and I nod even though he doesn't look at me. He continues, his face turned toward the curtained window and the stream of light warming the room. "Your mom lives in the city, and you have a little sister named Emme. You like people and you're always doing things for others. You love art museums for people-watching more than the art. You like exploring medieval villages and getting lost on purpose. You'll read anything you can get your hands on, and you'll try anything once. You're honest to a fault. You love Paris, wine from small, unknown chateaus, and chocolate. How am I doing?"

He looks toward me then, and the bed shifts at his movement, tilting me closer to him. The warmth of the bed and the coolness of the air brushing over my skin creates a peculiar sensation.

I nod. "That's all true, except . . ."

"What?"

"I've never been to Paris."

Max's shoulders fall and he leans back again into the bed frame, dropping his head against the wood. He stares up at the ceiling. His neck is long and lean, and his Adam's apple bobs as he swallows.

"Right," he says. "I took you there for the first time."

He took me there seven years ago, and apparently, we liked it so much we got married right away.

"You didn't try to steal the necklace, did you?"

I look over at Max, but he's still staring at the ceiling.

"I only ask because in my memories of you, you're honest to an appalling degree."

I smile. "That's what my mom says too."

He turns toward me when he hears the laughter in my voice.

"She says I have an inconvenient penchant for honesty."

He grins at my admission, a quick flash of white teeth. I'm more awake now. In fact, my whole body has woken up, and I'm glowy and warm and tingly like the vibrant, shimmery reflection of the sunrise on the golden lake.

"I know exactly what she means," Max says.

We lean toward each other—a smile in his eyes; a smile on my lips.

"I didn't steal it," I say, just to make sure he knows. "I don't know how the box opened, and I don't know how it ended up in my pocket."

"I believe you."

His warm breath, tinged with mint, tickles my upper lip. I blink. How did we get this close? An inch more and our lips will be touching. Neither of us lean back. Neither of us move.

"I did make the wish though," I say. "I'm sorry. I truly am. I took it back right away. Clearly, that didn't work."

Max reaches up, takes a strand of my hair, and tucks it behind my ear. His fingers drift over the sensitive shell of my ear and then down along my jaw.

"We'll figure it out," he says, his fingers resting on my cheek.

I turn my face into his hand until my lips connect with the tips of his fingers.

He draws in a breath, his chest expanding. *"Anna."*

I look up. His eyes are closed.

"What?"

He takes another pained breath. "I'm trying very hard not to find out if all my memories are true."

The corners of my mouth tug down. "What do you mean—?"

He clears his throat.

I notice the stiffness of his shoulders; the tightness in his muscles. I look down, noticing the hard line of him visible through his jeans.

"Oh. Ohhhh."

He opens his eyes and looks directly at me. "Exactly."

My heart does a slow flip in my chest and then a rapid beat, responding to the heat in his eyes.

My skin is hot, flushed, and I have the sudden wild urge to lift my nightie free and let Max recreate anything he wants. *Everything he wants.*

"I never wanted passion," he says, pulling his hand from my cheek. "I never wanted that kind of relationship."

I try to catch up with what he's saying, but it's like trying to do long division after drinking a bottle of wine.

"The kind in my memory," he clarifies. "I've always said passion isn't what I'm looking for. But apparently, it's what we have. Had. However you want to say it."

We have a lot of sex. That's what Max is saying. He remembers us having lots and lots of sex. Very good sex, if the tautness of his shoulders is anything to go by.

"Come to Paris with me."

I shake my head, snapped out of my chocolate-mousse, lust-filled imaginings. "Sorry. What?"

Is he asking me to Paris to recreate our first week together? Does he want a no-museum, sex-filled weeklong wrist-bound orgy trip?

He smiles, and that eager, happy-the-day-has-begun

look is back in place. "Like I said, I spent the night thinking. It appears I know you. It seems I like you. I think I can trust you." He lifts a shoulder in a small shrug. "We'll figure this out together. You made a mistake when you made that wish. Neither of us want this." He gestures between us. "I have an idea to fix it. All we have to do is fly to Paris."

"Paris?"

He smiles. "Paris."

I say yes. He's very convincing.

14

"CAN I ASK YOU A QUESTION?"

I study Max leaning back in the white leather club chair across from me. His ankles are crossed, he's absently twisting the gold signet ring on his finger, and until I spoke, he was contemplating the snowy white clouds outside the jet window.

We're in the air, soaring above the cloud line. Beneath us is a rolling white expanse of cumulus clouds intermittently broken with quick peeks at green fields stitched up with gray roads and patchwork towns.

I've never flown in a private jet before. Max has a number for his business, with three pilots on full-time standby. The larger jets fly between Geneva and New York or Singapore. The smaller, like this one, with only room for six passengers, flies shorter distances.

A flight attendant named Francesca warmly welcomed us on board. There's a bouquet of red roses on the varnished wood table next to the divan, and the floral scent fills the interior. Wine, cheese, crackers, and grapes are laid out. Francesca and both pilots recognized me, giving a cheery "hello" and "happy anniversary" and "how's your family?"

Max lifted an eyebrow at their familiarity, and I knew he was thinking, *This is mad.* It's the same thing he was thinking when Madame Blinken served us buckwheat crepes with cinnamon apples this morning and warned Max not to forget to take me by the flower market—the Marché aux Fleurs—to buy me freesias for our seventh anniversary.

He's taking it in stride though. For as many times as his eyes widen, the corner of his mouth twitches, or I see him thinking *how?* he rolls with it. He's a lot like this jet. Every time we hit a patch of turbulence it jostles, bumps, and then adjusts and smooths out. We've passed through a bit of weather, a few low-pressure areas, but all the same, the jet remains steady.

I've always admired that about Max. Over the years, when I've heard him on business calls, even in heated negotiations, he's always remained steady and calm. When someone attacks him or goes in a direction meant to trip him up, he always responds with logic and reasoning. Sometimes, if the situation warrants it, he shuts the caller down, but that's only after diplomacy fails.

Come to think of it, I'd never seen Max truly angry until he thought I was trying to steal the necklace. All in all, he's steady and solid, not fire and passion. At least that's what he strives for.

If what he says is true—that he doesn't want passion or romance—I might be the only person he's ever felt any passionate emotion for. Good or bad.

So I have a question for him.

"A question?" Max asks, and in his small smile I know he's thinking of last night, when he told me he'd rather I didn't ask him any questions at all. "Go ahead."

I glance around the cabin. The pilots are behind a closed door. Francesca is in the galley putting together a dessert plate with fresh berries, chocolate mousse, and whipped cream. She has a coffee tray on the wood counter, with a steaming silver pot of fresh coffee, a pitcher of cream, and a bowl of raw sugar cubes.

The engine noise gives a low-level hum, and across from the cushioned divan the news plays at a low volume. We're as private as can be expected. Still, I lean closer to Max, setting my hands on the smooth surface of the varnished wood table. The large round window lets in a spray of bright sunlight. This high in the sky, past the clouds, the sun is a brilliant white and the windows pull it in so that the light bounces off the white walls.

"This is personal," I say, giving fair warning. I keep my voice low.

Max leans forward, meeting me over our glasses of wine and plates of half-eaten brie and red grapes. "I wouldn't expect anything less."

I'm surprised at the teasing light in his eyes. I shift in my leather seat and clear my throat, giving myself a moment to tamp down the desire to clasp my hands to my chest and smile at him with hearts in my eyes.

"I was wondering, if you don't want passion, why did you ask Fiona to marry you? You love her. Wouldn't you have . . . ?" I trail off, not wanting to think about what they would have or wouldn't have done.

Max makes a small noise in his throat and leans back again. He thinks for a moment, considering my question. That's something I've noticed about him. He doesn't always answer right away. He takes the time to think about a question and then gives his best answer.

When he looks back at me, he says, "We're friends. That's all. Nothing more. Nothing less. I knew there would never be a spark. I didn't expect or want one."

He didn't want a spark? Didn't want the heat of passion?

"Why not?"

He watches me, his eyes a cool, deep brown, as smooth and tranquil as Lake Geneva on a moonless, windless night. "I realized early on that what most people call 'love' is just the fire of passion. It burns, sometimes out of control. But the hotter it is, the more quickly it snuffs itself out. When it's gone, the people are left with . . ."

He pauses, considering his words. "If they're lucky, they're left with third-degree burns, pain, and bitterness. But they'll have learned a valuable lesson, and hopefully they can move on a little wiser. If they aren't lucky, they're left with charred bones, ashes, and hatred for whoever they thought they loved. It's a terrible thing when the heat of the fire is gone and all that's left is cold, desolate reality. Passion isn't love. The point of flames is that they need fuel to burn. Passionate love uses people as kindling, and it consumes them until they have nothing left to give. And then. . ."

I lean forward, waiting for him to continue. My hands are curled around my thighs, my fingers pressing into my skin.

He shrugs. "My parents had two years of passionate bliss. Which is quite something, considering. Two years of passion, twenty-eight years of loathing. Was it worth it? They shouldn't ever have married. If my mother had stopped to consider that my father was a closet alcoholic with a penchant for violence, and if my father had stopped to consider that my mother was a raging narcissist with a penchant for lying, the mess of their lives would've been avoided."

"But then you wouldn't be here," I say. "If they didn't marry, you wouldn't exist."

He smiles, leaning forward again. "I suppose passion is good for something then."

I'm caught by the sunlight from the window reflecting off the deep pools of his eyes, catching the sparks of gold. We're close. Our hands rest on the table, inches apart. The cool, dry air from the overhead vent tickles my heated skin.

Beneath the table our legs are so close. All I'd have to do is move another few inches and I'd be able to run my calf along the line of his leg.

Max's eyes darken as if he knows exactly what I'm thinking. Maybe he does. He has seven years of memories. Maybe I've done something like that to him before.

"Ready for dessert?"

I break away from Max's gaze and give Francesca an overly bright smile. I make appreciative noises and thank her as she clears away the cheese and wine and then places the chocolate mousse and coffee in front of us.

Once she's gone I pick up my spoon, aware that Max has been watching me the whole time. I glance back at him, and when I do, he smiles.

I dip my spoon into the chocolate, skimming it over the surface. A little curl of chocolate balls on the spoon. Max stirs a sugar cube and then another into his coffee, and as he does, a lovely coffee-and-cream smell enfolds us.

"You have such a sweet tooth," I say, popping the chocolate mousse into my mouth.

Oh.

That's *good.*

My eyelashes flutter at the creamy, smooth richness.

Max smiles at the noise I make. "How do you know I have a sweet tooth? I was under the impression you don't have any memories of me."

"Oh." I dip my spoon back into the mousse. "Well. I don't. I just ..."

Max tilts his head, taking in the way I shift uncomfortably in my chair and look around the brightly lit cabin. He lets out a surprised huff of air. "You don't want to tell me something. I know this." He points his finger at me. "I recognize this. Tell me."

I sit still and frown at him. "I'd rather not."

"Please." He waves a hand. "Get it off your chest."

I scoff. I don't want to get it off my chest. I don't want Max to know how much I noticed him.

Finally, I shrug. "It's no big deal. It's just when you clean someone's house for years, you learn a lot about them."

He blinks as if this wasn't at all what he thought I was going to say. Then his expression takes on an interested light. "Really?"

I nod. Take a spoonful of mousse and shove it into my mouth. It's smooth and decadent and *so good.*

"What do you know about me? What have you learned?" he asks, staring at my mouth.

I lift my fingers to my lips.

"Let me." He reaches across the table and presses his

thumb to the edge of my mouth, watching me as he slowly drags it across my lip. A hot tingle runs across my mouth, and I clench my thighs together when a tight, needy insistence coils inside me.

Max pulls his thumb from my mouth. There's chocolate mousse on his skin. He takes it and slowly sucks the chocolate free.

"That is good." And then, as if nothing at all just happened, he says, "You were about to tell me everything you know about me."

"I was?"

He grins.

I set my spoon down, unable to eat while he's smiling at me like that. "Fine. As long as you remember I've been cleaning your house for years. Anyone would notice these things."

"Sure." He takes a sip of coffee and then places his cup back on its saucer.

"Well, you have a sweet tooth."

He nods and relaxes back into his chair.

I continue. "You love hazelnut and chocolate."

His eyes light with surprise.

"I clean your refrigerator."

"Ah." He nods.

"You drink coffee with cream and sugar"—I gesture to his cup—"and you rarely stop at one cup. You like to have a French press next to you while you read. You read a lot of books at the same time because you get bored easily and you like to keep your mind active."

He smiles at that, then he nods. "Go on."

"You enjoy British crime dramas, and although I can't be sure, I suspect you always know whodunnit before the show ends."

"Almost always. I'm not perfect."

I grin at that, and then I get carried away, because the way he's looking at me makes a warm, happy glow light in my chest.

"You like to listen to classical music while working. You never lose your temper, although you don't mind when other people do. You like Charles Dickens before bed, although I could never figure out if it's because you love how he spins worlds or because he puts you to sleep—"

"I like his honesty," Max says, watching me with increasing interest. "He was honest in his portrayals of people."

"That makes sense. I should've known. I always thought Freud was one of the worst things to ever happen to western literature. Before he came along, characters were living and breathing. They were flesh and blood on the page, you know? What they did, what they said— there were so many layers. And then along comes Freud, and people were no longer acting out of their own will or their own choices. Instead everyone was a puppet on the strings of past trauma. It scarred western literature. Truly. People aren't marionettes, jerked about by their mother's neglect or their father's abuse. We have free will. We have the ability to reason and choose and react or *not* react. By winnowing a human being's choices down to his past? Maybe that's a comforting view for some. Oh, he hurts others because he was hurt. Or she's scared to love because her husband died. One and one makes two. Red and blue makes purple. But don't you agree that one thing we should never forget is that people are infinitely more complex and our motivations are immeasurably more nuanced than any of us can ever know or explain even after the fact? Subsequent explanations can never do a human justice, and wrapping them up in a nice neat explanation, like "Oh, his mother was negligent," is a failing of modern times?"

I look at Max. He holds his coffee cup halfway between his saucer and his lips. I don't think he realizes he's still holding his cup upright. We hit an air pocket and the plane lurches. The coffee sloshes over the side and spills on his hand.

Max swears and sets his cup back on the saucer. I grab my napkin from my lap and dab at his hand.

"Thank you," he says.

I nod, dabbing at the coffee on his shirtsleeve.

When I'm done I fold my napkin into a square and set it on the table. "I got carried away."

"Don't be sorry," he says. "It's my fault. I was so involved in what you were saying that I forgot to set my cup down. I've often wondered why I like his characters so much. Now I know. I suppose I wish I was them, unburdened by Freud's specter."

He grins at me then, and I smile back.

"Don't worry, I won't think the only reason you don't want passion is because of your parents. I know there are plenty of other reasons."

"Oh?"

I nod, picking up my spoon again and taking another bite. "You like neatness. You like order. I've never cleaned another house where a bachelor makes his bed every morning with perfectly tucked corners. Where he hangs his towels, always puts his laundry in the hamper, stacks his dishes perfectly, and puts his fruit and vegetables in the proper drawers. You prefer things to be tidy. Passion isn't tidy."

"I'd agree with you, except I have a host of memories telling me I like untidy things very, very much."

"There's also the guilt you feel over your family's deaths," I say at the same time.

He glances at me quickly, a frown tugging at the corners of his mouth. "What?"

"Sorry. I shouldn't have said that."

The plane dips a bit, and we fly through the wispy confines of a white-gray cloud.

"No. Tell me what you mean. How you gathered that when we never spoke."

I look out at the fingers of the thin cloud leaving strands of condensation on the window. The chill air from the overhead vent licks across my skin. Max watches me, waiting for my response.

"Well. They died more than a decade ago. But the house . . ." I pause, trying to think of how to explain it. "It could be so full of life, but instead it's in this half-life stasis, as if living fully isn't allowed. Most of the rooms are covered in dustcloths and gloom. When you walk the empty halls, it almost feels like you should apologize for your footsteps making noise. The wine cellar, which clearly was once full to the brim, is entirely empty. In your brother's room there's a photograph of the two of you and the frame is shattered, and he looks like such a—"

"What?"

"Unfriendly sort."

Max's eyes crinkle as he smiles. "That's one way to put it."

"Yeah. I never met your family. Never saw them. I only know I'm not going to pretend that they're the reason you are the way you are. I'd like to give you more credit. I expect you can make your own choices."

"Unless a woman comes along and wishes me into marriage," he says.

"Even then. I've always thought no matter what happens in your life, you'll always be you. And you'll always have the freedom to choose."

The plane dips again, and my stomach rises and falls.

Max considers me, weighing my expression and my words. "I remember when I was twelve. It was my first year away at school. My brother and his friends, they were fourteen. I hung around them. They were already drinking, beating up weaker kids, breaking into the school after-hours, stealing things. I was sitting outside in the commons and my brother came by and said, 'Let's go. We're going to beat the crap out of this kid for showing us up in maths. You can help.' I remember that moment clearly because I knew without a doubt there were two paths in front of me. If I said yes, I'd be just like my brother. I'd become my dad. And if I said no,"—he lifts his shoulder in a small shrug—"they would hate me. But I wouldn't hate myself."

"You said no?" I ask, thinking about twelve-year-old Max, away from home for the first time.

Max nods. "I said no. My brother and his friends beat the crap out of me instead of the boy who showed them up in maths. They kept it up for years. But once I made that choice, I realized I had more choices in life than I'd ever realized. It wasn't inevitable that I'd be just like my father. Sometimes when I walk past a mirror and see the line of my nose or the tilt of my jaw, I see my father. I mistake myself for him. Years ago it always brought up an immediate self-loathing, but then I thought, 'Well, what can I do?' You can't change genetics. I'll always look like him. But I don't have to be him. That you can see that too,"—he gives me a swift smile—"I'm glad. I know our past influences us—you can't deny that. But we have a trump card, don't we? We have choice. I like that you see that."

I'm warmed by the light in his eyes, and I settle into the glow. "I've seen too many people come out of terrible circumstances and choose to be kind or do good to not believe it. Doing wrong is easy. Blaming someone or something else is easy. Choosing to do right? That's not always easy. Taking responsibility for your own life? That's not easy either. Most people would rather give that responsibility away to someone else."

Max tilts his head, considering me. "Is that what you've surmised from Dickens?"

I laugh. "It's what I've surmised from twenty-five years of living. But also Dickens. I started reading him after I saw all his books on your nightstand and I—" I cut myself off and a prickly heat stings my cheeks.

"What?" Max asks. "You . . .?"

I swallow. "I wanted to know more about you."

Max studies me, his expression searching.

In the silence Francesca strides to our table. She stops at my side, unaware of the currents running between Max and me. "We'll be landing soon. I'll clear this, shall I?"

"Thank you," Max says, handing her his coffee, his gaze still on me.

Soon our plates and cups are cleared and the large table is folded away. As the plane descends into the white mass of clouds, the cabin dims, the sun disappears, and I rub my arms in the sudden chill.

Max shifts in his seat, pulls his jacket free, and then hands it to me. "Here."

I take his jacket and rub my hands over the soft black leather. It's warm and smooth, and it smells like soft leather and Max's fresh-air scent. I slide my arms through the warm sleeves and pull it tight around my dress.

"Thank you."

"Anna?"

"Hmm?" I tug the jacket closer.

"Why didn't you ever speak to me?"

I glance quickly down at my hands folded in my lap. "I suppose . . ."—I look back at Max—"I was waiting for you to see me."

"How could I see you when you were hiding?"

I'm struck by his question, and then the plane is freed from the clouds. We're soaring above the outskirts of Paris. I let out a surprised puff of air.

We're north of the city, and it's spread out below us in shades of beige and sand and gray. From above the roads dart like arteries toward the heart of the city. It's a crisscrossing web of roads, old buildings, sinuous strips of water, and green parks. And there, standing regally in the afternoon blue, is the Eiffel Tower. My first view of Paris has taken my breath away. I think I'm in love.

"Isn't it beautiful?" I look back at Max. "Isn't it the most beautiful thing you've ever seen?"

Max's lips curve into a smile and he nods. "Yes."

I think about his question—*How could I see you if you were hiding?*—and I wonder, was I hiding? Is that what I was doing all those years? When I tied my hair back beneath my handkerchief, wore baggy clothes and big-framed glasses, kept my headphones at full volume, and never, ever, ever spoke to Max. Was I hiding? Would he have seen me if I'd asked him about Dickens or told him how much I liked his winter jewelry line with the emeralds and rubies, or if I'd told him I'd searched the city for the best hazelnut croissant and I'd found it at a little patisserie on the cobblestone paths outside the Saint Pierre Cathedral?

Is the reason Max never saw me because I never showed myself to him? All along I thought I was pressed up against the window of his life, never allowed inside. Maybe it wasn't a window. Maybe it was a door.

I lean forward and press my hand against the cool surface of the jet's window. As we fly lower to the ground I make out the outlines of roofs, the slow crawl of traffic, and soon the long line of the runway.

The jet kisses the ground, bumps, then settles. The buildings fly past in a blur, then the jet slows and smoothly pulls to a stop. I wait for my body to catch on to the fact that we're no longer moving.

After a moment I turn back to Max, pulling his jacket tight around my shoulders.

I'm in Paris.

We're in Paris.

I'm in Paris with Max.

"Thank you," I tell him. "Even if we're only here to reverse my wish. Thank you for bringing me to Paris. I won't ever forget it."

He smiles at me, a slow curl of his lips. "I expect that I won't either."

And with that, we've arrived.

15

———————

THE MARCHÉ AUX FLEURS IS AN EDEN BLOOMING IN THE shadow of Notre-Dame. The centuries-old flower market is a riot of colors and sweet fragrances on a tiny island in the middle of the River Seine. The Ile de la Cite, the little island, is at the heart of Paris.

Max brought me here directly after landing, claiming he didn't want to disappoint Madame Blinken. It doesn't matter that he'd never met Madame Blinken before my wish brought her into his life; he was adamant he'd bring me to the market and find a bouquet of freesias. "We'll explore," he'd said. He'd let me lose myself in the city and he'd stay by my side.

We have an appointment late in the afternoon at The Musée des Arts Décoratifs, but until then, I'm free to fall in love with Paris.

As I wander through the narrow, flower-strewn paths, I wonder, what better way to fill the heart of a city than with a garden of flowers?

The air is perfumed with the seductive scent of antique roses, the sweet, sunny scent of blooming azaleas, and the cheery, light perfume of delicate gardenias. Happy calls of, "Bonjour, madame" and, "Oui, oui, oui," and, "Merci, madame," echo through the orangerie stalls of the flower sellers. Iron supports hold up great glass ceilings, and the open-air stalls let the cool spring breeze blow the dreamy aroma through the flowering paths.

Sunlight paints the yellows brighter, the pinks softer, and the reds a more vibrant shade, so that every lily, every daisy, and every rose becomes the most beautiful flower I've ever seen. I'm in a dreamland and Max is here with me.

I grin over at him, eyeing a wooden shelf full of hand-painted ceramic vases and a display of potted succulents. He lifts an eyebrow when he sees my smile.

I squeeze closer to him as a group of women chattering in French push past us. We press against a tall lemon tree, the glossy yellow globes are full and ripe, and the sweet scent teases the air between us.

"Why didn't I ever come here?" I ask him. "To Paris."

He grips my arms and tugs me closer as a bearded man pushing a dolly full of oxeye daisies trundles past. Overhead windchimes tinkle, and there's a shout of irritation as the bearded man knocks a display of lavender sachets over as he wheels past.

I ignore the commotion. Instead I'm caught by Max's grip on my arms, and the friction of his legs pressed to mine, and the careful kiss of my chest against his. I tilt my chin to look up at him. This close I can see the sun shining on his hair, turning it a golden-tinged black. I can see the gold striations in his brown eyes, like little bursts of sunshine. I can smell the fresh-air, deep-woods scent that is the opposite of the heady floral scent combing the air around us. I swear I can almost feel his heartbeat.

Although the crowd has thinned, I don't step back, and Max doesn't let my arms go.

"I don't know," he says. "Maybe you were waiting for me to take you."

I smile at that. "Maybe. But I think it's probably because ever since I started working, I've never had two days off in a row. I always thought if I went to Paris I'd want to stay for at least two days. But"—I shrug—"it seems wrong to spend money only on myself when I could use it to help my family."

"You clean six days a week?" he asks, narrowing his eyes. "You haven't taken a holiday in seven years?"

"I like my job," I say defensively. Then I remember that Dorene fired me, and I add, "Liked. And I like helping my family. I don't mind not going anywhere. It's just as fun having a picnic in the park with my friends or taking a swim at sunset with Emme or watching old movies in the courtyard with Dorene. Besides, when I read a book I travel to new places. Just think, it's like I've already been to Paris because I read *A Tale of Two Cities*."

I smile up at him, then I slowly step back. Max reluctantly lets me go, but I can tell he doesn't want to drop the conversation. For a man who works seven days a week and spends most of his free time locked in his home office, he is surprisingly bothered by my work habits.

I push past a display of bright pink azaleas and enter an enclosed shop lined with terracotta pots full of herbs —lavender, rosemary, basil, and sage. It smells like a culinary escape, and I smile at the herby scent.

The light shines through the glass ceiling in a golden spiderweb pattern.

The proprietor, a small man with a quick smile, nods when I kneel to rub the prickly, needlelike leaves of the rosemary.

"You said you'd feel guilty doing something just for yourself," Max says in a low voice, stooping next to me. "But if it were your mom or your sister who wanted to do something that made them happy, what would you say to them? What would you want for them? If your mom wanted a trip to Paris, what would you tell her?"

I shake my head and stand. I walk toward the next open-air flower stall, full of hanging wicker baskets, crystal prisms, and wind chimes. They tinkle and the prisms throw rainbows across my path.

"I know what you're saying," I say, "but it's different."

"How is it different? How is it that you can want happiness for someone else but not want the same for yourself? How can you give others what they want but feel guilty taking anything for yourself?"

I turn quickly, and Max stops a few inches from me. "What are you trying to do?" I ask. "I can't change my life."

He holds up his hand. "You have the choice to do anything you like."

"You think I should have already taken the train to Paris?"

He shakes his head. "No. I think you should've said hello to me before yesterday."

"And what would you have done if I had?"

He smiles and then leans down and takes a paper-wrapped bouquet of freesias from the flower display. "I'm not certain," he says, holding the red and pink tinged blooms toward me. "Asked you to dinner? Begged you to join me for a coffee and a croissant? Purposely spilled my coffee, then automatically felt like an ass for spilling my coffee and asking you to clean it up just so I could see you? Hmm. Or I would've never spoken to you again, because I tend to avoid anything that smacks of passion. These are for you."

He holds the flowers out to me, and the scent of strawberries, citrus, and floral notes surrounds me. I take the bouquet and the paper crinkles in my hands. "Thank you."

"Freesias are the seventh anniversary flower," he says, and there's a teasing light in his eyes.

After he pays for the flowers, we wander down a narrow path toward the open-air of the Parisian sidewalks. It's a beautiful late-spring day, and the rumble of a passing delivery truck echoes off the stone walls and the narrow streets. Through the trellised plants and the glass walls I can make out the spire of Notre-Dame.

It's calling me, like the bells are ringing and I can't help but turn and stare.

"If you avoid anything that hints at passion," I ask, "then why are you giving me flowers? Why are you being—?"

"Nice?"

Max's eyes crinkle with his smile as we draw into the open city air. The dreamlike scent of Eden is replaced by the crisp exhaust and the stone-tinged air of city.

"Right," I say, clutching the flowers to my chest. I drop my nose to the blooms and take a long, happy inhale. "No one's ever bought me flowers before."

When I look up, Max is staring at me with a line

between his eyebrows and a wrinkle on his forehead. "Now that is just sad."

I scoff. "Why?"

He shakes his head. "As you know, everyone deserves flowers *at least* twice in their life."

"What? When you're born and when you die?"

He laughs in surprise, and when he stops he's grinning at me. "Three times then. And your wedding doesn't count."

I take another sniff and let out a happy sigh. "Fine. One down, only two bouquets to go."

Max sticks his hands in his pockets and then glances around the tree-shaded street, looking toward the spire of Notre-Dame.

"I guess you've forgotten. I'm being nice because I like you. Even though you shackled me with a wish and thrust me into this daft, weird world. I like you. It's a failing I have, liking you. I can't seem to help myself."

We smile at each other, and then he adds, "Besides, I have seven years of pseudo-memory full of turbulent, amorous passion. I'm surprised by the fact that I survived it. But here I am. Seven years married."

A motorcycle rushes past, its engine roaring and bouncing off the glass, iron, and stone of the surrounding buildings.

"Did you ever think," I ask, studying the now quiet Parisian street, "about how the worst thing imaginable is a life lived without love?"

Max steps closer, and at the same time I step closer to him.

"And since Paris is the city of love," I continue, "a life without Paris is unimaginable."

"Impeccable logic." Max holds out his hand, palm

outstretched. "Would you like to get lost with me? In Paris? Just for today?"

He's asking more than he's willing to say. But I hear his meaning anyway.

"Yes, please."

He smiles.

I take his hand.

16

———

We begin at Paris Point Zero. It's a small circle with eight triangular points set into an octagon set in paving stones. Max tells me it's from here that all distances in Paris are measured. Paris Point Zero is hidden under a massive line of people waiting to enter Notre-Dame, and most of them trod over the stones without looking down.

Max claims that if we're going to get lost, then we might as well start at the heart, in the center, at the very middle of the maze.

"Do your worst," he says, giving my hand a squeeze.

I grin at him as a stiff spring breeze tugs at my dress and whistles around the stone walls and spires. The cobblestone area in front of Notre-Dame is crowded, and even though I'm standing close to Max, holding his hand, I still feel jostled and jarred.

I spin in a circle and Max shifts with me. I keep turning until all the stone and spires and gargoyles and sky have blended together in a dizzying swirl. Then I stop and thrust my finger, pointing away from Notre-Dame, along the lazily flowing Seine, down the Parvis de Notre Dame.

"That way," I say, wobbling on my feet.

Max tugs me close. "Not back to Notre-Dame to see the Crown of Thorns or catch Quasimodo at the top of the tower?"

I shake my head. "If I go that way, I won't be lost, will I? And what's the fun in that? If you already know what you'll find, then there really isn't any point in going."

Max studies me, and even though there are about a hundred zillion people whirling around us, jockeying for pictures or jostling in line or cutting across the cobblestones, he makes me feel as if we're all alone.

"I don't know," he finally says. "I have to admit, I prefer familiarity and comfort. I like going to destinations where I know exactly what to expect. I like people who are constant and true. In my experience the unexpected never brings anything good."

A car horn cuts across the noise, and Max's eyes flicker as he looks toward the stone bridge straddling the Seine.

It's interesting. I thought I knew Max. I thought I knew his habits, his personality, his likes and dislikes. But every minute with him, something new unfolds. I wonder how much we'll discover about each other, spending the day together.

How much can you learn about someone in a day? And at what point do you stop looking and decide you know everything there is to know? That belief is never true. You can't ever know *everything*. But at some point people become comfortable with each other and stop looking for the unexpected and only see the expected.

Right now, though, everything is unexpected.

Even the way Max rubs the back of his neck and wrinkles his brow at the truck honking again then rumbling down the street, back toward the flower market.

When he turns back to me, he gives a small smile and absently runs his thumb over the back of my hand.

"I think," I tell him, enjoying the way his thumb kisses my skin as gently as a spring breeze, "I'm going to give you a gift."

"Really?" His thumb stills, and I lean closer.

"Yes. Today you gave me Paris. In return I'm going to give you the joy of surprises. I'm going to help you delight in the unexpected. That way, from now on, you can have at least one time in your life that the unexpected brought you something good."

He smiles at that, his eyes crinkling at their corners. "Lead on."

Above pigeons flutter against the clear blue sky, their wings beating like an elated heart, echoing across the stone. I grin and pull Max with me, clasping his hand.

After we cross the street I tug Max toward an elegant sandstone building called the Hôtel Dieu. Inside the courtyard there's a beautiful Italianate garden with a maze of shrubs and blooming flowers set against stone archways, long stone sunlit galleries, and twisting stairways.

The courtyard is quiet, a contrast to the crowds and noise outside Notre-Dame. A fat bumblebee buzzes past, landing on a deep red geranium. The garden smells like soil and wet mulch and spring blooms.

"I like how they called this the Hotel of God," I say, taking in the stairs curving around us as if they're leading up to the heavens.

"It was quite common to call Catholic charity hospitals God's hostel," Max says with a wry smile.

I laugh. "That's either morbid or lovely."

"Morbid," Max says.

"Lovely," I decide.

We grin at each other.

"You could say," I add, "that Earth is God's hostel and we're all here for a short stay until we arrive back home." I nod toward the manicured garden. "Earth. God's Hostel. Don't get comfortable—your stay is short."

Max laughs and nudges my shoulder with his. "How is that not morbid?"

I shrug, breathing in the fresh garden scents. "I don't know. I think it's comforting. Sometimes things in life can seem really awful, but I think that's only because of the immediacy of them. If you give yourself the grace of distance and the idea of eternity, then what seems so insurmountable, so hard and heartbreaking . . . well, it's not. It only feels that way because it's this moment. But no moment lasts forever. I like that."

"This is why you have a degree in philosophy."

"I do?" I look at him in surprise.

Max blinks at me, his forehead wrinkling. "Don't you?"

"No." I shake my head. "I deferred my admission once my stepdad left. I started working and then . . . there never seemed time. I was accepted to the school of arts." I smile at him, wondering. "Philosophy? What would I do with philosophy?"

Max tilts his head. "You run a nonprofit. It started as a community soup kitchen, the Open Heart Kitchen—"

"Because my family loves feeding all our neighbors," I say, delighted.

"That's right." Max grins. "And then you realized you could do more. It expanded into a community resource center. There are classes for adult literacy, computer literacy, resume and CV assistance, mentorships . . ." He trails off, catching my expression. "What?"

I let the bouquet of freesias sag in my hands. The paper crinkles against the edge of a manicured shrub. "The fake me seems a lot more amazing than the real me."

Max frowns. "Aren't you one and the same?"

I consider this. If you're walking along on the path of life and then you split in two, and one of you takes the right fork and the other takes the left, are you still the same person? Or do the experiences along the way change the contours of your soul? Experiences can influence your personality and your choices, but do they change your soul?

"You're right," I say finally. "It's still me. I'm me either way."

"I hope so," Max says, pulling me out of the Hôtel Dieu and the manicured gardens. "Because, if I'm being honest, I like the me I see in my memories too much to attribute him to someone else. I'd like to take a bit of credit for his good sense."

"His good sense?"

"My good sense." Max nods.

We step out onto the street and I lick my pointer finger, hold it up to the wind, and then point in the direction the breeze is blowing from. "That way."

Max grins. We wind through the streets, wandering past quaint stone houses, painted medieval-looking arched doors, and window boxes overflowing with spring flowers. There are brightly painted cafés in blues and reds and yellows, with iron balconies and ivy trailing up the walls. They smell like melting butter, simmering stocks, and freshly baked bread.

Narrow cobblestone alleys twist between buildings. There are bright street signs on the stone walls, with hanging glass lanterns and mopeds parked on the sidewalks.

Carved into one stone wall is a pretty stone dove caught in flight. "Look at the dove," I say, smiling at Max. "That's beautiful."

He points at the plaque beneath the dove. "Have you heard the story?"

"No." I peer at the plaque.

"Ah. It's a famed legend, actually," Max says. "This dove is one of a pair. In the thirteenth century, one of the sculptors working on Notre-Dame lived here with his two doves, a male and a female. When a flood swept through the city, the house collapsed. The male dove escaped, but the female was caught in the rubble. Every day the Parisians watched as the male dove returned day after day to bring food to his mate. He never abandoned her, and eventually, she was able to escape. The sculptor carved this in honor of their love."

Max's voice is a low murmur, barely discernible above the noise of people passing on the sidewalk and motorcycles whirring by. I lean close to hear him, and when he finishes speaking, I realize I'm pressed so close he could circle his arm around me, lean down, and press his mouth to mine.

"That," I say, "is a beautiful story."

"You're a romantic."

I take a step back and start walking again, winding down the narrow alley, past more cafés with wooden shutters and scents of wine-braised meats and yeasty breads.

"I am. I admit it. I'd like to think that if someone I loved needed help, I'd come back day after day until I knew they were okay."

He smiles, and we turn randomly down another cobblestone alley drenched in shade and cool gray stone.

"You're constant," he says.

I shake my head. "Constantly unexpected."

He smiles and then stops in front of a great black arched double doorway. Above the door is the carved face of a man and stone scrollwork. On a plaque above the shuttered window is an inscription for Heloïse and Abelard. The plaque claims they lived here together.

"*The* Heloïse and Abelard?" I ask.

"You know of them?"

"Who doesn't?" I ask, frowning at the stone house. "I prefer the doves."

Max raises an eyebrow. "Why?"

"I don't know. Don't you?"

He considers this, rubbing his chin in mock thought. "Let's see. What do I prefer? Saving my love from starvation or . . . falling in love with my young student, and when she gets pregnant, secretly marrying her?"

"Don't forget the castration," I say, smiling sweetly.

"Bloodthirsty." Max's eyes narrow. "See, this is what I mean. Passion led to castration. Abelard and Heloïse had a passionate affair. She got pregnant. They secretly wed. Abelard got his testicles sliced off. Heloïse was sent to a convent for the rest of her life. They exchanged letters for years but never saw each other again. How sad is that? I'd rather keep my testicles, thank you very much."

"I don't know," I say, pondering the plaque. "Perhaps he thought it was worth it."

"Trust me. He didn't."

I smile up at Max. "Are you sure? Maybe the sex was really, really good."

"Would you live in a convent for the rest of your life for one night of passion?" Max asks.

Because of the line of his brows and the serious bend of his mouth, I take my time considering the question. Would I spend the rest of my life locked away for one night with someone I loved beyond reason? Someone I considered the other half of myself?

"Yes," I decide. "I would."

Max raises his eyebrows.

"I don't think it was just sex or just passion. I think it was more. If I got to experience that *more* for even one night? Yes. I think the light of that one night could burn bright enough to make all the other remaining nights seem like day."

For a long moment we both stare at the house Abelard and Heloïse supposedly shared their love in. And then I pull Max along the road and we continue winding across the Ile de la Cite.

Around every corner there's a surprising sight. The sunlight escaping the shadows of a cloud to glint over the gold-tipped fence outside Sainte Chapelle. And once inside, the lower chapel with its vaulted ceilings that reminds me of lying in the grass at night under a canopy of stars. And then in the upper chapel, where the sun streams through a sea of stained glass so that it feels as if you're standing inside a rainbow, trying to catch your breath.

We catch the time at the oldest clock in the city. It's nearly 1 p.m. So Max closes his eyes, spins us around, and picks a direction, and we stumbled happily into the cutest café I've ever seen. It's an old stone house on a narrow street, with a profusely blooming wisteria covering the walls and climbing to the roof. The purple blooms fall like grape clusters from the vine and the lovely spring smell fills the street. There are café tables outside, spread among potted flowers.

Max can't resist the sweet butternut soup with hazelnut chips and the terrine with porcini mushrooms and pistachios. I can't resist the frites soufflés, which are golden twice-fried potato wedges, perfectly puffed and perfectly delicious.

Max carries the food in a take-out bag and I carry the bouquet of freesias, now hanging a bit limp in my hands. We walk west along the Seine until we finally reach the end of the island, and below, there's a green triangular park with chestnut and maple trees and a few benches.

"There," I say, pointing to a large weeping willow with its boughs bending over the Seine. "I want to go there."

I'm just not sure how. We're high above the little park. The stone bridges with their arches spanning the water connect the island with the rest of the city. Tour boats with tourists enjoying the sunshine and the spring weather sit on the top decks and snap photos as the boats chug past. The sound of cars rushing over the bridge and music echoing in the stone tunnels bounces to us. Birds in the maple trees sing, and there's the sound of laughter from a group of tourists leaning over the river.

"I love weeping willows," I say, staring at the giant tree.

Max nods. "All right. I can get you there."

He tugs me across the Pont Neuf and then halfway across the bridge, near the entrance to the Place Dauphine and a statue of King Henri IV, he takes us down a set of steps leading toward the Seine.

Under the shade of the hanging branches of the weeping willow we find a spot on the stone. I hang my legs over the sloped stone wall and bask in the sun streaming in long golden ribbons through the curtains of the weeping willow.

The Seine flows below us, a blue-brown full of currents and ripples that churns from the motoring of boats and eddies. A crisp breeze blows off the water and tickles my bare legs. Max settles next to me and pulls the dishes free from the take-out bag.

The butternut soup is a beautiful golden orange. The terrine is pretty with its spring-green pistachios. The frites are perfectly puffed potato purses. In a moment that shows his absolute brilliance, Max pulls two bottles of sparkling water from the bag and a ramekin of crème brulée.

We eat in silence, enjoying the savory flavors and the sun and wind on our cheeks. We take turns dipping our spoons into the soup container. Our fingers tangle when we reach for the frites soufflés.

Across the river and through the leaves, I can make out the façade of the Louvre and a line of buildings that are so Parisian in their architecture I can't help but smile.

"This has been the perfect day," I say, scraping my spoon across the crème brulée dish. "Thank you for getting lost with me."

Max smiles over at me, setting his spoon down.

"Maybe you were lost, but I knew where I was the entire time."

"Oh."

His eyes light and he leans close. "I was with you."

I give a surprised smile. "You know, you can be surprisingly charming. I never pegged you for a charmer."

"Of course I'm charming," Max says. "I'm a Barone. Everyone in my family, even the worst of us, is charming. It's in our DNA."

He says this almost as if he sometimes wishes he could be something else.

"Then say something not charming. Go ahead." I wave my hand, giving him permission. "Dare to be unexpected. Be un-charming."

He stares at me, his gaze catching on my lips. "I want to kiss you."

I shake my head. "That's still charming."

"Anna."

"Max?"

"I'm not being charming."

I blink. The sun filters across us. A tour boat glides past, tourists snapping photos of the weeping willow and the low bridges. A pigeon pecks at the stones nearby. A woman laughs, sharing a moment with her lover.

The cool breeze teases my skin and a warm ripple flows over me until my lips are tingling and I'm leaning closer to Max.

He watches me, his eyes burning with a yearning that makes my stomach flip and my heart flutter wildly.

I grip his shoulders, clasping the leather of his jacket in my hands.

"If you knew what I was thinking . . ." he says as if it will scare me off.

"Do your worst. Surprise me."

He spreads his fingers over my cheeks, tilts my face toward the sun, and then takes my mouth as if I've given him permission to conquer the world.

17

———

I think I finally understand why Max avoids passion. He's an unlit powder keg, and one stray spark will cause a massive, city-destroying explosion.

That one spark is a kiss. Just a simple kiss.

I've had plenty of kisses in my life. Closed-mouthed pecks. Cautious, curious first-date kisses. Open-mouthed, exploring, will-we-won't-we kisses. Boring kisses. Wet, sloppy kisses. Gross kisses. Nice kisses.

Mostly, if anyone had asked me before today what I thought of kissing, that's what I would've said.

Kissing is okay. Kissing is nice.

Nice.

There is *nothing* nice about Max's kiss.

The second his fingers stroke across my cheeks and his mouth touches mine, all pretense, all pretend, all polite disappears.

He makes a low sex noise in his throat—a rumble that shoots straight at me and hits me so suddenly I'm inflamed.

He slants his hot mouth over my lips, diving in as if I'm the first and last woman he'll ever taste. He's feasting on me. His fingers dive into my hair, and then he grabs a fistful and tugs my mouth closer. I gasp at the sting of his fingers in my curls, and at my gasp he bites my lower lip and thrusts into my mouth.

I'm invaded by him. He thrusts and tangles his mouth with mine, biting and nibbling, retreating and then invading again. My skin is hot, flushed with the glow and taste of him. Crème brulée, hazelnut, and cream. The sweat on his skin, the salt on his lips, the scent of him wraps around me and I'm dizzy with the onslaught of his mouth.

"Hell," he whispers against my lips, and then he licks the seam of my mouth, pulling his tongue across my lips. "You taste better than my memories. How can you taste better?"

I bite his lip, not caring if I taste better. I've never tasted him at all.

He swears then plants his hand on my sacrum and pulls me on top of his lap, positioning me so I'm straddling him. He presses his palm into my lower back, and I rock against him. He's hard. Very. And when I press against the length of him I let out a soft shudder that he captures with a groan.

We're at the edge of the Seine, under a weeping willow's ribboning light, kissing for the first time. Around us couples picnic, friends walk the bank, and tourists glide past in tour boats. The city is bright and noisy and crowded. But all of that disappears with the press of Max's hand to the curve in my back and the heat of his mouth against mine.

My dress falls around my legs, leaving my thighs bare and scraping against Max's jeans. The lace of my underwear rubs him. We're hidden by the long curtain of the tree's leaves, in our own secret world where kisses are more erotic and explicit than any sex I've ever had.

There's something happening here. Something I've never experienced before.

I'm vibrating, glowing brighter and brighter. I'm drunk on this kiss, dizzy and spinning, floating out of myself. I take my hands from the contours of his leather jacket and send them under his shirt, moving up along the bare planes of his abdomen.

His muscles flex under my questing fingers, and beneath me he thickens even more, his hips rolling in a lazy move that matches the thrust of his tongue.

My breath is tight, my heart gallops in my chest, and my skin is so sensitized that everywhere Max touches me lights up and sparks.

I press my fingers to the flat of his chest, where his heart thunders under my palm.

He pulls his mouth from mine. His lips are red and wet from the trace of my tongue. The light in his eyes is a violent, burning fire. His chest shudders as he draws in one deep breath after another.

I stare at him, still dizzy. Still aching.

He presses a kiss to the corner of my mouth, his stubble roughly scraping my skin. "If you knew how much I want you in this moment, I think you would run."

I shift over the hard length of him, my thighs clenching in response to the tight heat running through me. "I think I have a good idea."

"Darling. You have *no* idea."

At his rough growl I sink against him, and he twitches beneath me, the thrust of him involuntarily rising to meet me.

"This is the first time in my life," I admit, slowly pulling my hands out from under his shirt, "that I've nearly had sex in public."

At my admission Max's eyelids droop and his gaze burns again. "My mind is telling me this can't be real, but everything else is telling me it is."

Beyond the curtain of the tree a woman's sharp laugh sounds, cutting through our conversation. Max shakes himself, reawakening to the day. He pulls his hand free from my hair and glances at his watch.

"We have to go," he says, frowning at the time.

"Time to unmarry?" I ask, shakily climbing off his lap.

My limbs have that strange half-asleep pins-and-needles feeling. I'm heavy and clumsy and tingling. My face is tilted toward the stone and the river and I'm braiding my hair, smoothing my dress, but when Max doesn't answer I look back at him.

He's watching me braid my hair, a low flame burning in his gaze. "What happens if this can't be fixed? If my theory proves false?"

I pause, letting my fingers fall from my braid. "I . . ." My heart stutters, shudders, and then thumps along again. "I hadn't thought that far ahead."

Max nods. Then, in a smooth motion, he stands and holds out his hand.

I take his outstretched hand and he pulls me up. A sparking current travels along my hand, up my arm, and crackles over my skin.

"Never mind," he says, keeping ahold of me. "It'll work. By tomorrow we'll be strangers again."

He doesn't sound exactly happy when he says this, but I only nod.

Then he gathers the remains of our meal and I pick up the sadly wilted freesias, the flowers drooping toward death with every passing hour.

18

———————

THE MUSÉE DES ARTS DÉCORATIFS, ALSO KNOWN AS MAD, is located in the most northwestern wing of the Louvre, although it's not part of the Louvre Museum. Outside is the sprawling Jardin des Tuileries with its formal gardens, monuments, ponds, statues, and tree-covered pathways. The park is dotted with sunbathers, picnickers, tourists, and locals, all out for a sun-filled stroll. I want to hunt down the Rodin pieces at the western end, but Max tugs me along to MAD's entrance.

The stone façade is a soft, creamy beige, with a dozen statues standing in alcoves looking down on us as we enter the arched doorway. Every time I enter a great museum I'm stunned by the magnitude. The scale of the marble columns, the enormity of the arched ceilings, the grand marble staircases, and the sea of marble tiles and marble ceilings and marble . . . my gosh, how much marble can there possibly be in one building? Inevitably I crane my neck up and up and up, until I'm slack-jawed, staring at a perfectly rounded ceiling, a magnificent chandelier, and, of course, more marble.

But then I always lower my gaze and come back to ground-level, where masses of people intermix in a wave of museum confusion. The marble makes museums cold, with an icy stone breeze that never leaves the air even in the deepest heat of summer. The light is bright, almost harsh, and the noise is jarring. Voices echo off the marble, heels click on the mosaic tile, and every sound is magnified in the marble confines.

Still. It's gorgeous.

I stay close to Max as he leads us up the grand staircase to the second floor. Even in the white marble sterility of the museum, a tight, tingling awareness passes between us. Every now and then, as we pass a tour group or a large family, I move close and my hand or arm brushes against Max. When we touch, he tenses, his shoulders tighten, and he takes in a restraining breath as the air around us crackles. At the top of the stairs he takes my hand and holds it in a firm grip. As he does, he looks at me with a single eyebrow raised as if he's waiting for me to protest. I don't.

He nods then and turns toward the Galerie des Bijoux, our destination.

Usually, when I go to museums, I love to sit on a bench and people-watch. There are always the usual suspects. Mom friends pushing strollers, chatting while their babies sleep. Families on vacation, the parents grim-faced and determined to see the museum or die trying. Art students, quirky or mysterious, leaning against columns sketching in their notebooks. Retirees getting their daily step quotas in. A couple on a first date. An exhausted family of five, glassy-eyed after seeing their thousandth art deco vase.

My favorites, though, are the older couples—the ones in their eighties sitting on a bench together holding hands, pondering a painting. I like them the most.

"People-watching?" Max asks, slipping me a small smile as we walk across the glass footbridge spanning over the marble entrance hall.

I forgot. He knows I love museums for people-watching more than for the art.

"Maybe," I say. Then, when he gives me an amused smile, I admit, "Yes. Am I that obvious?"

"Only to me. I've seen you—" He shakes his head, cutting himself off.

I have to admit, it is strange. He's seen me, but he hasn't. He's my husband, but he isn't. He knows me, but he doesn't.

"You're easy to read," he says, looking down at me.

Suddenly I'm dizzy again. I don't know if it's from the pressure of Max's hand in mine, the shimmery sensation pulsing through me, or the fact that we're walking across a footbridge high above the ground in a marble palace.

"I like that about you," Max says. "You think you do the unexpected, but . . . when it counts, I know what you'll do. You'll do the right thing. There isn't any guessing. You put your family first, always. You try to make others happy, always. You're warm and kind. A little shy. A lot cautious. A romantic. You like people. You do what's right." He reaches up and touches the line of my jaw. "You're very expressive. There isn't ever any guess about what you're thinking. It all shows in your expressions."

My heart thuds and flops around in my chest, and the

lustrous glow that was coating me sizzles and pops and falls to the marble floor twenty feet below. If I'm easy to read, does that mean he knows? He knows I fell in love at first sight? He knows I pined after him for years? He knows I have all that love for him tucked in a corner in my heart, hidden behind a closed door? He knows the only thing he has to do is knock and I'll open it for him?

He knows?

Max drags his finger along my jaw. "In seven years I've never known you to lie."

"I can't lie," I admit. "It knots my stomach until I can't eat and can't sleep. It's easier to tell the truth."

Max nods. His hand pauses, cradling my cheek. A family pushes past, leaving us suspended above the great hall.

"I have a question."

"Yes?" I ask.

"Tonight," he says in a low, scraping growl.

I nod. Sway toward him. "Yes."

I grip Max's hand, afraid the dizzy rush cascading through me will cause me to stumble and then tumble headfirst off the suspended footbridge.

"If nothing else. If never again. Tonight," he says, his words low, dragging over me like calloused hands spreading my naked thighs open and delving higher and higher.

I nod, my tongue thick, my blood pulsing in a steady thrumming beat. "You want to make love?" I ask, and the question comes out as a whisper in the giant, echoing white marble hall.

Max's expression tightens, his gaze burning into mine. "I want to make you come so hard you forget your name."

Holy crap.

He's not finished. "I want to bend you over and bury myself so deep that when you scream your orgasm they hear you at the top of the Eiffel Tower. While you're still senseless, I want to lick you and taste you until you're begging for more, so that when I flip you over and work you, you'll *wish* you could stop coming. But sadly, that wish won't come true. You'll keep coming until I tell you to stop. Which won't be until the sun comes up. *That's* what I want."

Oh my word. Max Barone is a dirty talker. Smooth, charming, put-together Max Barone has a filthy mouth. And apparently, I find that wildly, unbelievably attractive.

"Holy . . ." I stare at him, wide-eyed.

His eyes narrow and he searches my face, looking for hints at how turned-on I am. The pinkening heat in my cheeks, the hard points of my nipples visible through my dress, the tightness of my shallow breath. I'm flushed. I'm out of breath. I'm . . . imagining.

When my cheeks feel as hot as a furnace Max smiles.

It's a wicked, happy, triumphant smile.

"I agree. To . . . to . . ." I trip over my tongue and then say in a rush, "All of that."

His smile breaks into a grin. A delighted, eager, wolfish grin. It's as if he's an apex predator anticipating the first juicy bite of a fresh kill. It's as if he's been starving himself on scraps and bits of old meat for his whole life and I've just offered him a fleshy, passionate bite of me.

I stare at him as wide-eyed and naïve as a deer, struck dumb by a pair of headlights.

I have a feeling a night with a passionate Max will be like standing naked under the onslaught of a hurricane.

As we stand there imagining tonight, the same feeling overcoming me as when we kissed, a woman strides across the marble, her heels clicking hurriedly on the floor.

"Monsieur Barone? Madame Barone?"

I break eye contact with Max and glance at the smartly dressed, well-put-together woman.

It's three o'clock.

It's time for our appointment with the conservatrice en chef.

It's time to get unmarried.

19

———

As we walk through the Galerie des Bijoux, I can't help but slow my pace to gaze in wonder at the glittering jewels and centuries of adornment encased behind the walls of glass. There are hundreds of necklaces, bracelets, brooches, rings, tiaras, and more. It's hard for my gaze to land on any one piece; instead my attention jumps from diamond to ruby to gold to silver as if I'm a beam of light reflecting off all the glittering surfaces.

"The collection spans from Middle Ages to present day." Edith Cloutier, the chief curator, waves a hand at the long glass wall to our right.

She's a small, neat woman in a black sheath dress that sets off her matching art nouveau bracelets, necklace, and earrings. She's left her clothing as flat and unobtrusive as possible to set off the art of her jewelry. Since I spent an inordinate amount of time researching the jewelry industry all those years ago, I recognize her set as Henri Vever—one of the most well-known Parisian art nouveau jewelers from the Gilded Age. She has a particularly beautiful yellow enamel, gold, and ruby pendant in the shape of a winged woman on her breast.

"We have twelve hundred pieces displayed. More than five thousand in our entire collection." She gives another flick of her fingers toward a glass case holding a diamond and sapphire diadem from the 1800s.

I blink at the sparkle of the stones as they catch the light.

Edith turns to look back at us, still moving quickly through the collection, her heels clicking briskly on the floor. "But you know that, having contributed many pieces over the years."

She speaks with a southwestern French accent, which to my ear has a more Spanish or Catalan feel, where the silent "e" is still pronounced, and so is the "r."

She speaks French in an almost singsong voice, slowly swinging through all the syllables in every word. And wow, do I appreciate it. The Swiss French I'm used to is spoken more slowly and uses different words and phrases than Parisian French. Since we arrived this morning I've struggled to keep up with the pace of the language. It's as if the city, so fast-moving, has caused the people who live here to shorten all their words to keep up with the rush. They swallow sounds, drop the "e" and the "i," shorten sentences, and hide the "pas," so I can't tell whether anyone means yes or no. It's left me in a sort of daze, and I'm incredibly grateful Max somehow has the ability to drop his native accent and blend seamlessly with the city.

So Edith, with her singsong accent, is a welcome relief.

She guides us through the restricted section, where the historical methods of jewelry production are explored, and then into a small, windowless, white-walled room with a round table, four chairs, and a decided lack of sparkle.

"I'm grateful you could arrange this on such short notice," Max says as Edith gestures for us to take a seat.

"It isn't a problem." She waves away his thanks. "It will only be a moment. I'll retrieve the parure. Make yourselves comfortable."

Once her footsteps have faded down the hall, Max pulls a chair free for me, its legs scraping against the ground. It's quiet in this small room. Cold. Without thousands of diamonds winking at me, I finally know where to look.

I sit and Max settles next to me.

I breathe in the scent of his warm leather jacket, the lingering trace of fresh park air, and a hint of freesia. Max has been holding them for me, unwilling to give them up even though they're fading fast. Now they're on the cushion of the chair, tucked under the table.

Max smiles at me—a long, slow, happy smile that pulls me back to his words on the footbridge. His promise. His lips curl as I draw in a shuddering breath.

Sometimes when you take off a thin gold necklace, you drop it on top of your dresser, and almost magically it coils into a spiral, wrapping around itself. That's the feeling I have right now. There's a shimmering gold chain dropping inside me and coiling in a tight spiral at the base of my spine. It glows and pulses and shines.

Max makes a soft noise at the look on my face, and then he moves his chair close and presses his thigh against mine. At the pressure I nearly climb on top of his lap again and straddle him, just like under the weeping willow.

Max slowly takes my hand, threads our fingers together, and then rests our joined hands in his lap.

He's dark. His black hair is longer on the top than on the sides and his stubble is already thick from a half-day of growth. His features are hard-planed, with a sharp nose and a square jaw. His gaze is direct. He said he'll always know what I'm thinking, but right now he's easy to read too.

He wants me.

He wants me with a heat that burns.

I can't decide if it's a wish come true or if it's the worst possible outcome.

My heart alternates between quick, fluttery beats and slow, aching thumps.

Tonight I'm going to lay myself bare. And tomorrow, all the heat and passion? It'll likely be gone. I wonder whether Max's theory —that passion burned out leaves only ashes and pain—or my theory—that one flaming night can light the rest of your life—will prove true.

Only time will tell.

Max strokes my palm in a slow circle and a tingle works its way up my arm. The dry, cold air of the museum is replaced by a flushed heat.

Neither of us say anything. The sounds around us are loud. The creaking of the chair when Max shifts. The rustle of my dress when I move closer to him. Max's long exhale. Heavy footsteps in the hallway. A murmured conversation as colleagues pass. Every sense is heightened. Hearing. Touch. Smell. Taste.

I can still taste his kiss on my lips. It tastes like addiction.

I glance at him out of the corner of my eye. He leans

close and says sotto voce, his words vibrating in the shell of my ear, "Do you remember what to do?"

It takes me a moment to understand what he's asking. He isn't talking about kissing or sex or how two bodies come together. He's asking if I remember what we discussed on our hurried walk from Pont Neuf to the museum.

"Yes," I say. "Of course."

Then the already familiar sound of Edith's brisk walk clicks down the corridor. We turn toward the door as she enters the room carrying a large burgundy leather case.

"Here we are." She smiles broadly for the first time since we arrived.

She slides the leather case onto the table and then sets white archivist's gloves, jeweler's tweezers, and a loupe on the table.

I lean forward in my chair, taking in the antique parure case.

"This is one of the finest parure sets in our collection," she says proudly, "although unfinished, of course, as you have the necklace."

She darts a quick questioning glance at Max, and I can tell by the gleam in her eye that she'd give up wine and chocolate forever if it meant she could add the necklace to the museum's collection.

"Madame Barone, this is the first time you've seen the set?" she asks as she opens the case.

"Yes—"

I would say more, but all my words flee like leaves in a windstorm. I let out a stunned exhale.

"Beautiful, no?" she asks. "We were very lucky to acquire this set."

"Beautiful" is an understatement. I thought the

necklace was the most gorgeous piece of jewelry I'd ever seen, but alone, the necklace was like a gemstone fallen from its crown. It belongs here. Or these belong with the necklace.

The case on the outside is burgundy leather, and on the inside it's satin and velvet. Nestled in the confines is a glittering, winking, startling set of sapphire jewelry that is more than 250 years old. In a word, it's dazzling.

"You said you had history to share." Edith looks to Max.

He nods, stroking the sensitive spot in the center of my palm. "Yes. This set, in Barone family history, is called the Bride's Parure—" He stops and looks over at me. "Do you know what 'parure' means?"

I smile. I do. Parure were one of my favorite things to research in my days of jewelry obsession.

"It means adorn. It's a set of matching jewelry meant to be worn en suite. Sometimes there were only a few pieces—a necklace, a ring, bracelets, earrings, a broach. Other times, they were very elaborate, up to sixteen pieces. Parure were very popular, especially in the Georgian era . . ." I trail off at the surprised look on Max's face. He wasn't expecting me to know anything about antique jewelry.

"I didn't know you were so well-versed," he says with a curious smile.

"Of course she is," Edith says, waving Max's surprise aside. "She's your wife. The last time you were here, Madame Barone and I had a delightful conversation about Queen Maria Amélie's sapphire parure."

"Ah. That's right." Max nods, the circling of his thumb over my palm slowing. "I'd forgotten."

He knows there was no last time I was here. I've never

met Edith before. But he smiles as if it's only natural I know all about eighteenth-century jewelry.

Edith gestures for him to go on. "Continue, please."

He takes a breath and looks over the sapphire and diamonds sparkling in the cold room light. "This set was completed in 1750 for my great-great, too many greats,"—he waves his hand—"Grandmother Marie Thérèse Chambray as a wedding gift. When King Louis XV requested"—Max's mouth tilts into an ironic smile, letting me know the request was actually a command—"that all precious gems and jewelry be given to the state to fund the Seven Years War, Marie Thérèse gave all in her possession except this set, which she hid for many years."

I lean forward excitedly. "Yes. That's why iron and cut-steel jewelry became so popular. They called it iron for gold. They upcycled nails, created iron chokers. Women wore iron jewelry to show support for military campaigns or as a substitute for the jewelry they gave up."

"We have quite a few pieces in our collection," Edith says. "Quite a few."

"Why did she hide these?" I ask.

"Wouldn't you?" Max quirks an eyebrow. "Perhaps slip it in a pocket?"

I kick him under the table and he lets out a soft grunt.

"I have a letter from 1759 from Marie Thérèse to her daughter," he continues, giving me a sidelong glance. "She claims to have hidden the set because it has unusual properties."

Edith picks up the loupe and holds it over the bracelets, magnifying the gemstones. "Rivière-style bracelet meant to lengthen the necklace if desired. Graduated and faceted oval-shaped sapphires varying from deep to vivid blue. Foil-backed collet settings, 18 carat yellow gold. Rose-cut diamonds, typical of the era. Tool-marks indicative of hand-carving."

She ticks off the attributes of the jewelry as briskly as her steps clicking down the hall, "Complementary brooch. Day-to-night earrings with the back-to-front European wire. The teardrop sapphire hangs below five rose-cut diamonds. Fine wirework with gold beads, stippled texture. The teardrop can be removed from the surmount for a day look. The tiara is"—she pulls the loupe away from her eye and glances back at Max—"stunning, but not unusual for this era and this caliber of piece."

Max gives an acknowledging smile. "Exactly. It wasn't the cut or the material that was unusual. It was what Marie Thérèse claimed the parure could do. She claimed in her letter that the parure granted its owner their fondest wish. If they whispered to the parure their heart's desire, the stones, the jewelry,"—Max shrugs—"*something* would hear them and grant their wish."

He looks at me then, and I see the glint in his eye, similar to the winking of the stones against the rich black velvet.

"Fascinating," Edith says. "You will share this document?"

Max nods but doesn't break eye contact with me. "I'll send you a copy."

"It's an interesting story," she continues. "It reminds me people will believe anything. Jewelry isn't magical. Not in the literal sense." She sounds amused.

Max isn't amused, though, and neither am I.

"Perhaps," Max finally says, looking back at Edith. "However, during the terror, the entire family was executed by the revolutionaries. The parure was stolen during the looting of Marie Thérèse's home. The only piece that wasn't taken was the necklace. Marie Thérèse placed that over her seventeen-year-old daughter's neck mere hours before Marie Thérèse lost her life. She gave her daughter, Thérèse, the necklace and a single wish. *Live.* Thérèse escaped France, made her way to Switzerland, and married Philippe Barone. Perhaps Marie Thérèse's wish for her daughter came true."

He lifts a shoulder. "Somehow the stolen parure remained intact, save for the necklace. It was passed down through the centuries, through collectors and families, until it came to you. Us Barones have kept the necklace and the letter."

"And you aren't likely to donate that to complete the museum's set," Edith says, reading his tone.

"No," Max says. "We won't part with it. However, I have recently acquired an acrostic ring you may be interested in."

Edith sits straighter, nearly vibrating with interest.

"What's an acrostic ring?" I ask.

"They're symbolic rings. The language of gemstones," Max says. "The gems form a line and the first letter of each stone spells a word. The ring I acquired, for instance, spells 'dearest.'"

"Victorian era," Edith says, and Max nods in confirmation.

"Diamond, emerald, amethyst, ruby, emerald, sapphire, topaz. Dearest." Max smiles at me.

I laugh, delighted. "That's lovely."

Max represses a quick smile. "I'll show it to you when we're back home. You can—" He cuts himself off, and the sudden awareness it's not *our* home and we aren't likely to be going back *together* sits like another person between us.

Edith doesn't notice. "Yes. I would like to see that," she says. Then, glancing between the parure and us, she stands and checks the clock on the wall. "I'll leave you for five minutes. I'll be right outside."

She leaves, closing the door behind her. As I don't hear the *click, click* of her heels I assume she must be waiting outside the room.

"Did you request alone time with the parure?" I whisper. "How?"

Max leans close and says quietly. "I've donated millions of francs' worth of jewelry to this museum. It's a small thing for them to do."

We both turn toward the parure. It doesn't feel the same as the necklace did. There isn't any of that spinning-in-starlight feel.

But then, with his free hand, Max reaches into his leather jacket and pulls a thin jewelry box from his interior pocket.

"You brought it with you?" I ask. "I can't believe you've been walking around Paris all day with a priceless necklace in your jacket pocket! Are you insane?"

Max opens the case and the sapphire and diamonds catch the light. "My *interior* pocket," he says.

I shake my head, my heart thumping. "Anyone could've stolen it."

Max snorts.

I pull my hand from his. Then, at the cold that seeps back over me, I lean against him, pressing my arm and leg against him.

Max fits the white gloves on and then lays the pieces together, completing the set.

I lose my breath. "It really does look like a river of light falling from the stars."

"It's the rose cut and the foil backing," Max says.

"Right. The rose cut was for catching the candlelight."

Max gives me a quick look, a frown at the edges of his mouth. "I've forgotten," he says. "What was the copper-zinc alloy often used . . .?"

"Pinchbeck," I say, lost in the glitter of the necklace.

"And how were diamonds cut in the 1700s?"

I know this one. "In thin slivers, more for surface area and sparkle than symmetry. Not at all like today."

"And what do you prefer—the girandole or the pendeloque earring?"

"The girandole."

"And your favorite jewelry house? Cartier, Boucheron, Chanel, Van Cleef & Arpels, Mellerio, Lorenz Baümer—"

"Barone," I say without thinking. And then at the taut, heated silence, I look away from the necklace nestled next to its family.

When I look at Max, his shoulders are tight, his jaw is tight, and there's a coiled energy compressed and ready to spring.

"You like me," he says, his voice low and tight.

My skin tingles at the energy crackling off him. "Yes?"

I bite my lip, realizing too late what I've given away.

"You learned about jewelry because you like me."

I start to deny it, but he squeezes my hand.

"Admit it. You learned it because you like me."

He's wrong. I didn't learn about jewelry because I like him. I learned about it because I love him.

"Yes," I say. "I researched all about jewelry because I liked you."

He catches the past tense. "Like," he corrects.

I smile. "Like."

He nods and his shoulders relax. "Make your wish. With the parure together for the first time in centuries, it will come true." Then, eyes narrowing, he says, "To be sure, I'll make a wish too."

I nod and clasp his hand tightly.

Then I lean into the swirl of the gemstones and the pull of their sparkling allure and whisper, "I wish everything was back to the way it was. I wish Max and I weren't married."

Because I'm holding his hand, I feel Max's stillness when I make my wish. The way his breath is held and the way his muscles tighten. And then, when I stop speaking, I feel his inhale.

Finally, he says, "I wish . . ." He turns back to me and glances at my mouth, then back to my eyes. There's conflict in the hard line of his mouth and the tilt of his jaw. Then he shakes his head and says, "I wish everything was put to rights."

His words drop between us and the sapphires and diamonds seem to lose their luster. Before the light shining on the facets set a sort of song in the air; now the room is cold and silent.

Outside the door a loud group passes, talking animatedly. They say hello to Edith and she responds, right outside the door. I'm aware that any moment she'll open the door and take the parure away.

Max lifts the necklace and sets it back in its box, sliding it into his interior pocket.

Suddenly I'm cold and tired, as limp and droopy as the freesias resting on the chair next to me.

"What do you think will happen?" I ask, glancing around the small confines of the room. "Will we wake up back in Geneva, everything as it was? Do you think we'll even remember this? Will you remember me?" A panicked twinge sets up in my chest and I clutch his hand. "Do you think you'll forget this and think I'm a thief and a liar again? That if I come to you, you'll call the police like you threat—?"

"Anna," Max says, shaking his head. "Don't worry."

"That's easy for you to say. You aren't the one who would end up in prison."

"But if I forget you," he says, "isn't that another sort of prison? I'll be sentenced to never knowing what I'm missing."

My lips part on a small, surprised exhale. "Does that mean—?"

"I hope I don't forget this," Max says. "It's been unexpected."

"In a good way?"

"In the best way."

We smile at each other, then Edith opens the door, here to collect the parure and send us on our way.

On our way out, back through the marble halls and echoing chambers, down the grand staircase, I can't help but think about the fact that no matter what happens tomorrow, we still have tonight.

20

———————

THE SUN IS A BRIGHT WHITE ORB IN THE BLEACHED BLUE sky, hanging like a glittering diamond over the Jardin des Tuileries. I blink into the light, letting my eyes adjust to the startling reality that yes, I am in Paris, and yes, it's as wonderful as I always imagined it would be.

Although I can't quite decide if it's wonderful because it's Paris or if it's wonderful because I'm here with Max.

Little spots dance in my vision as I take in the sun glittering off stone and statues, and Max takes my hand in a firm, welcome grip. The spring breeze teases us, the cool air kissing my cheeks. The shadows are lengthening beneath the museums and monuments, reaching across the cobblestone and dipping toward the stretch of trees spanning the park.

I shiver as we walk, because although the sun is warm and the air is more temperate than the museum, there is still a bit of late-spring chill in the air. The unfurling red and yellow tulips, the pearl string of pink flowers on the redbud trees, all shout that spring is here and summer is rushing toward us. There's a soft, subtle floral perfume and green metal chairs are spaced about on the crushed limestone, tempting people to sit, relax, and enjoy the changing of the seasons.

A white-haired couple sit in a pair of green chairs reading a newspaper together under a pink magnolia tree. As Max and I pass, the woman glances up, notes our clasped hands, and gives me a knowing smile, as if to say, "Ah, young love!"

I can practically hear the birds singing and the strains of an accordion playing "La Vie en Rose" while she imagines me and Max gliding into the sunset of dusky pink clouds, fluttering rose petals, and romantic amour.

My chest thuds hollowly and I give a tremulous smile back, feeling somehow as if I've lied to a woman I don't know and I want to apologize for the mistake.

But then we're past the couple and Max gives my hand a squeeze.

"Thank you," he says, and when I glance at him in surprise he lets out a sharp laugh at my expression.

"What? Why?" I ask, looking around. We're in the mecca of tourism, within shouting distance of the Louvre and in the shadow of the the Arc de Triomphe. There's an odd juxtaposition of serene park and fragile tulips quietly reaching toward the sun, clashing with the thousands of people that hurry through every day on their way to the next monument.

"For today. I've had . . ." He glances across the short, cushioned grass, the crushed limestone and naked, weathered statues, back toward the Seine and our little island interlude. "A wonderful time."

"Are you feeling sentimental? Already regretting the end of our marriage?" I ask, trying to keep the mood as light as the candy-pink petunias dotting the flower bed we're passing.

But who am I kidding? Petunias aren't light—they're one of the hardiest flowers around. If you want a flower that survives, you pick a petunia. They barely need any attention; they aren't fussy at all. Just add sun, some water, and voila, you have a flower that will bloom for you all summer long. Fine, a bit of deadheading is necessary, but don't we all need to let go of what's not working every now and then?

"What are you thinking?" Max asks, "You have the strangest expression on your face."

I wrinkle my nose when I look up at him. "I just realized I'm a petunia."

"A petunia? The flower?"

I point at the bright pink blooms. "There are some flowers that are fussy. That need coddling. That need constant attention. The soil has to be the perfect pH. They have to be fed composted fish brains, alfalfa meal, or a generous helping of manure . . ." I wave my hand, shooing that away.

"So you're telling me you don't need to be fed manure?" he asks, his lips twitching.

"No. I've never been one to appreciate being fed a load of crap." I grin. "I'm just . . . easy. I don't need a lot in life. I don't need a big house or lots of money or constant adoration. It doesn't take much to make me happy. For instance, for years I loved—" I'm about to say that for years I loved him, and all it took was standing in the partial sun of his presence, the remnants of his life, for me to fall. But I cut myself off just in time and instead say, "The small things. That's a petunia. Just sun, water, a bit of food, and they bloom beautifully all summer long.

But"—I narrow my eyes thoughtfully on the flower bed—"I was only wondering if maybe it'd be better if I was a rose. Or an orchid. Let me tell you, orchids are the worst to care for, but people love them. They're obsessed. There are clubs for orchids, fan sites, societies. It's like the harder something is to care for, the fussier it is, the more people love it. Maybe that's what I'm doing wrong. I'm a petunia when I should've been an orchid. People notice orchids. They don't notice petunias."

Max stops. Pulls me to the side of the path under the shade of a chestnut tree. The leaves rustle in the wind, whispering above us, and the light dapples over Max's face, darkening his eyes.

"Let me get this straight," he says, his mouth tugging down. "I tell you I've had a wonderful time today, that I want to make love to you until you're senseless, and you tell me you think you should be someone you're not?"

His voice comes out in a rough growl, and I swallow at the hard cast of his jaw and the intensity in his gaze. I try to say something, but the only thing that comes out is a short, surprised puff of air.

"If it wasn't clear before," he says, "I like you. You're not a damn petunia. You're a woman."

The way he says the last word almost sounds as if he's saying "you're my woman."

"But . . ." I pause, licking my lips at the dryness in my mouth. "You don't want me. Not *really*. Tomorrow—"

"Maybe I won't want you tomorrow," Max says sharply, gripping my hand tighter. "Maybe tomorrow I'll go back to being lonely and regretful and wishing I could find a woman who fits me as comfortably as your hand in mine. Who the hell knows what will happen tomorrow? Maybe I'll forget you and you'll forget this. You're right—I didn't want you before. But you can't stand there and tell me I don't want you now."

Max and I stare at each other underneath the soft shade of the chestnut tree, dozens of people passing by on the path beside us. Yet we're captured in the shade and the light, breathing heavily, a battle going on between us.

"I know you want me," I say, and when I do, his eyes flare. "I want you too," I admit in a whisper, "but I don't know that it's real. So tonight . . ."

When I trail off, Max steps closer, the heat of him pressing against me. "I know my own mind," he says. "I may be experiencing more feelings since you walked into my office than I have in years, but I know my own mind. I know what's real and what isn't. This is real." He holds my gaze for a long moment. "This is real."

Then he drops his mouth to mine, brushing his lips over me. His mouth is featherlight, as gentle as the breeze whispering across a petal in the afternoon light. "Tomorrow," he says against my lips, "this may not be real."

He presses another kiss to me, his tongue tasting the seam of my mouth, his lips drifting over mine like an ancient mariner exploring the seas, guided only by his instinct and the stars. "But it's real today and I've always thought the best way to live, is in the moment."

I sink into his mouth, gripping his jacket. The hard line of the jewelry box knocks against my knuckles. The necklace. The reason for all this.

"You won't regret it?" I ask. "Tomorrow?"

"Let's promise each other that whatever happens, neither of us will regret anything."

I look up at him, my breath shaking. The shadow of

the chestnut tree falls over him, painting him dark and tempting.

I have to tell him. I can't continue down this path without telling him. I can't promise I won't regret tonight if I don't.

I've been afraid, worried what he'll say or think, but the fear of regret is stronger than either of those worries.

"Max. The reason . . ." I pause, and he presses a kiss to the corner of my mouth. "I . . ."

He traces his mouth over my lips, tasting me.

"The reason I wished on the necklace is because three years ago . . ." I pull my mouth from his, setting my hand on his chest.

"Three years ago?" The edge of his mouth lifts.

My cheeks heat and a prickly-hot flush tickles my skin. Behind us, on the path toward the Arc de Triomphe a woman laughs loudly and a group of teenagers shout, shoving each other teasingly. I drop my hand from his chest.

"I met you," I say finally.

He nods. "Yes. By the way, was it you who left me soups and dinners on occasion? In my refrigerator, with a note on how to reheat?"

I swallow, my heart thudding along painfully. "Yes."

"Mmm. I always thought it was your partner—"

"Dorene."

"Right. Dorene. I like your onion soup. Wine or—"

"Whiskey," I say.

He nods. "And the books in the library. Sometimes the one I was reading—I always laid them flat, pages spread—I'd come back and they'd have a slip of paper bookmarking the page instead. It would be cut with crinkle edges."

"Laying them flat ruins the spine," I say, indignant on the book's behalf.

He grins. "It *was* you. And the scent of chamomile that lingered on my sheets. I thought it was the detergent, but—"

"It's aromatherapy. For healthy sleep. If you don't like it—"

"I like it." He takes my hand and places it back on his chest, inside his jacket, so that I can feel the strong beating of his heart and the heat of his skin through his shirt. "The weekly vase of flowers in the entry?"

"Me." I look to the side, avoiding his eye.

Max takes my chin in his fingers and tilts my face back up. "The fresh cakes of hand-milled soap laid out on freshly laundered towels?"

"Me," I whisper, my throat raw.

"The hazelnut croissants last Christmas? They weren't from your company?"

"No," I admit.

He nods, his thumb brushing over my chin and then lighting on my bottom lip. "I ate them all in one sitting," he says, smiling. "I glutted myself on them. I devoured them."

My breath is tight in my chest and it feels as if I'm breathing through a straw. I can't get quite enough air.

"One last question," he says, his voice low and melodious. "Did you ever lie in my bed? Strip the sheets, strip yourself, sprawl naked on my mattress and touch yourself?"

"No!" I cry, all the air rushing from my lungs.

"Shame," Max says, dragging his thumb over my mouth.

"You're disturbed," I say, my voice shaking. "I'm a

professional. I take my job seriously. Well, I did until I was fired."

Max grins, and as I keep talking his grin widens even more.

"How could you even ask something like that? How could you think that—?"

"And did you or did you not watch my crime-show episodes and leave the playback a good ten seconds after where I'd left them?"

"What?" I say, struck dumb.

He gives me a wolfish smile. "Admit it. You piggybacked on my streaming."

"Did not!"

"Mm-hmm."

"I . . ." I frown, giving him a no-nonsense look. "Maybe once."

He quirks an eyebrow.

"Twice."

His eyebrow rises higher.

"Fine. At most, six times. I had to watch until I found out how Sean escaped from—"

He starts to laugh, his chest vibrating with mirth under my palm. I push at him and he pulls me close, wrapping his arm around me and holding me tightly.

I stand stiffly. "It's not funny."

"It isn't at all," he agrees. "All these years, you were an essential part of my life, and I didn't even know it. You were wrapped in every part of my day and I didn't even know your name. It's not funny at all."

He brushes a kiss across the top of my head and I relax against the solid wall of his chest.

"All those years I thought I was alone, and all along, there you were, making sure I ate well, saving my books from neglect, leaving bookmarks and flowers and scents to make sure I had a good night's sleep. I thought I was alone, but I never was. Not for a minute."

I bury my face against the leather of Max's jacket, breathing in the soft scent, feeling the rise and fall of his chest. His hand tangles in my hair, scraping against the back of my neck. A warm thrumming hums through me like the awakening of the soil in spring. I feel as if I'm ready to bloom under the sunshine of Max's words.

I stretch up to him, raising my face to his, and admit, "When I first saw you, I thought it was love at first sight."

He stares at me for a moment, searching my gaze, feeling the weight of my words. "You didn't know me. You knew nothing about me."

"It didn't matter."

He nods and then asks, "You don't feel that way any longer?"

"No."

I don't think it was love at first sight. I *know* it was love at first sight. I don't think I loved him. I *know* I love him.

"Love at first sight is a fickle thing," he says, acknowledging its loss. "It's a lot like passion. Here today, gone tomorrow." He plays with my hair, the long curls sliding through his fingers and catching the dappled light. "Is that why you made your wish?" he asks, releasing my hair to let it fall back to my breast. "It wasn't to live in my wretched house or have a vault of jewelry at your disposal. It was for the idea of love?"

"You think I'm a fool."

He shakes his head. "I think I'm a fool."

"Why?"

"Because even knowing you're as constant as the north star, I'm still scared of how much I want you. I still want out of this upside-down world where I'm seven years married."

My stomach falls to the crushed limestone and flops around in the leaf-laced shade at our feet. I watch it gasp for breath and then die a slow death.

"We still have today," I tell him. "Tonight. You can be as passionate as you like. Tomorrow it'll all be wiped away. You'll be alone again. I'll be on my own. We might not ever meet again."

He shakes his head and reaches up to grip my wrist. "Don't. Promise me that when this is over, if I don't remember, you'll come to me and—"

"What if I don't remember either? Besides, you'll think I'm crazy. You'll kick me out of your house. You'll call the police—"

"Make me listen," he says.

"I can't make you do anything."

"You can make me do whatever you want. I'd . . ." He trails off, his gaze landing on my mouth. "I want to know you in our other life. I want the chance to get to know you there. To kiss you. To bring you flowers. To take you out to dinner. To meet your mom and sister. I want the chance to see if you are the choice I would make. I'd like to give you the sun and the rain and the . . ."

"Composted fish brains and alfalfa sprouts," I say.

"Exactly." He restrains a smile. "I'd start a fan site. A club. But I wouldn't let anyone else be a member, because I don't like to share."

I smile at that. "Are you saying that even though I wished you into a topsy-turvy marriage in an upside-down world, you still like me? You still want to know me?"

He dips his chin, and when he looks at me, his lips

soften and he smiles. He holds up the crinkled bouquet of freesias. "Do you see these flowers?"

I nod. "Getting a bit sad, aren't they?"

"They're our timer," he says, eying the drooping petals. "While they're still limping along, we're going to enjoy the hell out of ourselves. Come morning . . ." He shrugs. "Who knows? But meanwhile, you've never been to Paris. I'm going to take you on a whirlwind tour of all the romantic places—Montmartre, Sacré-Coeur, the Eiffel Tower—"

"But—"

"—kissing you in each spot. Imprinting a memory, so that even if our minds forget, our bodies and our souls will remember. So that the next time I see you I'll have a choice. And hopefully I'll make the right one."

I blink at Max, dizzy and stunned at his announcement, the scent of freesia swimming around us.

"Where to first?" he asks.

I'm swept away by the fire in his eyes. "Not the bedroom?"

He laughs and pulls me out from under the chestnut tree, back into the sun.

21

———————

In my mind Paris is a series of snapshots, a camera held aloft while Max kisses me breathless. Each kiss draws me tighter, so that as the blue sky shifts to a rosy, flower-petal hue, I'm practically shimmering in the last rays of the setting sun.

Generations of lovers have walked hand in hand through the city of love, and I'm wrapped in the magic.

Max strokes my cheeks under the Arc de Triomphe, nibbling on my bottom lip with surprising gentleness.

He teases me beneath the Eiffel Tower, his fingers threading through my hair, his body hard against mine. He plies open my mouth and draws out little gasps and quick breaths at the stinging pleasure.

Then he feeds me hazelnut and chocolate macarons from the famed macaron bar on the second floor of the Eiffel Tower. He wipes my mouth of the hazelnut crumbs and then, with hungry eyes, devours the flavor from my lips.

In Montmartre we climb the 222 steep stone steps

through the garden to the Sacré-Coeur. The steps are lined with pretty lampposts and leafy green trees shaded gold and pink in the dusk. Below lies a sprawling view of Paris, with street musicians playing an evening serenade, the romantic notes flowing in and out of the cool breeze and winking in time with the lights of the city flickering to life.

Montmartre is full of charm. Narrow, winding cobblestone streets, sex shops and cabarets, trinket and T-shirt peddlers, and caricature artists, and at the crowded steps where people climb to the basilica or drink wine in the grass as the light falls to night, flirty men chat up pretty women, and all the while, musicians play romantic songs.

On each stone step Max kisses me, or I kiss him.

Step.

Kiss.

Step.

Kiss.

It's a game at first, a laugh.

222 kisses to the top.

But then, after ten quick steps and ten quick pecks, Max stops, grabs my hips, and presses me against him for a languid, tingling, hang-on-or-your-legs-will-give-out kiss.

At step twelve, I pull his lower lip into my mouth and bite his soft smile.

At fifteen, his hands roughly span my hips as he moans into my mouth.

At thirty, he kisses the length of my collarbone.

Fifty through sixty, he kisses the tips of every one of my fingers. The press of his lips burns into them, leaving them glowing like the light of a firefly.

In my whole life I've had perhaps thirty or forty kisses. We pass that number and then keep climbing. The further we rise, the more all those other kisses are buried and forgotten, and all that's left is Max's mouth on mine, over me, on me.

At 112, I drag my mouth over the rough stubble of his jaw and then suck on the pulse beating wildly in his neck.

At 160, he kisses my closed eyelids.

At 200, he's tired of stumbling up the steps, his mouth on mine, so he lifts me in his arms and settles my legs around his middle.

My dress falls around my legs. Max's fingers dig into my thighs, pressing hungrily into my flesh as he takes another quick step toward the Sacré-Coeur.

For step 212, my hands dig into his shoulders, his fingers massage my thighs, and his tongue tangles with mine, thrusting then withdrawing.

At 222, he's kissed every bit of me. My fingers, my palms, my wrists, my collarbone, my neck, my eyelids, the shell of my ear, the backs of my knees, the insides of my thighs. My mouth. Goodness. My mouth.

Anywhere that is bare and uncovered by my dress, he's kissed.

Most of his kisses were chaste. Just his mouth on my skin, his gaze direct and watching as he lowered his mouth to me. Those chaste kisses chased over my skin and combined to drag me down into a whirling maelstrom of need.

With each step up, he dragged me further and further, heightening the sensations running over me and through me.

And now, on the last step, beneath the white rounded tours of the Sacred Heart, Max stares into my eyes. His mouth is wet, his lips red and slightly swollen. His gaze is glowing with the same heady, drunk-on-kisses, I-want-to-climb-inside-you feeling that is overwhelming me.

I reach up, thread my fingers through his thick hair, and pull his mouth to mine. His mouth is hot, still tasting of hazelnut and chocolate and thick desire. I press myself closer to him, my legs wrapped around his middle. He's hard against me, and as he strokes my mouth and we attempt to imprint ourselves on each other, a tight tingling travels down my spine and pools at the space where we connect.

"Take me to bed," I whisper against his mouth. "Please."

His arms flex and he drags me closer, a ragged breath escaping hot against my mouth. "You still haven't kissed me in front of City Hall, Palais Garnier Opera House, on the bridges spanning Canal Saint-Martin—"

I clutch his shoulders and stare into his eyes. "Max."

"Anna?" The corner of his mouth lifts, his gaze burning hotter. My lips tingle and ache for him to set his mouth back on mine.

"I've seen enough. Now I just want to see you."

The rest of his mouth lifts into a wide, happy smile. "You don't want dinner first?"

"Max!"

He laughs and then carries me back down all 222 steps.

22

Max's Paris home is in the 16th arrondissement, near Trocadéro. It's old, beautiful, and has a distinct old-money feel. The sandstone building is as stately as a Parisian museum, six stories high and wrapped in gorgeous iron balconies. Chestnut trees line the sidewalks, and after the noise and color of Montmartre, the quiet elegance of the sedate street sets off a rebellious buzz inside me.

Max's hand shakes as he unlocks the front door. I shiver at the look he casts me, my insides vibrating, my skin tingling.

When the door swings open I step through, and the lights automatically come on, set to dim. The space is open, hushed, and looks so much like the decorating at the Barone estate that I can't help but smile. Tall ceilings, chandeliers, ornate plaster molding, intricate paneling, nineteenth-century art, spindly-legged furniture, and luxurious rugs. The marble-floored entrance gallery sweeps into a wide sitting room with velvet-cushioned furniture and a chaise longue situated in front of a wall of windows that lead onto the iron balcony.

The tall gold satin curtains are drawn back, and right in the center of it all, there's a view of the Eiffel Tower. It's glowing, lit up like a Christmas tree. A beacon in the night.

Max shuts the door, and at the click of the lock we're enfolded in a quiet, expectant hush. He steps next to me, not touching me. But I can feel the heat of him; hear the quiet whisper of his indrawn breath.

"When you said you wanted my scream to be heard at the Eiffel Tower," I say, nodding to the shining lights reflecting off the windows, "you weren't kidding, were you?"

He's quiet, and when I finally look up at him I find he's watching me.

My breath catches and my heartbeat picks up, racing through my chest. I've seen that look before. It's the look my mom gave my dad, right before we took him to the hospital for the last time. It's the look Dorene has whenever she watches the opening credits of her husband's movies in the courtyard, the volume turned up high.

It's the look I imagine I had the first time I saw Max.

"Anna," he says, his voice a deep, insistent plea.

"Yes," I say, agreeing to everything in his eyes.

And then there isn't anything separating us anymore. I drop the bouquet of freesias and it hits the floor with a whispered sigh. Our mouths clash with a violent need. The teasing, fire-lit passion of the Montmartre steps is gone. Now it's as if our mouths are at war, fighting to win and to be won.

I grapple with his leather jacket. He shoves at my dress. I yank free his belt. He tugs my dress over my head.

Cold air hits my skin and my nipples pucker. He swears and grabs my breasts. He cups their heaviness in his palms and pinches my nipples. I bite his lip. Lick the inside of his mouth. Shove his pants down his hips.

My bra. His shirt. My lacy thong. His boxers. All gone. Casualties in our haste, and in our fight to touch and to feel and to be.

We're a battle of hands and mouths, tugging and tasting, and I'm breathing so hard I can't catch my breath.

I trip backward, falling against the wall. My bare back hits the cold plaster and Max falls over me, pressing me to the hard surface. He grabs my wrists, holding my arms over my head, and drops his mouth to my neck, to my fluttering pulse, and then to the hard points of my breasts.

I arch into his hot mouth and cry out when he sucks —hard—then bites down. Then he frees his mouth with a slow pop and blows hot air across my stinging nipple. There's a sharp, hungry pulse between my legs and I strain against his hold.

He looks up at me, his eyes glazed and hungry. Then he smiles so wickedly my heart nearly leaps from my chest. I clench my legs together at the insistent, needing pulse.

"You taste like sunshine," he says, "and wishes come true."

"You don't like my wishes," I say, straining at his hold on my wrists, wrapping my ankle around his calf and rubbing my leg down the rough hair on his. I shiver at the feel of him.

"Tell me what you wish for tonight." He drops his

mouth to my other nipple, takes a hard suck, and scrapes his teeth over the sensitive point. "Tell me what you wish and I'll make it come true."

I close my eyes, unable to look directly into his gaze. In life, sometimes you run across something so beautiful that you can't look directly at it. It's as if the beauty tears at something inside you. The beauty is so astounding, so shattering, that you have to look away. In this moment, with his mouth worshipping my breasts and his gaze telling me he'll grant my every wish, Max's smile is the most beautiful thing I've seen in my entire life.

The Eiffel Tower, Notre-Dame, Sacré-Coeur—nothing can compare.

He's so beautiful that I can't breathe, my heart has lost the ability to beat, and the corners of my eyes sting as tears leak from their edges. He's too beautiful to look at.

"Anna? What?" He straightens, releases my wrists, and pulls me to him, kissing the salt pooling at the edge of my lips.

I shake my head, my mouth trembling against his. "I'm afraid to ask."

"Tell me and I'll do it. Anything."

I open my eyes finally. He's waiting, his hair falling across his head, the stubble on his jaw dark after a day of growth. He smells like the city, fresh air, spring sun, and the hand-milled soap I lay out for him every week. On my lips I taste him—sweet, insistent desire.

"I want . . . I want a night I'll never forget."

He smiles, wide and wicked. "Anna, darling. I'm going to give you a night you remember even into your next life. You want passion?"

I nod. "Yes. Do you?"

He draws his fingers across my jaw and tucks a strand

of hair behind my ear. "For the first time in my life. I want it all. Damn the consequences."

"What consequences?"

He grins. "None. There are none."

Then he grips my hips and lifts me. I straddle him and he strides through the living room, down a long, antique-strewn hall, to a large bedroom. There's a giant four-poster bed in the center of the room with a white silk canopy. On the nightstand is a photo in a gilt frame of me and Max at our wedding. He glances at it and lets out a small scoff.

He carries me to the bed, flips the photo face down on the nightstand, and says, "This night is about us. Not that."

I nod, my throat tight.

Then, as if we've both given ourselves permission to let go of everything except the wish of this moment, we collide.

I grip Max's bare shoulders, press myself against his length, and send my mouth over his lips. He sinks to his knees, hitting the thick rug, and drops me to the bed, my calves hanging over his shoulders.

And then, with a ragged breath, he sets his mouth to the heat between my legs. There isn't any build up; there isn't a slow tingle or a throbbing spark. No. The second his mouth hits my clit and he takes a long, hard suck, I arch my back and scream.

The orgasm rips through me, tearing me in half as I come and come and come. I claw at Max's shoulders and he grabs my wrists, pushing them and me back to the bed as he continues to suck and bite and pull so the orgasm that began doesn't stop—it just keeps building and growing—until I'm mindless with the sensations tearing through me.

Max's rough stubble rubs against the insides of my thighs, his fingers release my wrists and reach up to grip my hands in a tight hold, and he thrusts his tongue inside me. He's rough, insistent, a mirroring of the kisses we've shared. When his tongue invades me I cry out again, clamping down, wishing he were inside me so I could feel myself around him.

He's tasting me, sucking and biting and licking, and I can feel his hot breath as tremors flow through me. I grip his hands and try to pull him up.

But he shakes his head and says, "Not done," in a greedy, hungry voice. "Been reminiscing about this taste, and it's better . . . how is it better? You're so sweet."

He sucks me again, humming against me, and when I lift my hips involuntarily he lets go of my hands and thrusts a finger inside me, then another.

I toss my head, driving down on his invasion. "More," I say. "More, more, more."

My toes are curling, my spine is tingling, and the blood pumping in my veins has taken on a throbbing pulse that echoes my heartbeat. It's as if my veins are contracting and pumping pleasure through me in great, violent pulses.

Max swears as I come over his hand. I scream raggedly again, my voice raw and husky.

The mattress is soft underneath me, the satin sheet slippery and wet from my sweat and my coming. Max lifts me then, pushing me back onto the bed. He presses his mouth to mine and his lips are wet, sweet, and hot.

I'm buzzing, so sensitive that everywhere he touches me I light on fire like dry kindling set to flame. He presses his body over mine, pushing me into the mattress. His legs are muscled and rough with hair, and they scratch my bare legs, sending a shiver over me. His chest, solid and muscled, has a dusting of hair that scrapes my sensitive breasts and just-kissed nipples.

He's hard, full, and thick. I reach down and wrap my fingers around him. He's satin heat, and when I clench my hand in a tight grip he pulses and leaps in my hand.

Max's jaw clenches and he yanks in a shuddering breath as he stares down at me.

Then I gently push him, and he rolls with my touch, flipping our positions so I'm on top and he's helpless beneath me. He's covered in perspiration, the wetness of my orgasm, and the flush of sex. I make my way down his abdomen, kissing his taut skin, the line of his muscles, the trail of hair leading down.

And then I lick the moisture at the tip of him. His hips jerk up toward me and he makes a strangled noise. I grip the base of him and wrap my mouth around him.

He tastes salty and sweet, and as I lick around his length his hands dig into my hair, and he lets out another indistinct sound.

"Anna, Anna, Anna," he says, until my name has blurred into one long *annannanna*.

I take him deep, the tip of him pressing against the back of my throat, and he fights his urge to thrust and bury himself, holding still beneath me as I suck and lick and taste.

I can feel him growing thicker in my mouth, and as I tilt my eyes up to look at him I see ecstasy on his face. His mouth is upturned, his eyes glazed, and he's watching me as if I'm his dove, his Heloise, his heart.

I pull my mouth free, my lips tingling from the

suction and the feel of him, and when I do, he grabs me and flips me beneath him.

"The first time," he says, "I want you to come here, in this bed, so that if I don't remember you, I'll come back here and dream about this moment. But the second time? What do you want? I want your hands spread on my desk, your ass in the air, as I come in you from behind. The third time?"

"Do you have a garden?" I ask. "I want . . . outside."

I gasp as he sends his length gliding against the sensitive nub of my clit.

"I have a balcony," he says. "We could open the doors, let the stars in. And in Geneva . . ."

He trails off, pausing over me. I'm sure he was going to say that in Geneva he has acres and acres of land with countless spots to have sex for all of nature to see.

There's almost a flash of regret there, so I quickly press my mouth to his, tugging him by the hair to pull him in for another deep, luxurious kiss.

Finally, with his length dragging over me, he says, "In Geneva there's a folly in the woods. A ruin with stone columns and a mosaic floor, open to the sky. The columns are perfect for tying someone up and licking them until they scream."

"Sounds lovely," I say, dragging my hands over his lower back, pulling him along me.

"It does," he says, lost in the rhythm of moving along the outside of me.

The slow, teasing build that was lost before is there now. It shimmers and glows, and I reach out to meet it.

Max reaches toward the nightstand, pulls a condom on, and then settles his tip against me.

"Anna? Yes?" he asks, whispering my name.

"Yes," I say, arching up to him.

He lets out a shuddering breath and then looks into my eyes as he slowly pushes forward, stretching me. I tilt my hips at the feel of him. He keeps my gaze, watching my expressions, reading my every emotion.

He pulls his tip out and slowly thrusts back in, a millimeter at a time. The slow build is nearly too much—I want to grip his hips and pull him inside me in one quick, hard thrust. But no matter how much I tug, how much I roll my hips, Max keeps up his slow invasion so I feel drugged on the pressure of him, on the clasp of my insides around him.

As he thrusts deeper I cry out, clenching, riding on a wave of mounting pressure. When Max feels my muscles clenching around him he makes a harsh, hungry noise, and then his slow, careful control breaks.

He thrusts into me and the hurricane I predicted is unleashed. Max thrusts into me as I come, screaming into the sheets.

"I feel you," he says. "I *feel* you. You are the sweetest thing I've ever felt. I can't—"

Then his voice is cut off and he's pressing a bruising kiss to my mouth. He grips my hips, tilting me, so that when he thrusts in again he hits a spot that has me crying out incoherent words.

I grip him, coming against him, as sweat runs down his forehead, down his chest, and the sounds of begging and pleading and loving and worshipping blend together in a single wish. *More. More. More.*

And then—*I love you.*

I say it first, somewhere in between *yes* and *please* and *more* and *I can't* and *you can.*

"I love you."

I say it first.

And then, if I thought Max was unleashed before, my words cause an explosion. He flips me over. I grab the wooden headboard and he grips my hips, holding me from behind, spreading me out beneath him as he thrusts and thrusts and pushes me higher and higher. And then he's off the bed, standing, and he's pulled my ankles over his shoulders, tilted my hips, and he's pistoning into me, hitting that spot, and I'm screaming as I come.

And then he's over me again, his eyes glowing in the lights of Paris as he looks down at me, burying himself inside me. He grips my hands, holding me close, and we're touching everywhere—touching so deeply I think he's touched my soul.

"Anna," he whispers against my mouth, "I was wrong. One night with you." He thrusts again, losing his rhythm, his words coming out ragged and raw. "One night with you. I'd give up anything."

Then he reaches down and strokes my clit, and with my name on his lips I light up like a line of stars, like a rivière necklace, like a wish in the glowing fire of a burning candle.

He gives one final thrust—a desperate, needing, shaking plea. I clench around him as he comes, driving into me, calling my name.

As we slide down, our hands entwined, our legs tangled, our hearts thumping wildly, one against the other, Max presses a kiss to my mouth and pulls me against him, wrapping me in his warm embrace.

23

WE'RE WRAPPED IN THE DEEP SILENCE OF NIGHT, IN THE contentment of the early hours and the hush of moonlight before dawn. A soft glow cascades through the bedroom window, reflecting the lights of Paris and casting a rosy, dreamy luminescence over the bed.

Max's arms are wrapped around me, and I lie sprawled naked across his chest. His breath is steady, his chest rising and falling in a soothing rhythm as he strokes a hand through my hair. His heartbeat thumps against my chest, and I pull in a breath, drinking in the cloaked night air full of the memory of freesias, slick bodies, and deep kisses. The cotton sheets are warm, soft, and tangled around us.

The neighborhood is quiet, the old stone building is quiet, the bedroom is quiet. It's strange how quiet a city can be in the deep of the night. Yet without the noise and the color and the sights, it's easy to get lost in the way Max's fingers tangle in my hair and how his exhales fall in warm puffs across my skin.

I'm lulled and floating in a euphoric afterglow. I don't know if I've ever been so relaxed, as if I'm floating down a lazy river, lounging on an inner tube in the sun, Max cradling me in his lap as I drag my fingers through the cool water and he kisses the edge of my mouth.

Earlier, when I said "I love you," I claimed I said it first. But what I really meant was I said it and Max didn't.

Instead he made love to me. In the bed. Bent over his desk. Against the wall, with the balcony doors flung open and the sounds and scents and sights of Paris falling over us. In the shower, with hot jets of water spraying over us and frothy soap suds sliding over bare skin. In the kitchen, after we devoured a plate of hazelnut croissants and sipped burning liquor from a fifty-year-old bottle of Dalmore that Max said he'd been saving for the right moment.

Ten hours of making love. With his mouth. With his hands. With him thrusting desperately inside me. Max told the truth on the footbridge in the museum. He kept me coming all night long.

And now, with two hours left before sunrise, I can feel our time slipping away. Draining like grains of sand through an hourglass.

Never in my life have I wanted the sun to never rise—until now.

"I almost wish tomorrow wouldn't come," I say, my eyes drifting closed at the soothing rhythm of Max's hand stroking through my hair.

He makes a soft sound, his chest rising beneath me. "It will work out. Don't worry."

I open my heavy eyelids and stare out the window, past the rooflines and the tops of dark chestnut trees, toward the Eiffel Tower.

"I know our wish will work," he says, his chest rumbling with the deep baritone of his voice. "I felt something there, like I was spinning. A strange whirring, an odd tingling."

"Like you were flying?" I ask, wondering why I didn't feel anything—not like I did the first time.

"That's right." His hand trails over the back of my neck, his fingers playing over my spine.

"I felt that the first time. In your library," I say.

He presses his mouth to the top of my head, feathering his lips over my temple. We've touched each other so much tonight, explored everything, yet this intimate, casually gentle kiss makes my chest squeeze tight.

"Tired?" Max asks.

"Mm-hmm," I murmur, pressing my face into the pillow of his chest.

"Tomorrow, in case I don't remember you . . ."

I nod, my cheek scraping against the hair on his chest.

"I'm going to tell you something I've never told anyone. If you tell me this, I'll listen. All right?"

I lift my head and look into his eyes. They're shadowed by the muted dark, barely catching the glimmer of the lights outside. But still there's a warmth there, and the knowledge that tomorrow he might not know me or remember this. He might not like me. In fact, he might dislike me. Quite intensely.

"Okay," I say, my voice raw from the night of crying out in his arms.

He shifts me so we're sitting up, leaning against the dark wood headboard. The room is just as opulent as his home in Geneva. Lots of antique, elegantly carved wood, brass and gilt, and sumptuous fabrics. I know for a fact the interior design and the furniture was passed down and Max, being Max, left it as it was. He's a traditionalist in a lot of ways, and he values family and history and consistency. Even, I suppose, when family and history and consistency let you down.

"You know my father drank?"

I nod and he looks away, out the window, over the city.

"Living with an alcoholic, as a kid, it's like this nightmare where you're walking across a field full of landmines. Every day you wake up and you're shoved into this field, forced to walk across it, and you can tiptoe, or you can run, but either way, you have to do it. Sometimes you make it across with no explosion. Other times you step on a mine and it doesn't detonate. But then some days the explosion is violent, and you break an arm or blacken an eye, and your ears are still ringing days later. But it's not the landmines that are the worst. It's the fact that every day you have to stand at the edge of that field and walk across it. There's no escaping it. You have to keep walking, keep living it, over and over and over. And every day, you don't know what's going to happen. You have no control. You have no idea which step will set a landmine off."

He stops, his jaw tight, the muscles in his chest hard. I press my hand to his heart, feeling the slow, steady beat. "I'm sorry. I'm sorry I couldn't have walked it with you."

He smiles down at me, the hardness in his eyes softening. "I'm glad you didn't. I'm glad you weren't there. I hated so much. The only thing that matched how much I hated was how much I loved. Can you imagine? Loving so intensely, hating so much. It was too much for a kid. All those emotions bottled up inside. I promised myself every day that when I was eighteen I'd escape. I'd make my own way." He shrugs. "I didn't. It turns out I loved my family more than I thought. Love, even in small portions, is enough to defeat an ocean of hate. So that little light, it took me back. After university I returned home, the dutiful son to my father, the loyal younger brother, the loving son to my mother. And then, on a ski trip I was meant to be part of, all three of them were caught in an avalanche. They died."

He shakes his head, his expression a mask concealing his heart. "I was never afraid of the violent outbursts, my parents' passion, my brother's cruelty. What I was afraid of was that I saw myself in them. I saw that if I wasn't careful I could be just as violent, just as cruel. Every one of us has the capacity for cruelty—it's there inside us all. Every day we choose whether we'll live in the shadows or the light. I saw that more than most, because in myself I saw my father, and I saw my brother. So when I decided to let my family rest in peace, when I decided to let them go, I made myself a promise."

I look into his eyes. His steady, direct gaze. *This is important,* his dark eyes say. *I've never told anyone,* his expression says.

"I wrote a letter and buried it in a cognac bottle under a pile of rocks at the folly. I'm meant to break it if I ever falter. Read it and remember."

"Falter in what?" I ask, my hand curling against his chest.

The air between us is thick, heavy and full of the yearning memory of last night.

"I promised myself I would never love so deeply that I could hate in equal measure. I told myself that if I ever found myself embroiled in passion, I would step back. I would walk away. I reminded myself of all the good things in life—all the constant, pure, *good* things that didn't involve a field full of landmines or a love that was like a wooden boat crashing against a rocky shore, over, and over, and over again. The letter is there. I want you to remind me. And then I want you to tell me that I was wrong. Love isn't the opposite of hate. It doesn't have room for hate. It's pure and compassionate and forgiving and full of grace. It's constant. It's quiet. It's loud. It's steady. It's the night sky full of a million blazing stars. It's the first snowflake landing on your outstretched palm. It's a hand gripping yours in the dark, holding on when you're certain you're all alone. And passion? It isn't anything to be afraid of when it's rooted in love. Tell me that, Anna. Please? Will you promise to tell me?"

I lean forward and rest my forehead to his, looking into his eyes. I can see stars there now, the reflection of Paris's lights in the deep brown. The warmth of him sinks into me. The fear that tomorrow, all this will be forgotten.

I may have wished to be married to Max, I may have wished for his love, but I could never have wished for this. Because while I thought I knew him—while I thought I loved him—I never knew that I was only sitting at the shore of this love. After today, I'm sailing on an ocean of love and it spans as far as I can see. I could spend a lifetime exploring; a lifetime sailing this sea.

"I promise," I whisper. Then louder, "I promise."

He smiles, relief flooding his eyes. Then he pulls me down to the bed, the sheets rustling beneath us, the mattress rolling, and gently kisses me, quietly loves me, until we fall asleep to the soft, seeking, golden light of dawn.

24

I WAKE TO BRIGHT MID-MORNING LIGHT SHINING OVER THE bed, once again tapping insistently at my eyelids. I'm floating in a blissful state of half-sleep, half-waking and I squeeze my eyes tighter, burying my face against the soft pillow.

The plush bed is warm and cozy, the sheets wrapped around my legs. There's the sound of a dove outside, cooing to the morning. I smile at the familiar scent of Max on the sheets, mixed with our night of lovemaking and . . .

I open my eyes.

The white silk canopy is above me.

I'm still in Paris. In Max's bed.

This isn't where I'm supposed to be. I thought I'd be back in Geneva.

I sit up in bed, yanking the white sheets over my naked breasts. My hair falls over my shoulder and goose bumps rise on my skin at the slight chill in the air. Outside the window the sky is the deep cerulean blue of late May, shining over the elegantly curved roofs of the stone townhomes across the street. The soft coo of the mourning dove sounds again above the noises of a neighborhood waking. But inside Max's home it's quiet.

I shiver and slowly glance around the bedroom.

There are plenty of things I didn't notice last night in the heady blur of lovemaking. The large bed sits in the center of the bedroom, the wood frame a rich walnut, ornately carved. The walls are dove-gray with plaster panels and thick crown molding, with beautiful plasterwork on the ceiling. There's an antique crystal chandelier, of course. Glossy wood floors—again, of course. The thick, luxurious silk rug Max dropped to his knees on last night and pulled me to his mouth. Matching nightstands, a chest of drawers, a wardrobe, and tasteful oil paintings of the idyllic French countryside.

Then my eyes are drawn away from the furnishings to the door.

It's Max. He strides into the bedroom, a small smile curving the corner of his lips.

I can't deny it.

My heart gallops like a racehorse after the starting shot. I didn't know how scared I was about this moment, how fearful I was that he'd have forgotten what we did, or that he'd hate me again, until this very moment.

The flood of relief knocks me flat and I sag back against the headboard, my hold on the warm sheet wrapped around my breasts flagging.

"Good morning," he says, his voice rich and melodic, tinged with a smile.

He's dressed already. His black hair is wet and glistening from the shower, the thickness smoothed back.

He's in casual clothing, barefoot, a day's worth of stubble darkening his jaw. He has a breakfast tray in his hands. There's a plate of tartine smothered in butter and glossy, jewel-red jam, and a French press full of steamy black coffee next to two white mugs.

I stare at Max, at the tray of food, my heart thumping wildly in my chest.

It's the way he's looking at me. Like *I'm* breakfast. Like last night wasn't enough and he's very, very glad we're still here together and not back in Geneva.

He remembers me.

He still likes me.

"Morning," I say. It comes out as a squeak, and I blink at him, scooting back on the bed.

He grins at the noise I make and then lifts an eyebrow at how I'm still clutching the sheet to my chest.

He slides the tray onto the nightstand and settles on the bed next to me. The scent of coffee and cherry jam swirls around us, sweet and pungent. The bed tilts as he moves close, and the sheets scrape over my bare skin, drawing out more goose bumps.

"Why are you blushing?" Max asks with a smile. "Was last night . . .?" He trails off, his eyes going sleepy and happy. Then he threads his hands through my messy morning hair, tugs me close, and brushes his warm lips over mine.

I'm sore and achy, and there are places on my body that I didn't even know could be sore—yet at the heat of his mouth on mine there's a sudden hard, demanding throb. My eyelashes flutter and I lose my grip on the sheets, baring myself to Max.

He makes a hungry noise and scrapes his hands over my nipples, covering my breasts with his palms. That steady shimmer I'm already addicted to spreads over my skin.

"Did I mention how much I love you?" Max asks, trailing his mouth down my throat to my collarbone. His stubble scrapes over me, and I shiver when he rolls a nipple between his pointer finger and thumb.

But then his words sink in.

Love.

Max just said he *loves* me.

I said it first. And this morning he said it too.

I grip his shoulders as he pulls me onto his lap. The fabric of his clothing scrapes against my thighs as he tugs me close, settling me against his hard length.

"You . . ." I gasp when my nipples scrape against his shirt. "You love me."

It's a statement, but also a question.

But then I look into his eyes and I can't deny it. Max brings his mouth back to mine, nibbling at my lips. He tastes like café au lait, demerara sugar, and cherry jam, as if while making our breakfast he tasted the coffee and stuck his finger in the jam jar, licking it clean.

He's kissing me like he loves me. But even more, when he pulls back, leaving my mouth wet and buzzing, he's looking at me like he loves me.

No. Like he adores me.

Like I'm his Venus. His one true love.

Like he would die for me.

"Why do you sound so surprised?" he asks, tilting me back on the cloudlike bed, laying me bare on the mattress.

He settles over me, his legs cradling mine, his hands busy working magic.

"But—" I gasp when he manages to flick me *just right.*

Then I say, "But . . . we're still here. Are we . . .?" I gasp again, losing my train of thought for a moment when Max moves his finger in a lazy circle, causing a heat to spread through my abdomen and then lower.

"Of course we're still here," he says, giving me a conspiratorial grin. His eyes are clear, happy, and intent on pleasure.

"But . . ." I close my eyes. "Are we . . .? Did our wish work? Are we still married?"

Max makes a noise in the back of his throat and sinks on top of me, pressing me into the cushiony bed. He smells so good. The soap he used reminds me of what we did in the shower last night. I drag in a deep breath. Outside the dove coos again and the morning light shines a bit brighter.

"We're still married?" I ask again, gazing up at him.

He presses a gentle kiss to my mouth.

"I hope so," he says, gruff laughter in his voice. He takes my wrists in his hands, binds them in his grip, and holds them over my head as he starts to rock into me. "This next bit might be awkward if you weren't my wife."

He grins down at me as if he's planning very, very wicked things.

And—

I freeze.

Beneath the warmth of Max's body, in the heat of his bed, with the sun spreading over me, I go cold.

All the fuzzy, floaty, blissful orgasmic ecstasy that I woke up to disappears in a sudden, unexpected pop. That shimmery heat running through me? Now it's ice. It's prickly and cold, and I'm frozen.

When Max and I wished on the parure I believed that when we woke up we wouldn't be married anymore. I thought we'd be sent back to Geneva, back to how we were. I even worried Max might not remember our time together and he might hate me again.

I wished for us to not be married. Max wished for everything to be set right.

Is this setting things right?

Was his wish granted?

Or is this the second half of my wish?

I wished Max and I were married. I wished Max loved me.

Max stills. His hips stop rolling and his hands loosen on my wrists. He looks down at me, a line forming between his eyebrows.

"What's wrong?" he asks, his expression searching, his deep brown eyes concerned. "Anna, love? What is it?"

Oh no.

No.

Max looks like he'd happily take a sword to the chest to make whatever is upsetting me go away. He looks like his only wish in this life and the next is to love me and make me blissfully happy.

"You *love* me?"

"Always." He smiles happily, his dark brown eyes warming. "Forever."

"Oh no."

He laughs. "Oh yes."

"Oh no!"

He's in love. *In love* in love.

Not a normal "will you marry me?" kind of love, but a love potion, drugged, obsessed, want-you, need-you *in love* kind of love.

He lowers his head and tries to brush another sweet

kiss over my mouth. I turn my head and his lips run over my cheek.

"We're married," I say, staring at the photograph on the nightstand—the one from the night before. It's me in a wedding dress, Max at my side.

"The best seven years of my life," Max says into my neck, nuzzling at the frantic beat of my pulse. "Marrying you was the best thing I've ever done. Happy seven-year anniversary, darling."

Oh no. What have we done? "Please tell me you're kidding."

He laughs. "No. You've always been the best part of my life. Why would I joke about that?"

"Max."

He's still over me, pressing me into the bed, his hips settling over mine. I tug at my wrists, still held in his firm grip. He lets go and I put my hands to his chest, pressing at his warm, solid muscles.

"Anna."

I shake my head.

"Do you remember your other life? The one where we aren't married. The one where I cleaned your house."

He gives me an incredulous look. "What?"

A knot forms in my belly, twisting my insides into a queasy ball.

He doesn't remember.

He's lost who he used to be.

He's lost seven years of his life.

Somehow the wish we made yesterday didn't make things better; it made them drastically, horribly worse.

"I love your sense of humor," he says, grinning down at me.

Before, Max was unique. While everyone else

believed he and I had been married for seven years, Max remembered both the new reality and the old.

Now I'm the only one who remembers that none of this is real.

I've lost him.

"Max. I'm not joking."

He nods and then drags his fingers over my cheek. "Okay. Breakfast first, and then we'll do what you asked. We'll get busy making our baby."

And *that* is when I shove as hard as I can, pushing Max off me and out of the marriage bed.

25

———————

Apparently, it is absolutely impossible to convince someone of something if they are convinced something else is the truth.

Me telling Max we aren't married is met with the same disbelief as if I'd told him the sky was green, trees could talk, or that I didn't like kissing him. All of those are obvious lies of such a huge proportion they're incomprehensible.

Exactly like it's incomprehensible we're not married, madly in love, and wanting to try for a baby.

"We're not married," Max says flatly, disbelief coating his words.

He insisted on breakfast, and since I've never been able to think on an empty stomach, I agreed. We moved the tartine and coffee to the kitchen, and while Max pressed fresh orange juice and cut up a few apricots, I threw on one of the chic dresses I found in the wardrobe and quickly braided my messy bed hair.

"That's right. We're not married," I say.

A spray of sunlight falls over the breakfast table, settled beneath a large window in the bespoke kitchen. It's a cheerful, brightly lit space with long stretches of white marble counters, hand-crafted cabinets, and hand-milled brass fixtures. There's a crystal bowl full of ripe apricots, fragrant peaches, and nectarines on the counter. A vase full of sunny yellow tulips. It's just about the prettiest kitchen in existence, and last night, while we were eating, drinking, and making love, I didn't appreciate its charm.

"You made a wish on the Bride's Parure and then. . ." He holds his hands out in front of him in a "voila" gesture.

"Exactly." I lean forward, the scent of toasted baguette and cherry jam tickling my nose. "Exactly. If we go back to Geneva, maybe we can figure out what we missed. We can reverse this. Why . . ." I frown at the look on his face. "What?"

He smiles and tilts his head. The way his lips curl makes a sweet, apricot-flavored ache roll through me. For a moment I get lost in the way he looks—black hair, sharp nose, rough-cut features that flicker from stoic and stony to playful and sweet in a millisecond.

"Darling. If you've changed your mind about a baby this year, that's all you have to say. We can wait. I married you. Whether we have children or not, it's life with you that I want." His gaze goes bedroom-eyed and intimate, and I almost melt into a puddle and drip from my chair onto the glossy wood floor.

"Gah," I say, then I realize *gah* isn't a word.

Max's smile widens and he flashes his teeth, all happy, as if everything is settled. He picks up a slice of apricot and sets in on my plate. "Have some apricot. It's delicious."

His fingers are glossy and wet from the juices. He watches me as he licks the liquid from his fingertips.

Is it hot in here? Yes. It's definitely hot in here.

I grab my cloth napkin and fan myself. The white of the cloth waving in the air is like a sign of surrender, as if already I've accepted this as my new reality.

Well, the heck with that.

I shove the napkin back into my lap. "Max."

He quirks an eyebrow.

"We are not married."

He nods, pouring me more coffee from the French press. A puff of steam rises between us and the arabica scent fills the air.

"If not the baby," he asks, "then . . . is this foreplay? Like when we play grumpy boss and her naughty secretary?"

"What?" *Grumpy boss and her naughty secretary? Me and Max play what?*

"Professor and failing student? Are we role-playing this morning?" He looks at the ceiling, considering this and rubbing his chin. "This could work. We're not married. Which means—" He looks back to me, his expression lighting up.

"No," I say. "No. I'm not role-playing. I'm not joking. I'm not suffering from a delusion. I'm telling you, we're not actually married. This isn't reality. This is a wish. The myth of the Bride's Parure was true and . . . Stop laughing!"

His laugh is deep and mellow, and the rich notes reach down into my belly and turn me inside out. Have I ever heard him laugh before? Really laugh? I've heard him make sounds of amusement, give small, careful laughs, or speak with a smile in his voice. But I'm not sure I've ever heard him laugh with his entire body.

His shoulders shake, he leans forward with obvious glee, and his mouth twists into the most delighted smile. There are things in life that are infectious—the flu, annoying songs—and apparently, Max's laugh.

Everything in me lights up at his laugh, and I want so badly to join him. It's as if he's let go of everything, dropped all his worries and fears, and is as light as a ray of sunshine. And he's asking me to join him.

He stands then, crosses the small space between us, takes my hands, and pulls me up. When I stand he tugs me against him.

I hit his chest with a small thud, and then he wraps his arms around me.

His eyes are still brimming with laughter as he looks down at me. "Did I mention today how happy you make me? You always make me laugh." His hands spread over my back, holding me close. "When we met—"

"At the art museum?" I ask, wondering if he has the same memories as he did before.

"Yes," he says, his hand stroking along the curve of my back. "I knew within seconds of seeing you that I was going to marry you. It was love at first sight. Luckily, you didn't make me wait too long."

Oh gosh. He's giving me that look again. The "I love you till death" look.

The hard part is I've always wanted him to look at me like this. I just wanted him to do it of his own free will. For three years he saw me cleaning his house. There was never any love at first sight. He loved Fiona, not me.

"What about Fiona?" I ask.

"Fiona who?"

When I first made the wish, Max told me he'd called Fiona and she'd said, "Max who?" He was devastated. She'd been his best friend for nearly a decade. And now he doesn't remember her either.

"You love her."

"I love you," he says.

"In the real world, you love her."

"Impossible."

I step back, breaking free of his arms. "No. It's not. In the real world, I clean your house and you . . . you ignore me. There wasn't any love at first sight."

"If I saw you, no matter what reality we were in, I loved you. Trust me." His expression says he's so confident of this fact there's no way I'll change his mind.

I drop my head, looking down at the wood floor sparkling in the late-morning sun. My shoulders fall. "This isn't right," I say, my fingers curling into my palms. "You don't love me. You think you do, but you don't. You never had a choice." I look back at him—at his concerned expression and his wrinkled brow. "You and I both know what's most important is having a choice."

He reaches out, brushing a strand of hair behind my ear. "Not true," he says. "There's no choice in love. The second I saw you I fell hard. The only choice I had was whether or not I was going to acknowledge it, and then, what I was going to do about it."

I shake my head. "I wish that were true."

He takes my hands, unfolds my curled fingers, and clasps them with his. "It is true, no wish needed."

My chest feels hollow and his words echo around it, banging off my ribs and knocking into my heart. They hurt.

Maybe he does love me. Maybe after last night he did. But he never said the words. He made his choice. He told me to come to him, remind him of his letter, remind him of what love was. But that was when he expected to forget me or to forget that he liked me.

What am I supposed to do now, when the opposite of what we believed would happen did?

I wish I could ask his advice.

I clutch his hands and he smiles down at me. I'm struck by the fact that our pose right now is just the same as it was in our wedding photo on the nightstand.

In Max's mind we've been together for seven years. He's my friend. My confidant. My lover. My husband.

Maybe I *can* ask him for advice.

"If you did believe me," I begin, "that this isn't reality and we aren't truly married. That we didn't really speak until a few days ago. What would you do?"

He thinks for a moment, his thoughts flowing, his mind working. Then he finally asks, "Was I happy in this other reality? Were you?"

"Happy?"

He nods. "Were you happy?"

Heat creeps over my cheeks as I think back. *Was I happy?* I thought I was. I loved my family, my friends, my job. *But was I happy?* Perhaps there's a demarcation between acceptance and happiness and I didn't realize the difference between the two. Like Max said before, I was all in on making others happy, but for some reason I hesitated when it came to doing things for myself.

"I think I have my answer," he says, studying my expression. "And me? If this other world is real, was I happy?"

"I don't know," I admit. "You seemed lonely. You were often . . . alone."

"I didn't have anyone?" He seems to find this idea unfathomable.

I shake my head. "Not after Fiona turned down your marriage proposal."

He lifts an eyebrow. "I was turned down?"

"Shocking, I know," I tell him, unable to hide a smile.

He smiles back. Squeezes my hands. "Then if I were to give you advice, I would say . . . stay. Don't try to fix this. I'm happy. You're happy. I don't want to go back somewhere where you're not."

My heart gives a painful hard thud in my chest. "Even if this isn't real?"

He gives me a heartbreaking smile. Around us the sun lights up the cheerful kitchen, and outside a late-spring wind blows, whistling jauntily over the old stone.

"Who's to say what's real and what isn't?" He leans forward and brushes a kiss over my mouth. His lips taste of cherries and apricots.

He wants to stay. But if he remembered his old life he wouldn't want to. I know this because he felt that way only yesterday.

When Max pulls away, he smiles. "There. How did I do? I always enjoy playing out your philosophical debates. You keep me on my toes."

Wait. "What?"

He frees my hands. Gives me a crooked smile. "I quite like the 'not married' angle. What do you think about me chatting you up in a bar, using terrible pick-up lines, and then coming home for some hook-up, one-night-stand sex? We haven't done that in years."

And that's when I realize, if we're going to get out of this mess, I'm going to have to figure it out myself.

26

───────

What do you do when all your wishes come true?

This is the question I contend with as Max winds through the narrow stone streets of Saint-Tropez. The Mediterranean sun bounces off the seashell-pink, butter-yellow, and sherbet-orange buildings and slides over the red-tile roofs. All the old stone and stucco houses are light and bright against the sharp blue sky. We're in the center of the town, where the old fishing village and the luxury beach resort come together in a marriage of irresistible charm.

For years my mom wanted to bring my sister and me to the French Riviera. It was her dream holiday. Emme's too.

The azure water, the pebbled beaches, the sandy ones. Vibrant, wine-deep sunsets spilling over rustic fishing boats bobbing next to sleek yachts. Cool sea breezes blowing through open doors in an old stone house overlooking the harbor. Picnics on the beach.

Painting on the boardwalk. Lazy mornings, afternoons that draw out like treacle, and sunsets that last for hours.

Anytime there was a show on television about the French Riviera, my mom would watch it, the remote clutched in her hand, her eyes glued to the screen. She would drink in the panoramas of crescent-shaped beaches and turquoise water, glistening white hotels and rustic villages. The fig and olive trees, the oranges and lemons growing in the bright sun. The villages adorned with flowering pink bougainvillea, fragrant jasmine, and golden mimosa.

Somehow, instead of representing a stretch of beaches and harbors along the coast, the French Riviera began to represent something else.

Freedom.

If we ever made it to the French Riviera, it would mean my dad's hospital debts were finally paid off. It would mean we had enough money to spare to take a trip to the beach. It would mean my mom had vacation time. *I* had vacation time. It would mean we'd finally decided that instead of always doing what was practical and right, we would do something impractical and perhaps wrong. Just because we wanted to. Because it was a dream.

If we ever made it to Saint-Tropez, we would know we'd climbed out of what happened after my dad died, we'd discarded what happened after Emme's dad left, and we were finally free.

It was a years-long dream, and now we're here.

The car tires vibrate over the cobblestone, and I turn my face to the open window, breathing in the subtle hint of seawater, jasmine, and spring breeze. The sunshine flashes through the tile roofs and the tightly clustered three- and four-story old buildings. The street is narrow, twisting through an old part of town, leading down to the harbor. Even here I can feel the cool air rising off the water, winding through the sunbaked streets. It echoes like the sound of motorbikes, engines, people, and sea birds, all calling out in the late afternoon.

The sun has sunk into the stone and it warms the village like a tight embrace. I let the cool air drift over my face and drag through my hair.

Max squeezes my hand. He has one hand on the steering wheel and his other holds mine, resting on the shifter.

There are five days left in our "anniversary" weeklong holiday. If I wondered what life would be like married to Max, I don't have to wonder anymore.

One second it's like being wrapped in a warm hug, my head resting on his shoulder, his arms around me. The next second it's like flying, or perhaps like falling, a giddy rising of my stomach. And finally, it feels like home. Not the home you're waiting to leave, but the place you're meant to stay.

After our breakfast I didn't broach the subject of my wish or the unreality of our marriage again. Max had plans for the day. Once the tartine was eaten and our coffee cups were empty we did the dishes, and as Max washed and I dried, he regaled me with stories about the inspiration behind the latest line Barone was developing for next winter and his progress on wooing a reclusive visual artist for a new collaboration.

"It'll be like Picasso, Dali, Koons—they all worked in jewelry," he said, his enthusiasm sloshing suds over the side of the sink as he scrubbed jam off a plate.

And then, as we walked to a market hand in hand, he asked for my thoughts on whether he should continue working with a diamond supplier out of Canada or shift to Australia. He asked me as if I was intimately familiar with the intricacies of his business and he would take my thoughts on the subject as seriously as his own.

Once he'd picked up fresh cheese, herbs, pasta, and wine I asked what our plans were. He told me this week, the only plans we had involved eating delicious food, strolling the streets of Paris, and making love at least three times a day. After all, we hoped for a baby by next summer.

That was when I knew we couldn't stay in Paris. First, because if we stayed here it would be increasingly difficult not to give in to Max's slumberous expressions and take a weeklong tumble into bed. Second, because I would hate myself if I used Max when he didn't remember the truth. And third, because Max would hate me too.

So.

No sex.

No. Sex.

Which meant I needed a distraction. Away from Paris. Away from the romantic city of love and our secluded love nest.

Back to Geneva?

When I mentioned going back to Geneva Max looked at me as if I'd suggested eating dirt.

But then my mom called and said, "Anna, I hate to ask this, but I don't know what else to do. Can you come?"

And thank goodness Max already knew I can't ever refuse when my mom asks for help.

So here we are, here I am, in Saint-Tropez. The place of dreams.

All I have to do is help my mom, avoid making love with Max, and figure out how to reverse my wish.

Easy.

27

———

The villa my mom and Emme are staying in is the light pink color of saltwater taffy. It lines the water, next to a rainbow of pastel buildings adorned with quirkily colored shutters and caps of tile roofs. It's close enough to the center of town that there are families lounging on the small sandy cove, kids digging in the sand, and a few couples spread out on the flat rocks, lounging in the slanting sun.

The sea is so vibrant, ranging from bright turquoise to deep indigo, that I have to blink a few times to let myself adjust to the vivid colors. It's almost too much, how pretty it is. Even the sound of the waves breaking against the craggy rocks and the scent of seagrass and sand—it's all so *pretty*.

"It's almost too beautiful," I say, giving a sigh at a white sailboat sliding past. The boat is a smooth stone, thrown and skimming the surface.

Max holds my hand, pulling me along the road

toward the pink villa at the edge of the water, the last in a long line of homes perched above the cove.

"Funny. That's how I feel about you," he says, giving me a crooked smile. "The first time I saw you, I thought to myself, 'She's so beautiful it hurts to look at her, but it'd hurt even worse to look away.'"

The breeze kicks up and tugs at us, pushing me closer to Max. My cotton dress blows in the wind and Max's short black hair flips over his forehead, covering his eyes. I reach out and push it back, and when I do, he grabs my wrist. My pulse flutters beneath the warmth of his hand.

On my right is the sea, with its sun-bleached sand, scattering gulls, and gently rocking waves. To my left is the pretty taffy homes standing against the pale blue sky and falling sun. In front of me is Max, looking like all he wants to do is kiss me under the sun to the melody of the sea.

Charming, I called him.

And he said, "Of course I'm charming, I'm a Barone."

But this is more than charming. My stomach flips and I keep my hand still as he slowly strokes the fluttering pulse in my wrist, his fingers shackling me.

"I don't want to look away," he says. "That's love, isn't it? When I wake up, you're the first person I want to see. When I pick up the phone, you're the person I want to talk to. When the day is done, you're the person I want to wrap my arms around. If I told myself seven years ago, when I saw you for the first time, that that's what I would feel today . . ." He lifts a shoulder in a small shrug. "I'd call myself the luckiest man in the world."

He turns my hand until my palm is facing him and presses a hot kiss on the sensitive center. Then he drags his mouth over my wrist, his eyelashes fluttering as his eyelids drift closed. His mouth leaves a hot trail over my skin, sparkling like the sun reflecting in sharp white points off the cool water.

His mouth is soft, wet, and his stubble scrapes me like sand dragging across naked skin. At last he sets his mouth over my pulse and gives a hard suck, leaving behind a wet claiming that burns as his mouth leaves me.

I'm flushed and dizzy. The sea breeze strokes over me, cooling my skin and licking me with salty air and effervescent mist. For a moment I wonder if I should scramble down the rocks and jump into the sea to cool the boiling heat in my blood.

"Are you always like this?" I ask him, dazed by the dazzling effect of his mouth. I struggle for the proper word. "So . . . complimentary?"

He flashes me a quick grin, which appears and then recedes as quickly as the waves crashing over the small sandy cove.

"No."

My shoulders fall.

He laces his fingers with mine and then drops our hands, pulling me along the road again. "Most days I'm worse," he says, giving a wink.

My face burns, like I've been lying on the beach all day and the sun has left me pink and hot.

He takes in the heat in my cheeks and his smile widens. "You love me." It's not a question; it's a happy statement born of confidence and years of intimacy.

"Yes," I say, not bothering to deny it. It doesn't matter which reality we're in, that remains the same.

"It's a good thing we have five more days. There are so many things I want to do to—"

"Max! Anna!"

It's a high-pitched, joyous shout. I turn sharply and watch in wonder as my little sister flies out of the mint-green front door of the villa. She races down the sidewalk, hopping and bouncing like a kid let loose in a toy store.

She looks so *happy*.

She's barefoot, beach-tanned and freckled, with sun-streaked brown hair. Her shorts and navy-striped top are the picture of coastal living. I gobble up her appearance, noting the smudge of indigo watercolor on her cheek and the paint on her fingers.

I grin, my heart ready to burst. My baby sister, the artist.

Max knows what she's going to do before I do, because he releases my hand, and when my sister launches herself in the air he catches her and quickly spins her around. She lets out a delighted shriek and a wild laugh.

Max laughs and then drops her gently to the ground, where she knocks into me, folding her arms around me. I let out a gust of air, and over Emme's head Max grins at me.

"You're here," Emme says, her face buried against my dress, her voice muffled under the waves and the wind. "I missed you and Max. It's been weeks!"

Max reaches over and rumples Emme's hair. "Hello, Emmeline. What sort of plans do you have for us today?"

Emme releases the tight hold she has on me and turns to Max, her face glowing with anticipation. "Everything! Now that you're here, we're going to do everything! Oh! I want to show you my watercolors. Mom says they're my best ever, but she's—"

She grabs Max's hand and drags him back toward the

front door, her excited chatter snatched away by the wind. Max shoots me a look over his shoulder—a happy grin and a quick wink.

My heart sort of tumbles out of my chest at that grin.

I hadn't thought for a moment about what it would mean for my sister if Max and I were married for seven years. But here in this world, that means Max has known Emme since she was a baby. She's grown up with Max in her life. Clearly, they love each other.

I stare after them. Emme scrambles onto Max's back for a piggyback ride. Her laughter carries over the sea breeze, and I smile as she tugs on his shoulders, pointing toward the citadel, an ancient fortress over the city, and then at the sea, where a rustic fishing boat bobs in the water, and finally, toward a pretty medieval bell tower rising over the village.

My mom finally makes her way outside. She carefully picks across the concrete, hobbling on crutches in an unpracticed gait. I study her carefully. Even though her right leg is in an air cast, she looks healthier and happier than I've seen her in years. The deep wrinkles and signs of fatigue she held in Geneva are gone. Instead the stress lines have transformed to laugh lines and she has an air of energy blended with contentment. She's a bit like the birds wheeling through the sky, floating effortlessly then diving lightning-quick to the water.

"That man is going to make a wonderful father," she says by way of greeting. She stares after Max and Emme picking their way down the rocks toward the little cove beach. It looks like they're taking a beach detour before Emme's watercolor tour.

My mom reaches out and wraps me in a hug, the

crutches knocking against me. She laughs as we both wobble on the pavement, then I hold her tight.

"Hi, Mom," I say, my lower lip wobbling. All of a sudden, everything hits me. My mom is happy. Emme is happy.

My mom finally has her dream.

Yet . . .

We pull apart and she studies my expression. She catches the wobble in my lip.

"What's wrong?"

I shake my head. "Nothing. I'm just really, really happy to see you."

She smiles, the wind blowing her short, curly hair about. "I'd hug you again, but I'd probably fall over. These crutches aren't as easy as they look."

At that I wave to Max and Emme and then usher my mom back inside to find somewhere for her to elevate her ankle.

"I tripped, slipped, fell backward off a boulder, and landed in a patch of prickly pear," my mom says once she's settled on a padded chair on the balcony, her foot raised on an ottoman. "I'm more embarrassed about the prickly pear than the broken leg. Did you know, the nurse had to remove thirty-two prickers from my derriere?"

I restrain a smile.

"Thirty-two," she reiterates. "And then, bless him, he asked me out for a glass of wine."

I snort. "Love is in the air."

She waves that away. Then she looks out over the cove, where Emme is directing Max in building a sandcastle with a moat. He's pulled off his shoes and rolled up his jeans, but even so, the bottoms of his jeans are soaked with seawater.

When he sees me looking he holds a hand up in a wave. Emme shields her eyes with her hand, squinting through the sun, and then she jumps up and down and points to the sandcastle. I hold up both hands in a thumbs-up.

"So," my mom says, picking up a glass of iced fizzy water.

I do the same. The glass is cold and the condensation runs in rivulets over my fingers. The fizz hisses and sparkles and little bits of peach and raspberry float in the water, mixing with mint sprigs. I take a drink, and the sweet of the fruit and the bite of the mint perfectly match the smooth sea breaking against the rocky shoreline.

The cold drink bubbles over my tongue, and then I swallow the sweet juice.

"So?" I ask, smiling.

"What's happened with you and Max?" my mom asks, setting her glass back on the little balcony table.

I nearly drop my own glass, but then, after giving my mom a quick look and clutching the glass more tightly, I carefully set it on the table.

"What do you mean?" I ask, my voice a little too high.

My mom gives me a considering look. She's in the sun. It splashes over her and paints her in bright Mediterranean colors. I hold still under her inspection, but every now and then I glance back toward the beach, where Max is piling sand in a barricade to stop the sea from destroying their fledgling sandcastle.

"You forget I'm an expert in marital discord and marital harmony. I've had both. There's something worrying you. And it's not something small. I know marriage, and I know you."

"Mom—" I shake my head.

"I thought you were too young when you got married. I was proven wrong. I thought you were from two different worlds and that it would never work. I was proven wrong again. I thought he didn't truly love you, that you were just a fling. I was proven wrong again and again. You've had your share of rough patches, but you two have always made it through." She nods, a firm jerk of her chin. "You have what your dad called a true connection. So"—she turns to me—"what is it? What's bothering you? Whatever it is, you'll work it out."

My face goes cold even with the sun beating down on me. What's wrong? That's easy.

"He loves me," I say, my voice coming out in a rough whisper. "That's what wrong. He really, really loves me."

My mom frowns, and over the water a lone white gull lets out a harsh cry. "And you don't love him anymore?"

"I do," I say. "I love him too."

She gives me a look then—one that tells me I'm not making any sense. I rub my hand along the rim of my cup, my finger sliding over the cold, wet surface. A bit of ice clinks as it shifts in the sparkling water.

"That doesn't sound like a problem."

"It will be," I say, "when he realizes he doesn't love me. That he never did. Or maybe he loved me a little bit, but that little bit was ruined by something I did."

"What did you do?"

I look out over the rugged coastline, the secluded cove, and the sparks of blue sea shining like a dream.

"I made a wish." I turn to her then. "Do you remember when I was little, how I always wanted to be a genie?"

Her eyes crinkle when she smiles, and she brushes her short hair back from her face. "You refused to believe me when I said humans couldn't grow up to be genies." Her expression softens. "You always wanted to make others happy. Your dad. Me. Your friends. Even strangers." She shakes her head and shifts her ankle on the padded ottoman. "I'm not surprised you feel guilty about making a wish for yourself."

"What?" I look at her in surprise. "I don't feel . . ."

Okay. Maybe I do.

Isn't that just what Max said?

"One of the most wonderful things about you is how much you care. But sometimes, as your mother, I'd like you to be selfish. To take the biggest piece of cake. To take the first place in line for the slide. Do you remember at the playground, all the kids would shove ahead of you, and you'd wait, sometimes for ten minutes, until no one was there to step in front of you? I never understood why you didn't feel deserving. Or was it that you felt others were more deserving?" She reaches out, taking my hand. My fingers are cold from the icy condensation of my glass. "Anna, you deserve love."

"I know," I say.

She squeezes my hand. "You may know here,"—she points to my head—"but maybe you haven't figured it out here." She points to my heart. "Let Max love you."

"But . . . he doesn't . . . he won't . . ."

"Let him love you. What's wrong with wishing for love?"

"I suppose I don't want him to love me if it wasn't his choice. I don't want to force him to love me."

She laughs and nods toward the beach. "No one can force that man to do anything he doesn't want."

I look toward Max again. He and Emme have finished building the sandcastle and are now knocking the sand from their feet as they climb back up the rocks. They'll be here soon, and then it'll be time for dinner and then bed.

"Adversity," my mom says, "either breaks people or makes them strong. Your husband had more adversity in his first twenty years than many people have in a lifetime. He's strong. Nothing could make him love you if he didn't want to."

"Not even magic?"

After all, that magic is what made my mom appear in Saint-Tropez, happy and well-rested even with a broken leg.

"I don't believe in magic," my mom says. "And if I remember correctly, neither does Max. In fact, didn't he say at your wedding that he didn't even believe in love until you came along?"

I don't know.

I don't know what he said at our wedding.

But instead of admitting that, I say, "That's right. He did say that."

She nods and takes a long drink of her peach and raspberry fizz. Down below, Max opens the front door and Emme shouts up to us, "We're back! Come see my watercolors, Anna!"

My mom smiles at me. "Thanks for coming. I only need two days. By then, I should be a little more mobile."

"Don't worry about it. I've always wanted to come to the French Riviera."

She gives me a strange look, then she shrugs and smiles. "Haven't we all?"

When Emme bursts onto the balcony I turn to find Max trailing after her. His hair is mussed from the wind and he smells like sand and salt. He gives me an intimate smile that makes a soft, sweet humming start in my belly and spread all through me with a luxurious warm glow.

He leans down and brushes his lips across mine in greeting. "You taste like summer," he says against my mouth.

Then we're pulled to Emme's art room, where we view dozens of paintings of sailboats, sunsets, and turquoise-studded seas. There's a boisterous dinner on the balcony, a sunset walk through old town, and finally, Max and I wish my mom and Emme good night.

In bed Max pulls me into him, my back curving into his front. He kisses my neck, his warm breath whispering over my skin and the sheets gliding over my legs. He's warm, the bed is soft, the curtains stir in the breeze, and through the open window the waves crash against the shore.

"Love you," Max says, his voice a low rumble in the dark, sea-lit night.

Everywhere his mouth touches shimmers like a star lighting in the sky. I close my eyes and fall into his whispered love.

The night is heavy with jasmine and the sweet perfume of flowering mimosa. Max brushes a hand over my hip, the sheets rustling, his mouth pressing a kiss behind my ear. Then he reaches out and clasps my hand.

I fall asleep in his arms, hoping that tomorrow all of this is gone.

28

———

It's not.

I imagine I'm still in Saint-Tropez, because while I was hoping this would be gone, in the secret place in my heart, I was wishing that it wouldn't.

I have to admit, when Max brushes a kiss over my mouth and says in a sleep-tinged voice, "Morning, love," there's a traitorous leap in my heart before it sinks with the realization we're still together and Max still isn't himself.

Luckily, seconds after waking, Emme knocks on the third-floor bedroom door and shouts, "Can we go to the beach today? Mom said she needs rest and we should go out! Do you want to go? Yes or no?"

Max lifts himself up on his forearm and gives me a hooded look, his expression sleepy and hungry at the same time. His bare chest skims against my back and I feel his hardness pressing into me. He wore boxers to bed, I wore a nightie, and there is only a thin layer of cotton separating us. His hair is messy, his morning stubble thick and dark, and a stream of morning sun shines through the curtains, casting a golden glow over his bare skin. He makes a small noise in the back of his throat and strokes his fingers up my arm, tracing the spill of sunlight.

"You're beautiful in the morning," he whispers, his gaze following the steady progress of his fingers.

"Yes or no?" Emme shouts through the door.

"No," Max growls, too quiet for Emme to hear.

"Because I really want to paint the beach! Anna? Are you awake?"

Max brushes his hand over my nipple and it peaks under the slight pressure.

"Yes," I call, my voice a half-croak, half-gasp.

Max gives me a happy, self-satisfied grin.

"Do you want to go to the beach?" I can hear Emme bouncing up and down, her feet thudding rhythmically on the third-floor landing.

Max flips me over and executes a quick move where his legs cage mine and his arms pin me beneath him.

"Say no," he mouths, slowly shaking his head.

A slow throb rolls through me as he settles over me. His weight is delicious. Erotic. My eyes nearly roll backward in ecstasy. Which settles it.

"Yes!" I shout.

"No," Max says at the same time.

"What?" Emme asks.

I start to yell yes, but Max presses his mouth to mine.

"Hey!" I say, which he takes as an invitation to French, sending his tongue to quest over my lips and into my mouth.

"Anna? What?" Emme shouts.

"Yes," I say, the sound buried under Max's mouth.

"What!"

Max is laughing against my mouth. He's laughing, his eyes open, staring down at me with humor as he licks me into submission.

I do the only thing left to do. I grab the nearby feather pillow and whack him over the head with it.

Max laughs again and nips my lip. So I drive the pillow into his face, smothering his laughter. He rolls off me, his shoulders shaking.

"Yes!" I call, thwapping Max with the pillow again. "We'll be right there."

"Yay!" Emme shouts. "I'm ready!"

Max grabs the pillow, shoves it behind him, and gives me a satisfied smile. When he drops back to the bed, he crosses his arms behind his head, displaying an impressive amount of chest and shoulders. He tilts his eyes to the ceiling, looking incredibly amused and very happy.

Then there's the sound of Emme's feet banging down the three flights of stairs. It sounds like an avalanche of goats tumbling down a mountain.

We wait until the sound of her feet disappears, and then Max turns to me with a wicked grin. "Five minutes—"

"No." I back away, shoving the sheets aside and scooting off the bed.

No sex. Can't do it.

"Four?"

"No!"

"Ninety seconds. You know I can make you come in ninety seconds."

Oh. Um.

That sounds . . .

"No?" I say, but it comes out as a question, and Max knows it.

He gives me a confident smile and curls his pointer finger in the cutest "come here" gesture I've ever seen.

Oh gosh. My willpower—it's crumbling.

Stand firm, Anna!

I grab another pillow and hold it in front of me. "No."

Then, before Max can respond, the goat avalanche starts again, this time the pounding coming back up the stairs. Emme's back.

The look on Max's face is priceless. He looks like he was just told he can't have chocolate and hazelnut ice cream for the next year. I burst out laughing.

Emme bangs on the door. "Mom said she needs help, Anna! She's trying to make breakfast and she dropped a tray of eggs!"

"Why is she trying to make breakfast?" I call. "I'll make breakfast."

"'Cause she's hungry! 'Cause her body's tryna fix a bone!"

Max snorts. "My body's tryna fix a bone too."

I point a finger at him. "You. Shh."

He gives me an unrepentant sinner smile. *Unbelievable.*

"Coming!" I call.

"You're really not," Max says, a mournful note in his voice. He sits up in bed, the sheets pooling around his hips, then runs a hand through his messy hair.

"What?" Emme asks through the door.

"I'm coming!"

Max laughs again, his shoulders shaking. I throw the pillow I'm holding at him. He catches it, tosses it to the side, and says, "I wish you were coming. You could be. Wouldn't it be nice?"

Too nice.

That's the problem.

He looks like a devil, all dark and handsome, sitting in the pristine white bed, his tempting smile illuminated beautifully by the morning sunlight. I have to get out of here before I do something I'll regret.

I point a finger at him, giving him a "shh" look.

Outside the door Emme bounces up and down, the floorboards squeaking impatiently. Max smiles at the sound, his face softening.

"I can't wait to have kids with you," he says, switching from playful to solemn. I'm nearly knocked over when I see how much he means it. "I can't wait to meet our little girl with your heart or our little boy with your humor."

The look on his face scares me. It's that bowled-over-by-love look. The look that says he's so deep in love he'll never pull himself out of it.

"Anna?" Emme calls, saving me from responding.

I give Max an apologetic smile and practically sprint out the door.

29

———————

THE "BEACH" IS ACTUALLY A LONG TURQUOISE RIBBON OF hidden coves, secret beaches, and sandy isthmuses accessible only by foot or boat. Leaving the busy center of Saint-Tropez with its bustling harbor, throngs of tourists, and lively charm, I never would've imagined the string of quiet beaches hidden at the end of the peninsula.

The coast is raw, undeveloped, and untouched by the glitz and glamour only minutes away. It's like finding a raw gemstone, unpolished and uncut, and all the more beautiful because of it. If I could, I'd hold this stretch of coast in my hand like a pear-size sapphire and watch in wonder as the sun sets it alight.

Instead I have to be content with drinking in the way the light hits the shallow water, coloring it indigo, turquoise, and sea-green. I'm dazzled by the sea. Dazzled and dizzy. I feel almost like the coast is wooing me. The sea is a kiss, the soft mist spraying over my sun-heated skin. The murmur of the waves crashing against rocky coves is the teasing whisper of a lover tempting me to bed. The humid, heady fragrance of salt, windswept wildflowers, and seagrass is a perfume that plants memories of sweat-slicked nights spent making love.

Every rocky cove, every alabaster-sanded secluded beach, every spill of rollicking, wildflower-covered hill falling into rocky shore and smooth sand, has me tumbling a bit more in love.

If Max was stark and stoic in Geneva, a reflection of the barren nature of his estate, then here he's as wild and unpredictable as the white-capped waves rolling over the craggy rocks and playfully splashing anyone who ventures too close. He's shed all of the restraint he had in Geneva and is showering me with a sort of constant, open, unreserved love.

He's loose-limbed, athletic, as we climb over rocks, scrabble over outcroppings, and wind further along the coastal trail to more isolated stretches of sand. When we reach tall, jagged rocks he lifts Emme over them or helps her down, then he takes my hand, helping me over uneven ground. Sometimes he lets my hand go as soon as I'm back on even footing; other times he holds onto me a bit longer.

Now Emme runs ahead, the pack she's carrying full with tubes of watercolor, brushes, a palette, and her watercolor pad. It thumps against her back as she skips down the narrow trail, leafed by spiky plants, windswept grass, and an abundance of bright yellow and purple wildflowers.

Max runs his thumb in a circle over my palm, matching the rhythm of the waves. A delicious shiver travels up my arm and then settles in my middle.

"I've fallen in love," I say, and when I do, Max turns to me, his eyes crinkling and a questioning smile in his gaze.

"With Cap Taillat," I say.

I gesture at the giant sand-colored rocks extending into the sea, their surfaces smoothed and rounded. Earlier we passed the Plage de l'Amour, the love beach, where the rocks extending into the sea almost looked like a giant's hand reaching out to his lover. We passed coves with rustic driftwood structures built by families, and quiet beaches with sailboats bobbing just off the shore. We trundled over a narrow wooden bridge hung between two steep rocks, the turquoise sea sweeping out beside us.

"It's no wonder my mom always wanted to come here. I can't imagine anywhere more beautiful in the whole world."

Max looks out over the coast, toward Emme running ahead, excitedly pointing at the isthmus. It's a long, thin stretch of white sand nestled between two shores. On one side the water is sheltered and quiet, a smooth, tranquil sea. On the other, white-capped waves crash playfully against the shore. At the end of the wide strip of sand, a green-studded dune rises into the cloudless blue sky. The breeze tugs at my cotton dress and whistles around us, cooling the flush riding over my skin at Max's smile.

"More beautiful than Paris?" he asks, and in his question I see the memories of our first week there together, before we were married.

I don't remember that Paris, but I can see the reflection of it in his eyes.

"I think," I say, breathing in the humid, sea-mist air, "they're hard to compare. Paris is like a sapphire, round-cut, all fifty-eight facets sparkling and reflecting every bit of light—"

Max lifts my hand, kissing the tips of each of my fingers. He smiles as he works.

"—and Cap Taillat, I was just thinking, is like an uncut sapphire. Corundum," I say, naming the mineral that both sapphire and rubies come from. "It's rugged and raw and beautiful without any cut or any polish. It just is."

I flush as Max presses a final kiss to my hand. He doesn't let me go; he just tucks our bound hands next to his side.

"I love it here too," he finally says.

We both watch Emme for a moment as she runs out onto the strip of white sand and then dashes to the clear, shallow water on the calm side. She dips a toe into the water and then splashes, sending the water into the air in a wide, sparkling arc.

"I think," he says as we start down to the empty beach, "I like it here because it lets me forget all the polish, like you say." He smiles over at me. "I can go back to being unpolished. There is something to be said for Paris, Geneva, New York. Yet sometimes it's exhausting always doing or going or being. I like coming here, where the hardest decision is which beach we'll go to and which wine we'll have with dinner. It always seems here, in this place, we're allowed to love without reservation, because that's what a sea like this, a coast like this—what a place like this—expects. In Paris or back home, you can hide. There isn't any hiding here." The corner of his mouth lifts, and then he shrugs. "Is that what you meant?"

My heart trips over itself, crashing about, and I take in a rough breath. Without thinking about it I throw my arms around his middle and press my face to his chest.

He lets out a surprised huff of air and then wraps his arms around me, pulling me close.

He's warm from the sun and he smells like fresh sea air. I listen to the steady thud of his heart thumping against my cheek. He presses a kiss to my temple, then to the edge of my eye, and finally, he leans down to press a soft kiss to the edge of my lips.

"All right?" he asks.

I nod. "I'm okay. It just hit me. I had to hug you."

He lets out a low laugh and presses another kiss to my mouth.

On the beach Emme has opened her pack and is pulling out her watercolor pad and paint tray.

"How long do you think she'll paint?" Max asks, looking at the sun, nearing the zenith of the cloudless sky.

"Hours."

Max nods, a humor-filled light in his eyes. "I should've brought more food. More drinks."

He tucks me against his side, and then we start down the path for the last little bit until we reach the soft, sun-warmed sand. The wind whistles over it, leaving patterns that look like waves, and the grass bows beneath the breeze. A pair of gulls swoops overhead, and a few sailboats are moored far out in the shallows, but otherwise we're alone. The three of us have a strip of sand, a little Eden to lounge in and be grateful for. Uncut and unspoiled.

"Now that's a happy kid," Max says, nodding at Emme.

She's cracked open her paint and is stretched out on her belly, lying on the sand with a paintbrush in her hand and her pad in front of her. She's eying the sailboats, preparing to imprint their likeness on paper.

"I was wondering," I say, hesitant but asking anyway, "do you ever worry that you won't be a good dad?"

Max stops. Pulls me up short. We're only a few long shadows away from Emme, but the waves and the wind keep our words quiet.

It's interesting standing in the middle of the sea like this. The strip of beach is narrow; within seconds you could choose to jump into rough foaming waves, or instead dip into cool, serene waters. I've never been anywhere where two opposite choices are so immediate and apparent.

"No," Max says.

"No?"

He shakes his head. "No. I never worry. My father . . ." He shrugs. "You know this. He often told me, even when I was four, five, that he wished he'd stopped with my brother. He'd rather I hadn't been born. To him I was a mistake, a sort of representation of the prison of all his choices. My parents . . ." He looks down at me, his brown eyes solemn. "Some parents don't love their children. My parents certainly didn't. So no. I never worry that I won't be a good dad. Because whatever mistakes I make, whatever I don't know and have to learn along the way, it'll be okay, because every day I'll let my child know I love them. I'll say it, because a lot of the time, people don't know you love them unless you tell them. So I'll say it. And I'll show it. So no. I don't worry. I learned early on that not much else but loving mattered."

He gives me a small smile, and then, as the wind tugs at my hair, he reaches up and tucks a loose strand behind my ear. "Is that what's been bothering you?" he asks, lowering his hand. "Are you worried about me?"

I shake my head no and then change my mind and nod yes.

Max gives a surprised laugh and then grins. "Don't. Don't worry, love." Then he grips my hand, gestures at the wide expanse of the beach and the sea and asks, "Ready?"

To my right is the choppy water and the jagged rocks rising from the foaming waves. To my left is the calm, tranquil, turquoise sea. I have to step forward. I have to keep going. We all do. But I'm not sure if loving Max will lead to the heartbreak of a turbulent sea or the gentle love of tranquil waters.

If I keep on, will he hate me, or will he love me again?

"Ready," I say.

We spend the day in a sun-bleached, salt-soaked haze of soft sand and cool water and lapping sea. Sandcastles are built and destroyed. Paintings are created and pinned to the sand with sea rocks so they can dry in the sun. Cold bottles of Orangina and slices of baguette, creamy Brousse de Rove—the local goat's milk cheese—and small, juicy, jewel-red tomatoes are greedily consumed. Max soaks in the sun, turning sun-bronzed. Emme and I pinken and freckle. The sand tickles, the salt dries, and the breeze whips my hair into curly tendrils.

Max and I lie in the soft sand holding hands, the cool water tickling our bare feet, held at the edge of the tide.

"I love you," he says, staring into my eyes, his head turned to me, his cheek pressed into the sand.

Will he regret this?

Will he remember this?

Will he wish I'd never come along and wished this into being?

Like he said earlier, even for all the mistakes you're bound to make, you can still say, "I love you too."

That night, exhausted from a day in the sun hiking over the rugged, untamed coast, I fall into bed. I barely notice Max's arms come around me as I pray that somehow everything will be set right. This time I scour out that secret place in my heart, and I wish . . .

30

IT TURNS OUT THE REASON MY MOM LOOKED AT ME strangely when I said I'd always wanted to come to the French Riviera was because we've been coming here for years. Max's great-aunt and her fisherman husband lived in Saint-Tropez, and when his great-uncle passed, Max bought his aunt the taffy-pink villa so she'd have a house on the sea that she loved for the rest of her life.

She died before Max and I met, but Max kept the house because it reminded him of his funny, hilariously vulgar great-aunt, her quiet husband, and the long summer days when as a boy he'd sneak away from his family's vacation spot at an ostentatious resort and visit his dad's funny black sheep of an aunt.

Apparently, every summer we stay for a week or two while Barone Jewelry has a pop-up store in an old bougainvillea-covered mansion with a beautiful blooming garden in the center of old town. My mom mentioned every year, Max has created a special piece of jewelry for me and incorporated it into one of the collections.

The first year we were married, there was the Effiel Tower—for Paris—the design hidden in numerous bracelets and necklaces. Another year, one of the necklaces had a pendant in the shape of a tarte tropézienne, my favorite pastry in Saint-Tropez, a fluffy brioche cake filled with decadent vanilla and lemon custard and dusted with pearl sugar. The pendant brioche was 24-karat gold, and the sugar was diamonds. When my mom mentioned the tarte tropézienne, Max laughed at the memory of me eating so much in one sitting that I didn't have room for lunch or dinner. Then he went out and brought home a pastry box, just for me.

Another year, Max created a bracelet with opals for our time in Australia. There was the year with the sapphires for our sailing lessons on Lake Geneva. There was the necklace with a ruby heart for the year I started the Open Heart Kitchen, part of the community center that fed anyone who was hungry and in need. Now, it seems, there are a dozen Open Heart Kitchens around Switzerland. Another year, Max created a book charm for our shared love of reading Dickens.

Each year he hid a love note for me out in the open, where I was sure to find it. Maybe no one else knew the sapphires in the necklaces five years ago were a message from Max, but I did.

Well, at least, the me of this reality did.

So while every night I wish for this dream to end, during the days I love like Max asks, without reservations.

We stay the whole five days, meandering the cobblestone streets, exploring the churches, the seventeenth-century citadel, and the winding, narrow village lanes. One morning we wander to the Place des Lices, where white tents are bunched together, shading an open-air market. We find aromatic rosemary and marjoram, fresh, creamy goat's cheeses, mounds of finger-staining berries, baskets of sun-warmed nectarines, sweet clover honey, and sprays of fresh-cut, bee-tempting flowers.

When Max catches me looking at a bouquet of freesias, he asks, "Would you like—?"

"No." I shake my head quickly and turn away, walking toward a table of cured sausage and olives.

The freesias remind me of Paris; of the wilting clock of our time together.

At night we binge-watch crime dramas, trying to out-spoiler each other, writing down our guesses for whodunnit on scraps of paper at the beginning of the show. At the end we unfold our guesses. Whenever Max wins I toss a pillow at him; when I win he tackles me under him and tickles me until I promise between breathless laughs to stop bragging.

By the end of the week my mom is more mobile and agile on the crutches, her leg healing. My sister has filled the house with watercolors, beach stones, and driftwood. Max is relaxed, quick to smile, and quick to kiss. I'm humming from the little touches, Max brushing his hand over me as he passes, a whispered kiss when we meet in the kitchen, a hand held in the market. If this were my life, I'd be blissed out on sun, tarte tropézienne, and the way Max's arms wrap around me at night.

But this isn't my life. And the happier, more blissful each day is, the more a shadow seems to creep over me, until I feel a cold grip inside.

At night, and sometimes during the day, Max will kiss me just like he makes love—a luxurious, erotic teasing of my mouth until I'm practically vibrating with need. But always, I say, "Not now, no, not now." Then he'll press a final kiss on my mouth and wrap me in his arms.

The excuses are creative. No "I have a headache" for me. One night, it's "Too many tartes—I'll puke if I'm jostled during sex." Another, "I'm too sunburned to copulate—the sting is extreme." Then "The gory, gruesome crime drama left me too freaked to fornicate."

Finally, the last night, Max doesn't kiss me; he just pulls me onto his bare chest and we fall asleep to the sound of the waves and the cool kiss of the breeze.

And so, five days later, a week into this wish, I'm so deep down in love with Max that I know, of the two sides of the beach, I've headlong tumbled into the riotous waves, and I'm currently being bashed against the jagged rocks.

We fly from the private terminal at La Môle airport and land in Geneva, leaving my mom and Emme with a kiss, a hug, and a promise to see them soon at their stone cottage outside Geneva, when my sister is back at school after break and my mom is back to work. Now we're curling around the lake, nearly back to Max's—our —home.

I stare out the window, watching the sky paint the hills purple and the water a rippling gold. Geneva is a collection of fireflies glowing above the lake, lighting up in the deepening sigh of dusk. It's strange to be here, riding in Max's Aston Martin back to his austere, starkly beautiful estate, instead of taking the bus back to my square-roomed, windowless post-war apartment.

"Home," he says, a smile tugging at his mouth when he pulls down the drive.

My stomach dips as I take in the chateau, its windows lit and reflecting the warm gold of the setting sun, its weathered stone painted a sparkling pink. The flower gardens around the house, planted in this new reality, give a welcoming feel. Even the swifts swooping between the towers and the chimneys have a sprite-like, playful feel.

It's a home. It's really, really a home.

I know now what this feels like. I was making onion soup last night for dinner, whiskey poured into the pot, a loaf of bread in the oven, when the thought struck me right over the head.

The last time I made onion soup, after I was fired, my mom said I had a problem with honesty. She reminded me of all the times I'd made us take the bus back to the store or turn around because I realized a store clerk had accidentally given us too much change. One franc. Two. Ten. It didn't matter. What mattered was the money wasn't mine and it was wrong to keep it. I returned it every time. Because if I didn't, I would feel sick to my stomach, cold in my hands, and I'd worry until I did the right thing.

This wish. This marriage. Max's love.

It's the same thing.

The store clerk gave me too much change. It's not mine and I have to return it.

This marriage isn't mine, and Max's love isn't mine, and the longer I hold onto it without turning around, the worse it's going to feel.

Because it isn't right.

Max turns into the garage, pulls the car to a stop, and

kills the engine. "Happy to be home?" he asks, smiling over at me. "Back to work. I'll be late tomorrow night, but I imagine you'll be out late too, catching up—although I expect everyone did an excellent job while you were away—"

I set my hand on his arm and cut him off. "If you were at a shop and you realized they gave you five francs too much in change, would you give it back?"

Max lifts an eyebrow. "Of course."

I nod, wetting my dry lips. "And if it were one franc?"

"Still yes."

"What about a cent—something that seemed completely inconsequential?"

He nods. "Yes. Accounting is the devil. I wouldn't wish an unbalanced end of day on anyone."

My heart thuds painfully, sounding loud in my ears. With the engine off, the car is hushed and still. The air grows warm and heavy. The interior lights cast a cool glow over us.

"What if," I ask, "instead of a franc, you were accidentally given something more? A million francs. And, say, you were poor and had always dreamed of a million francs because of everything you could do with it. No one knew that it wasn't really yours, so you could keep it, enjoy it, experience . . . love. Would you? Or would you give it back?"

Max frowns, studying the light glowing over my face. He's thinking, taking his time with his answer. The leather of the seat is warm beneath me and the motor-oil scent of the garage spills into the car. It's a comforting, normal sort of smell, a normal sort of situation, sitting in a car with a man in a dimly lit garage.

Except this question is more meaningful than the usual driveway conversations.

I'm asking Max whether or not he wants me to give him up.

Because, let's face it, if I can't undo this wish, then I'm going to have to leave him.

This love isn't mine to keep.

I only wonder if he'll agree.

"I would know," he finally says, his voice thoughtful. "Perhaps no one else would ever know, but I would know. What I think of myself matters a hell of a lot more than what anyone else thinks of me. At the end of every day, I want to be able to say that I did my best, I treated others well, I told the truth, I didn't do anything that later on I'd be ashamed of. I'd return it, love. Even if it hurt to give it up, it'd hurt worse to keep it."

My throat is tight and raw, so instead of speaking, I nod. Finally, I swallow down the peach-pit-size lump and say, "That's what I thought."

"You'd give it back too." He smiles at me, reaching out and brushing a knuckle over my cheek.

"Yes," I say, knowing that even if I'm in this reality forever, I can't keep what isn't mine.

"Why the questions?" he asks, his hand lingering on my jaw.

I turn my face into his warmth. "Just wondering."

He nods. "Fair enough. Shall we go in? Have a late dinner? Make it an early night?"

At the smile in Max's eyes, I know he's imagining what we can finally do now we're back in our own home, our own bedroom, and our own bed.

We're back in Geneva. The dream is over. The freesia has wilted.

"Before we do," I ask, knowing what I have to do, "can I see the necklace from the Bride's Parure?"

31

————

I'm back in the library where all this began. A week ago I stood in front of the sapphire rivière necklace and made a wild, daring wish. It's hard to imagine the me of a week ago. Red-cheeked, tired, dressed in soapsud-damp jeans and a bleach-stained sweatshirt, hiding behind the belief that Max didn't see me, when in reality, I'd never let him see me. I was lonely—I see that now. I was scared to ask for love. And like my mom said, I was also scared I didn't deserve it.

When Max found me in the library and demanded I never set foot in this house again, that I never see him again, I didn't think we'd end up here.

Dusk has fled and the deep, inky indigo of night has saturated Geneva. The tall windows of the library show smudges of dark woods, black water, and the lights of the city reflected in the lake.

During the day the library is always bathed in sunlight, with golden specks drifting on streams of sun falling through the tall windows. Daylight makes the library feel open and expansive, with its walls of books, tall ladders, and stone columns. The tall plaster ceilings, the cheerful fireplace, and the groups of leather chairs clustered together always gave the room an elegant, bookish feel. Even the subtle paper and binding smell was hidden under the airy, open nature of the room.

But now, at night, all of that open, expansive elegance has disappeared. The dark windows shutter the room, and the quiet blankets the library in a muted hush. The room is sleepy, dreamlike. All the shelves of books feel like a warm hug wrapping around me, and the room is no longer expansive, but cozy. The padded chair by the window—the one where Max sat and read at night while having a cup of coffee—now there are two chairs, with a blanket on one and a stack of books by the other.

That's what's different about the library. It feels like a pot of tea and a tray of biscuits, a warm blanket, and a book next to the person you love. Before, it was a place to be alone. Now it's a place to be together.

Max unlatches the oil painting of Mont Blanc and swings it wide. Behind the painting there's a safe, and in seconds Max has pulled out the gold filigree jewelry case. I catch my breath as the light shines on the delicate violets and vines etched into the gold.

Max brought the necklace to Paris, but after our wish on the parure, when he forgot everything, it returned here.

"Why did you want to see it?" Max asks, snapping open the case.

"I wanted to make a wish," I say, not looking at the glittering string of sapphires, but instead looking at Max.

I'm trying to memorize him in this moment. The softness of his mouth, the relaxed set of his shoulders, the mess of his hair from running his fingers through it while we made our way home. I take in the warm, familiar intimacy in his gaze and the way he watches me as if he's constantly delighted I'm here and that he's here with me. I memorize the rough stubble on his face that scrapes over my cheeks when he kisses me. I take in the way he tilts his head and leans slightly toward me as if he can't help but move closer to me, even unconsciously. I take in the fresh air and leather smell of him, the steadiness of him, the goodness.

I've changed over the past week. But so has Max. Before he was as austere and stark as his home, with only quick flashes of the passion hidden underneath. Now, while he still looks the same—as beautiful as a glacier sliding into the cold depths of the arctic—there's more. The solitude of the arctic is gone, and instead it's the rugged, raw beauty of the Côte d'Azur. He's the turquoise sea, the rocky shores, the golden sands, and the turbulent waves. He's the sea-thick air and the hot sun rolling over the grass-swept dunes, *and* he's the stark, barren chateau alone on the edge of Lake Geneva. He's both and he's more. He's 222 kisses climbing to the Sacred Heart. He's a weeping willow over the Seine. A flowering Eden in the center of a city. A friend. A confidant. A hand held in the dark when you're certain you're alone.

He's my wish.

I didn't know that loving Max would feel like breaking apart. It feels so much like breaking that I don't know if I'll ever be able to put myself back together again. The rivière necklace is twenty-six sapphires, broken and cut gemstones wound together in a river of light. I wonder, is that what people are like? Are the breaks what make us beautiful? Has all of this been worth it even though it's going to break me?

"A wish," Max says, his voice a soft rumble. The corner of his mouth lifts as he watches me taking him in. "I didn't think you believed my family's myth. I don't."

He runs a finger over the black velvet embracing the necklace. "I always thought it was a nice story explaining why my lucky ancestor didn't lose her head. Nothing more." He looks back at me and smiles. "What sort of wish did you have in mind?"

I shake my head. My throat is tight, my face cold, and the air is so thick that I'm struggling to pull in a breath. "What would you wish for?"

"You," he says without having to think. Then he grins and says, "Since I have you, I'd wish you'd always stay—"

"I'm leaving," I say.

He blinks.

I don't think he can make sense of what I said, because his brow wrinkles, his lips turn down, and he shakes his head. "Where? Did Christine call about the center? You could . . ."

I have no idea who Christine is. This isn't about the community center. I shake my head and Max trails off, a question in his gaze.

My eyes burn and there's a pressure in the back of my throat. The library is as quiet as a tomb, closed-in and hushed. There isn't the magical, golden thrum that infused the room a week ago. Instead there's a heavy weight pressing down on my chest. My heart struggles against the pressure, thudding painfully under the weight.

I've felt this once before, when my heart stuttered under the weight of a moment. It was the night my dad died. I stood at the edge of his hospital bed, eleven years old, too scared to hold his hand and too scared to say goodbye. The nurse outside the room said, "It's time to say your goodbyes." But I thought—no, I believed— that if I didn't say goodbye then he couldn't die. Because my dad wouldn't leave without saying goodbye. He *wouldn't.*

So I didn't say goodbye. Instead I said, "I have to go to the bathroom. I'll be back."

I made sure my dad heard me. "I'll be back."

Because he wouldn't leave if I told him I'd be back. He wouldn't.

Then I ran down the hall to the bathroom, locked the stall door behind me, and got on my knees and prayed. And I prayed and I prayed and I prayed. And just to be sure, I made a wish.

An hour later, with aching knees and a tear-ragged throat, I crept back into my dad's hospital room. My heart stuttered and sort of caved in inside my chest. Because I'd been wrong. My mom was sobbing. And my dad had left even though I didn't say goodbye. He'd left even when I'd told him I'd be back. And most importantly, he'd left even though I'd prayed and wished that he wouldn't.

So, this time around, I want to say goodbye.

It's going to end—it has to end—one way or another. But when it does, I at least want to say goodbye.

"I don't know if you'll remember this," I begin, and when Max starts to speak I shake my head. "Don't . . ." I clear my throat. "Don't . . ."

Max steps forward, crosses the rug I cleaned just last week, and takes my hand. "Anna. What?"

I clutch his hand, feeling the warmth and the strength of his grip.

He doesn't understand. He has seven years of love behind him and he imagines a lifetime of love ahead. I don't know if we'll ever leave this reality, and I don't know, if we do, whether or not he'll remember this.

"I'm leaving. I'm saying goodbye," I say, my voice hushed in the stillness.

"I don't know what you mean," he says, shaking his head and gripping my hand. But he does, because his eyes are tight and his face is pale.

"I'm not sure what's going to happen tomorrow. Maybe you'll forget me—"

"Anna, what are you talking about?"

"Maybe you'll hate me—"

"Stop," he says, pulling me closer, tugging me against him. "Anna, stop."

But I don't. I can't. "Maybe you'll wish you never met me. Or maybe we'll still be here, and you'll still want me."

"I'll always want you." He grips my arms, and I can feel the shaking in his hands, the tightness in his chest, and the thundering in his heart.

"But if you wake up tomorrow, still here, still wanting me? Don't come after me. Don't come looking for me. Don't. This love isn't real." He starts to argue, so I shake my head. "It isn't. It isn't real. You didn't have a choice in it. I took your choice."

"Leaving is taking my choice," he says. "I don't understand. You aren't . . . you're not making any sense. We're happy. I love you. You love me." He pauses as if he's wondering if the love he took for granted actually wasn't true. "You love me?" he asks slowly. "Anna?"

I see in him the boy who wasn't given love, the man

who turned from love, and the man who in Paris asked me to find him and tell him that love wasn't anything to be afraid of. He trusted me to find him and love him and give him a choice in loving me.

His expression has clouded, doubt twisting through him, tinging the memories of the past seven years. Before the doubt can work its way into his heart, I say, "I love you. I loved you from the minute I laid eyes on you. And it's been growing exponentially ever since—so fast that you'll never catch up."

"Then why?" he asks, holding me tighter.

The weight of the library has deepened, the heaviness drawn into a slumberous breath, the last rattling struggle of a shuddered inhale. On the desk the rivière necklace gleams dully in the light, winking sleepy blue eyes.

"I can't keep this wish," I say, speaking to the gradients in the necklace. The soul-deep blue; the achingly vivid indigo; the yearning of a dark winter sky; the colors of wishes and love. "Tomorrow, if you wake up and we aren't married but you still remember, please know I'm leaving because I love you. I love you desperately, and if you . . . if you still feel even a glimmer of what you feel now . . . I'll be happy just to see you, to know. If you don't remember, I'll come. I'll risk your hate. I promised I'd show you your letter, so I will."

I look up at Max, and his brown eyes have taken on a frosted edge, icy like winter-blue. "Why," he asks in a hard voice, "wouldn't we be married?"

I swallow, my arms shaking as I wrap them around his shoulders. My vision is dark at the edges, the sparkle of the necklace a flash at the corner of the feathering blackness.

I reach out to the necklace, with my heart, with my mind, and I wish—

Let him go.

Let him love who he wants to love.

Let him go.

When I look into Max's eyes, the goodbye there for him to see, he makes a ragged sound and shakes his head.

"No," he says, spanning his hands over my jaw, cupping my cheeks. "No. Whatever it is, we can figure it out. Together."

He stares at me just like he did the first time we argued in this same spot. His gaze sears my mouth, and my lips tingle and ache under the need in his expression. He wants to kiss me—an angry, punishing, teeth and tongue and need-filled kiss.

Unlike last time, I let him.

No.

I kiss *him.*

I stand on my tiptoes and press my mouth to his.

He makes a desperate noise, his mouth ravaging mine, the heat of him imprinting on me. His hands spread over my face, tilting my mouth so he can plunge inside. He bites, swears, fights, and claims. And all the while I claim him back. I drag my hands over him, touching every inch of his face, his chest, his shoulders, his heart. With each ragged breath, each heated kiss, each desperate draw of my hands over him, and every whispered plea, I tell him, *I love you, I love you, I'm sorry, I'm leaving, don't forget, I love you.*

When he pulls away, shaking, wild-eyed, ragged-breathed, I back away slowly across the thick, luxurious rugs, through the elegant columned library, through the weight of air that feels as thick and as sharp as glass.

I stop at the library door and cast a last plea to the necklace. *Let him go.*

"Don't," Max says, standing in the shadows, expecting me to come back to him. "Anna. Don't."

I love you, I want to shout. *I love you.*

Instead I whisper, "Goodbye."

32

THE DARKNESS IS ABSOLUTE. I WONDER ABOUT THAT, BUT then I decide I don't care because the hammering in my head is extreme. I'm sure even a sliver of light would feel as if my skull were being cracked open and my brain shoveled onto a cutting board.

I wandered the streets of Geneva for hours last night, the dark churches, the tall spires not quite reaching the stars, and the old, watchful stone buildings keeping me company in my solitude.

At two in the morning, after haunting the streets for hours, I found myself at the edge of the water, looking up at the giant engagement ring glittering in the moonlight where it hung over the Barone showroom. The building was eerily quiet, the windows shuttered, the lights dim. Without the lights, without the glitter of gems or the promise of Max in his office upstairs, the building was an empty shell, a lonely reflection on the water.

I stood for a long time while the water lapped behind me, splashing quietly against concrete, the infrequent sound of a car's engine cutting through the silence letting me know I wasn't entirely alone. An insubstantial mist hovered at the water's edge and blanketed the air in a damp chill. Still, I didn't leave.

Not until I heard sirens in the distance. Then I looked to the east to find the Abry clock glowing with the time. I'd been standing there at the water's edge, in the center of the city, for nearly an hour. The streets were empty, the bridges quiet, the ducks and swans asleep. I'd not seen another soul.

I felt so heavy, as if my blood had been replaced with lead and it was impossible to move my arms or legs. There was a weight on me. It had started in the library with my last wish, and it continued to grow heavier with every breath.

It was the opposite of the glowing lightness I'd felt with my first wish. What else could it mean except that I was being pushed back down, shoved back into my life? I flew for a bit, soaring on love, and now I'm falling, not flying, gravity sending me back to earth.

The question is, when I slam into the cobblestones, will Max be there to catch me? Or will the wish, and all that came with it, wither and die as quickly as a wilting flower?

Will he?

Won't he?

Will I?

Won't I?

Those were the words that fluttered around me, thrown out on the wind, while Geneva slept. And then I hit a point of exhaustion so deep I stumbled across the empty street, grabbed the rough bark of tree to steady myself, tripped through the grass, and then collapsed heavily onto a wooden bench. I fell asleep, my eyelashes fluttering as I stared out over the black water smudged with evening lights, imagining I could make out the lonely, stark façade of Max's home.

And now, darkness.

Absolute darkness.

Geneva isn't this dark. I'd be able to see the sky, the stars, or the dawn. There are streetlights, city lights, the winking of a boat trailing through the water. So I'm not on the wooden bench on the water's edge anymore.

I moan, blinking into the blackness, the movement causing a sharp pain to ricochet through my head. My mouth is on fire, dry and sharply bitter. There's a queasy rolling sensation in my stomach, as if I'm in a boat, shoved in the hull, and I'm splashing up and down with the tossing of the waves.

Since this began, I've woken up in Max's bed in Geneva, in Max's bed in Paris, and now. . . I stretch my legs, wincing at the pounding in my head . . . Now I'm in another bed.

It's smaller. The mattress is floor-hard but still sags in the middle, the sheets soft and worn from too many washings. There's chamomile spritzed on the foam pillow, the scent barely noticeable. The air is still, the only noise the sound of my breathing and the heavy beating of my heart.

I know for a fact that if I roll over onto my stomach and reach up and to the right eighteen inches I'll find a lamp on a nightstand. If I flick it on I'll see a tiny, windowless bedroom painted bright yellow.

I'm back.

I'm home.

I let out another moan. Why is it that I feel as if I've

been hit by a delivery truck and had all the packages crash on top of me? It's like my body is reflecting my heart.

Except, if I'm back here, that means . . .

Max.

He's himself again. We aren't married and he'll be himself. Will he remember?

I jerk upright, hiss at the sudden pain, and then press my hand to my head at the wave of dizziness.

It doesn't matter. I kick aside the sheets and my old quilt and reach for my nightstand, feeling around for my phone. If Max remembers, he'll contact me. He may have already tried to call. If he hasn't, I'll go to him. I promised I would.

I finally hit the cold rectangle of my phone and grab it. I close my eyes for just a second, sending up a quick prayer. Not a wish. A prayer.

Then I turn on my phone.

The glow illuminates my bedroom, a cool blue light sweeping over the room. I squint at the light as it hits me, causing my head to throb with renewed vigor.

I grip my phone. Shake it to make sure I'm seeing it right.

Then I blink.

Blink again.

Nothing changes.

Max hasn't called. He hasn't texted. I'm certain he hasn't emailed.

My stomach drops, the queasiness increasing.

There isn't any reason for him to have called. There isn't any reason for him to see me ever again. There certainly isn't any reason for him to love me.

Why?

Because there was no wish. There was no Paris. There was no Saint-Tropez.

It's 7:13 a.m., five hours since I went to bed. Drunk on too many bottles of wine with Dorene and my mom after getting fired. I'm hungover. Terribly, horribly hungover.

Jobless. Heartbroken. And . . . stunningly . . . alone.

"It was a dream," I say, my voice cracking. The noise sets off a sledgehammer in my head. "It was a wine-induced, drunken stupor of a wished-for dream."

I let out a gasping half-laugh, half-sob. "It was a dream."

I drop the phone and it hits the bed with a dull thud. I was so surprised when I woke up in Max's bed with not even a hint of a hangover. Well, *surprise*. Here it is. Because none of it was real. *This* is real.

My subconscious made it all up. Three years of wishing for love and a sapphire necklace was all it took for my mind to create a fantasy.

But what if . . .? I look around my room, shadowed by the glow of the phone. There aren't any windows, there isn't any outside light, but what if there could be? What if I tried to talk to Max? *What if . . .?*

I shake my head, wincing at the sharp, protesting pain.

If it was real, then he would call—

My phone rings.

I screech in surprise. I grab it and scramble to my feet. There's an unknown number on the screen.

My heart pounds and my finger shakes as I answer the call.

"Max?" My voice wobbles and there's a quiet joy blooming inside me. *He called. He remembers. He—*

"Is this Anna Benoit?"

It's not Max.

The joy and the hope and the elation incinerate in an instant.

It's a woman, speaking in French, with a Genevan accent. In the background there are more voices speaking rapidly, and a mechanical beeping noise.

"Yes?"

"You are listed as the emergency contact for Dorene Laporte."

"Yes." I nod even though she can't see me, then I flick on the lamp at the edge of my bed. It bathes the room with a cold light, and I wince at the brightness. "What's happened?"

When she tells me, I throw on the first outfit I see—a dirty pair of jeans and a wrinkled sweatshirt on the floor—I shove my feet into a pair of sneakers, and I shout for my mom. Then I sprint down the building stairs and out into the too-bright morning sun with another wish chasing me down the street. *Let her be okay.*

I don't have much luck with wishes. All the same, I still wish.

Not for me, but for my friend.

33

____

For the first time in days the hospital room is quiet. Emme is asleep, curled up on the blue vinyl chair in the corner of the room, her arms wrapped around Bijou, her stuffed dog. My mom stepped out for a breath of fresh air, citing the need for coffee.

I almost went with her, but I haven't left the hospital in six days, and the thought of stepping outside and blinking into the bright sun, breathing in the early June heat, and facing the reality of Geneva without Max—I can't.

It feels like if I stepped outside the unchanging constancy of the hospital and acknowledged the movement of the city, then . . . I'd acknowledge that I have to move on too.

Geneva is moving, changing. In the week we've been here, the small window details a sky that has shifted from the wet blue of May to the blooming sunshine of June. The yellow tulips lining the sidewalk below have given way to a profusion of purple, fuchsia, and red petunias, spilling like a vibrant river over the flower beds.

I try not to look at them. Every time I glimpse the petunias I hear Max growling, "You're not a damn petunia. You're a woman." And then, "Let's promise each other that whatever happens, neither of us will regret anything."

I've acknowledged that none of it was real, but all the same, it *feels* like it was.

I can still smell the petunias in Paris. I can taste the hazelnut macaron on my lips as Max kissed me. I can feel his mouth teasing mine and his hands scraping over my hips. I can hear him laughing as he rolls me beneath him and presses me into warm sand, daring me to break free and jump into the cool water. I can see it all, just as clearly as I can see the petunias blooming outside, the June blue of the sky, and the spare rectangular buildings rising around the hospital.

All the same, it wasn't real.

What's real is the small square of this hospital room. The sterile white walls, the cords and machines, the ammonia-like smell, and the dry air that steals all the moisture from your skin and lips and eyes. The nurses that come like clockwork to check on Dorene. The food tray delivered three times a day: banana, bread, yogurt, hardboiled egg, cheese, green beans, beef.

The sounds of the hallway: a squeaky wheel on a janitor's cart, the heavy footsteps of an orderly, the whispers of a worried family, the loud hello of a phlebotomist come to draw blood.

Reality has winnowed down to a single room and the people inside it.

Max isn't here. There isn't any reason for him to be here, and there isn't any reason for me to think of him.

Sometimes I check my phone, expecting a call or a text from him, but then I feel like a fool because *it wasn't real.*

Even so, I look down at my phone. There's a text from my mom: *Black or with cream?*

Cream and triple sugar please, I send back.

Dorene shifts on the narrow hospital bed and glances at my phone. I drop it into my purse and stretch out my legs, leaning back in the hard plastic chair.

"Have you made a decision?" I ask, keeping my voice quiet so I won't wake Emme.

The poor kid hasn't been sleeping well. Not since Dorene was admitted.

I guess none of us have.

Dorene looks better than she did a few days ago, but she's still pale and worn-out, faded like an old black-and-white movie, tired around the edges. It could be the hospital gown. Even the healthiest person looks sickly in a hospital gown. Or it might be the rumpled bed, the taped IV line on the back of her hand—or maybe it's just the fact that we're all confronting—again—the frailty of life.

The last time I was in a hospital—fourteen years ago —I was scared of everything. This time around I was scared, at first, of losing Dorene. Then, when I realized she was going to be okay, I was only scared of not being there for her.

She only has me, my mom, and Emme. We're her family.

"I have," Dorene says, staring at the old portable television my mom brought from her apartment. It's the ancient TV/VCR combo Dorene has always watched her husband's movies on while sitting out in the courtyard, chain-smoking and quoting the rapid-fire dialogue.

For the past week she's been playing his movies nonstop, from early morning through the long night. The flickering static of the screen wavers in streams of light. At dawn and at dusk, when the golden in-between bathes the room, that flickering light takes on a ghostly feel, as if her husband exists in that movie light, comforting her from afar.

"What did you decide?" I ask, wondering what the future holds.

"You're still fired," she says, taking her gaze off the screen long enough to give me a smile. It's not as vibrant as it was in the past, but there's more strength there than there was a few days ago.

I smile back and impulsively reach out to grab her hand. Her skin is cold and dry, but her grip is strong.

"And?" I ask, scooting my chair closer.

She clicks her tongue, turning back to the screen. On it, her husband's most famous film, an angsty arthouse movie about a tragic love affair in the French Riviera, is at its climax. The hero is on the beach, frothing waves crashing behind him. He clutches his dead lover to his chest and shouts in torment and anguish at the heavens. Apparently, the week this film was released people were sobbing in the streets all across France.

"I told Julien he shouldn't have killed her," Dorene says, pursing her lips. "It's a terrible idea, doomed love. But he was adamant. '*Oh no, Dorene. Love is only potent if it is bittersweet. We only want love if it is pain. It is a sickness!*'" She scoffs and rolls her eyes as if she had this argument only yesterday. But then she turns and grins at me and I see the woman who stole a Bugatti and drove through Paris naked. The daring, independent woman who lived all sixty-three years of her life with relish. "The fool won his argument by dying on me. Would I have loved him this long if instead he'd run off with one of his actresses? Or if he'd fallen on hard times and turned to drink and bitterness? I don't think I would have. Although I can't be sure."

She shrugs and then scoffs again when the hero enters a bereaved soliloquy, berating the capriciousness of love.

"That isn't love," she says, pointing to the screen. "If Julien were here, I'd tell him that. Thirty years later, I understand. Perhaps if he'd made it this far he'd understand too. But it takes time . . ." She shrugs. "When you're young, it's easy to think you know what love is. You feel it so strongly. But . . ." She lifts her shoulders again and then leans back against the gray headboard.

"What is it then?" I ask, watching the dark-haired man weep over his lover.

"That?" Dorene points to the screen. "Possession. They wanted to possess each other. Own the other. What else? Need. An endless hunger needing to be filled. Lust, of course. There's nothing like a good swallow of some straight-up lust. Passion—"

I look at her quickly and she cuts herself off.

At her raised eyebrow, I shift in the hard plastic chair and rub at my arms, chilled by the cold hospital air.

"What?" Dorene asks, her expression probing.

She knows me too well. Seven years of talking every day, working together, has left her able to read me like a book.

I glance over at Emme, making sure she's still asleep.

She's tucked Bijou under her chin and her mouth is parted, her eyes closed, eyelids fluttering with dreams.

"I'm only surprised," I say slowly, "that you'd say passion isn't love."

Dorene pats my hand. "Someday you'll see."

We're quiet for a moment, Dorene watching the movie credits, me looking out the window at the petunias painted bright against the blue sky.

It was a dream, I tell myself. *It was a dream.*

Max never told me about his parents. He never told me how he felt about passion. He never asked me to—

A chill hits me so hard that the hairs on the back of my neck stand on end. Then my heart flutters and starts to race.

Max asked me to find the letter he wrote, to bring it to him, and to tell him passion wasn't love. What if . . . what if the letter is real?

Am I crazy to think it?

Would it be crazy to look for it?

"Yes," Dorene says.

I look back at her, my forehead wrinkled. I'm pulled back into the small hospital room with its white walls and sterile air.

Dorene looks at me curiously, waiting for my response.

"What?" I ask.

"Yes," she says happily, "I've decided. This was a wake-up call. I'm retiring." She waves her hand in the air as if she's drawing a line between her old life and the new. "Tomorrow I'm leaving for Saint-Tropez."

A flood of warmth, like sunshine on the beach, washes over me, replacing the cold. Dorene mentioned this, but I didn't know if she'd actually do it. As soon as she's discharged, she's packing a bag, hopping on a train, and leaving everything behind. No warning, no dallying. Just leaving.

"That's what we do when we die," she'd said. *"I'm just starting my stay in heaven a little early."*

I smile at her—a genuine, happy smile. "Good," I say. "I'll miss you, but I'm happy for you."

"You'll help me settle in?" she asks, worriedly smoothing the rumpled white hospital sheet. Maybe the clots in her legs, the clots in her lungs, forced her into a new perspective, but that doesn't mean she wants to do it all on her own. And she shouldn't have to.

"Of course I will," I say, wondering if Saint-Tropez will look anything like it did in my dream.

Dorene isn't the only one with a new perspective. For years I've been waiting for "someday." For that moment when I can reach out and grasp freedom. A stone cottage outside the city. A holiday in the French Riviera. The courage to talk to Max.

After getting fired, after Max (the real Max) telling me to never set foot in his home again, after Dorene's pulmonary embolism, and after my dream and my wish, I'm not the same. While Dorene was recovering and making her decision, I was making mine.

"We'll help you settle in," I tell Dorene. "We'll stay a week. Then I start my new job."

Dorene makes a disgruntled noise, but I shrug. I don't want to keep cleaning, and I'm not going to continue Dorene's business after she's gone. Instead I've accepted a nightshift job in the stockroom at the market where my mom works. During the days, I'm going to start working on plans for the first Open Heart Kitchen, based on my family's love of feeding anyone who needs a meal. I dreamed it, and I want it to be real.

"Well, a week it is," Dorene says. Then she smiles over at Emme. "I'll enjoy seeing what she paints. And you,"—she pats my hand again—"I'll enjoy seeing you relax. Flirt. I can say this, as I nearly died—"

"You did not," I say.

She holds up her thumb and pointer finger, holding them a half-inch apart. "Nearly."

I shake my head. "No."

She smiles. "Ah, denial. How sweet you are! As I said, since I nearly died, I can tell you, stop tiptoeing around life. Live, Anna. Steal a car, naked. Stay up until sunrise, dancing on the beach. Kiss a man who doesn't know your name." She lifts an eyebrow. "Live with passion, love with your heart. Now go away—I'm tired and I want to watch this next movie alone."

"Go away?" I ask.

She nods. "Go away. You've been here as long as I have, and I think that chair has attached itself to your rear."

I almost start to argue, but then I think about passion and love and . . . the letter. What if the letter is real? That would mean my wish was real. What happened was real.

I stand so quickly the chair squeaks against the linoleum. My muscles ache from sleeping in a pull-out vinyl chair/bed for the past week, my eyes are gritty, and I've not had a good long shower in days, but suddenly I'm exhilarated.

"I'm going," I say, glancing at Emme.

"I'll watch her." Dorene waves her hand. "Besides, Janice will be back with the coffee in five minutes."

"You're right." I grab my purse and rush toward the

door. I turn back when I reach the threshold to smile at Dorene. "I'll be back soon."

"Don't hurry," she calls, shuffling through the VHS tapes next to her bed. "I don't need you until tomorrow!"

I rush out of the room, down the long halls, through the lobby, and into the bright sun.

My heart races. My hands are sweating.

I grab a cab and then have it drop me off a quarter mile from the Barone Estate, where there's only the rippling lake, tall grass blowing in the wind, and the deep, leafy green of the woods on the eastern edge of Max's property.

Once the taxi is gone I hurry into the trees, picking my way through the loamy undergrowth shaded by thick pines. The cool air is full of evergreen and moss scents, the ground crackles beneath me, and an alpine thrush pipes a long, lone call through the muted woods.

I was right—the sights, sounds, and smells are all overwhelming after spending a week in the sterile confines of a hospital room. Even the snapping of a twig beneath my foot sounds loud. All the same, I hurry forward, hoping Max's story of the folly in the woods was real.

Finally, my hands shaking, my breathing loud in my ears, I drop to my knees. The damp, loamy ground bleeds a cold wetness through my jeans.

It's real.

I'm in the shade at the edge of a small ruin. There are eight stone columns, each about six feet tall, wide enough that you can barely circle your arms around them. They surround a twelve-foot-wide octagon with a mosaic floor. The gold, indigo, and azure tiles are faded and weathered, but the design is still clear. The mosaic is in the pattern of a lover's knot, just like the pendant on the necklace. The folly is open to the sky, just like Max said. It's surrounded by old pine trees and tall oaks, shaded by leaves and tall-reaching branches. Moss, pine needles, and leaves are littered over the folly.

"It's real," I say, my voice penetrating the hush of the woods.

Next to me, there's a pile of moss-covered gray rocks, just like Max said there'd be.

I shove them aside and they topple noisily to the leafy ground. My hands scrape over the coarse stone as I move the last of them away.

Then I dig.

The soft ground gives easily. Moss. Soft, gnarled roots. Dry pine needles. Decomposing leaves. I dig through the layers, my bare hands pushing aside the cold dirt.

At first I hurriedly dig through the soil. It's rich, mahogany-brown, and it smells like Christmas. I feel as if I'm unwrapping a present.

What will Max say when I bring him the letter?

Will he believe me?

Does he already remember?

The anticipation is almost too much to bear.

But then, after the hole is two feet wide and eight inches deep, I slow down. I slow my movements, calm my breathing, scrape aside the dirt, slower, slower, delaying the moment when I finally admit the truth.

Ten inches deep.

Twelve.

Fifteen.

And finally, I stop.

The soil is now dark brown, almost black, so hard-packed and full of thick, gnarled pine roots that I know no one buried anything beneath this point.

In fact, no one buried anything here at all.

The hole is empty.

So. It wasn't real.

For a week I've known it wasn't real. Since I woke up. I only let myself hope for a moment. But this confirms it. There is no bottle buried next to a folly in the woods.

I must have heard of these ruins from Dorene, or in an article about Max, or . . . I don't know. Somewhere, my subconscious picked up this tidbit and put it in my dream.

I lean back on my heels. My jeans are soaked and covered in black dirt and moss streaks. My hands are stained brown, my nails dirty. I hold out my hands and stare at them.

"What are you doing?" I ask them. "What did you expect to find?"

I shove the dirt back into the hole and then pile the rocks back on top. They clink together like markers for a tomb. This is me burying any last glimmer of my misguided hope.

I glance behind me, back through the woods, thickly leafed out and darkened by the shade. It's early evening and the shadows are growing longer, crisscrossing over the forest floor. I can just barely make out the stark gray lines and the cold stone of Max's home. Soon the setting sun will hit the walls and turn it a warm gold, but until then, it's lonely and gray in its solitude.

Max is back to being all alone.

Just like he has been for the past ten years.

I make a decision—I'm here, I may as well go all in. I stand and wipe my hands on my jeans, leaving dirt streaks on my thighs. There's a line of sweat on my forehead, so I quickly rebraid my hair and pat it down.

I don't know if I'll ever have the courage to do this again—to talk to Max—so instead of thinking or second-guessing, I hurry through the woods. At the lawn, under the open sky, I feel exposed and small, like a mouse below a hawk, but I keep going.

The estate isn't welcoming like it was when I saw it in my dream. There are no bright, blooming flowers, no gracefully curving beds, no glowing windows. It's back to its stark, austere, isolated beauty.

What will you say? I ask myself, trying to think up the words to explain why I'm here. *What will you say to him?*

I knock on the door, flushing when I see how much dirt is still covering my hands. I put them behind my back, clasping them there.

Maybe I should go. I could run home, take a shower, put on a dress. Then come back.

But I know if I turn around now, I might not come back. Not ever. But I have to make sure. Because if there's even a slim chance my wish was real, then I need to try. I promised.

But what will I say?

I'll say . . .

The tall wooden front door swings open. The hinges sigh, creaking as the door sweeps inward onto the marble tiles.

I stare, mouth open, eyes wide.

It's Madame Blinken. The housekeeper from my dream. Except . . . not.

She scowls at me, her eyes narrowing and her nose

flaring. She's just as neat and tidy as the last time I saw her, but she is not happy to see me.

"Is . . . is Max here?" I ask. Then, more confidently, "I'm here to speak with Max."

She sniffs and then looks me over, detailing every dirt smudge, every moss stain, and every drop of sweat and hair out of place.

"Monsieur Barone"—she emphasizes the "monsieur" —"is unavailable."

"Unavailable or not here?" I ask, looking past her at the brightly lit marble entry. The chandelier is casting sparks over the floor, the lights are shining, and there's a savory, herby smell coming from the kitchen.

Does that mean he's home?

Madame Blinken sniffs again and begins to close the door.

"Wait!" I say, suddenly desperate. "Would you please tell him Anna Benoit is here?"

Madame Blinken stops, the door half-closed. When I say my name her eyes widen, and I know intuitively it isn't because she's happy to see me or because Max told her to let me in as soon as I arrived. Instead her grip tightens on the door and her knuckles turn white.

"When I entered this position, Monsieur Barone informed me to call the police if his former cleaner, a woman named Anna Benoit, came here again. Am I to understand you would like me to call the police?"

She gives me a hard stare.

And I go cold.

There was no letter.

There is no Max. At least, not the Max I love.

I knew it. I did. But now I really know it.

"No," I whisper. "I don't want that. Tell him . . . please, tell him I'm sorry. I won't come again."

I stumble back, numb, cold.

I was wrong. I actually didn't know it before. Somehow I was still soaring, flying on the belief that maybe . . . maybe . . .

I turn, hurrying down the steps into the darkening dusk. When my feet hit the last stone I'm jarred, aching, broken.

And even though I know all my wishes have been used up, I make one more.

I wish for Max to be happy.

34

SAINT-TROPEZ IS JUST AS I REMEMBER. IT FEELS AS IF I truly was there. There are the same pastel-taffy houses, the same sea-salt scents mixed with blooming mimosa, the same turquoise sea crashing over sand and rock and spraying me with cool salt mist. The tarte tropézienne is the same, the soft brioche filled with the sweet, tart lemon and vanilla custard that burst over my taste buds like sunshine from behind a cloud. Everything is the same. Even the Barone pop-up store in the old bougainvillea-covered mansion is there.

I'd find it strange, except my mom says with enthusiastic conviction, "This is exactly like I've always imagined! I feel like I've been here a thousand times before."

Emme agrees, joyfully painting another watercolor, determined to leave Dorene with a lifetime supply of landscapes and still lifes.

I can't disagree with my mom or Emme. After all, we've watched about nine million travel shows and documentaries on the French Riviera. It would only be strange if we *didn't* feel like we've been here before.

So we help Dorene settle in. We find the best market, florist, and boulangerie, we cook and freeze soups to last months, we meet the neighbors, and we help to make her apartment a home. When we leave, I try very hard not to cry. My throat is tight and there's a terrible itching at the backs of my eyes.

"Allergies," I say.

Dorene scoffs and pulls me into a hug. "It's a shame you didn't kiss anyone while you were here."

I squeeze her tighter and then press my lips to her cheek. "There. Job done."

She swats me, and I smile and step back.

"You'll visit soon?" she asks.

Emme runs to hug her around the waist, and then my mom joins in. We promise to visit at Christmas. When we talked about it last night, six months didn't seem like a long time, but with this goodbye, six months seems to stretch out like an eternity.

As we leave, Dorene squeezes my hand a final time and says, "Be happy, Anna."

It's funny—that's the exact thing I wished for Max. It's what I've wished for everyone I love. I didn't know they were wishing the same thing for me.

I kneel down on the glossy concrete of the market, positioning the cardboard box so I can use the box cutter to open the top. It's the end of my first week at my new job and I'm starting to feel more comfortable. I've never worked at a market before. I've never taken inventory, stocked shelves, or had a dozen coworkers. I always thought my last job was physically demanding, but unloading boxes and unpacking products is hard work.

For the past week, once I've stumbled off the bus, I've mumbled hello to Emme and my mom as they've rushed out the door for summer camp and work and then I've collapsed into bed. I've woken up in the afternoon, refreshed and ready to work on my business plan for Open Heart Kitchen, and then, after dinner and wishing Emme and Mom good night, I caught the bus and headed to work again.

I've been so busy and so tired that I've not had time to miss Dorene. I've barely had time to miss Max.

No. That's not true. I miss him all the time. Even when I'm not thinking about him I'm missing him. There's this pressure on my chest that hurts. It's a hole, a phantom limb, a loss. But I'm refusing to acknowledge the pain of missing him, because if I miss him, then that means I miss a dream. A wish. A figment of my imagination.

So while I'm counting how many cases of dishwasher detergent I've unpacked, and as I'm breaking down cardboard boxes and tossing them in the compressor, I specifically do not think of Max.

I don't think of how he smiled right before he reached out to tuck a strand of hair behind my ear.

I don't think of how he took my wrists in his hands and held them over my head while he kissed me.

I don't think of the way he held my hand and talked with me about Dickens and self-determination and truth and honesty.

I don't think of all the things that are true in both real life and in my wish—that he loves reading late into the night, that he's loyal to his friends, that he loves crime dramas and has a sweet tooth, that he's levelheaded and thinks before he speaks, that he's brilliant at what he does, and that he's alone.

For three weeks I haven't thought about any of that. And while I haven't thought about any of it, I've missed him.

Every second of every day.

I miss him.

It's eight o'clock at night, and outside the store the Geneva sky is fading to the soft denim-blue of dusk. It was warm today, one of those balmy June days that precede the heat of July. But inside it's cold. The freezers and refrigerators send chilly drafts throughout the store. The overhead fluorescent lights shine like a never-ending sun, bathing the aisles in a cold white light.

In an hour the market will close and then the real work will begin. But until then, I'm in the baking aisle, unloading a carton of baking chocolate.

So far, this is my favorite aisle in the store. The market is a gourmet specialty shop, so there are all sorts of interesting products from all around the world. But I have to say, I prefer the sweet to the bitter or the sour. I like stocking sugar more than chicken or canned sardines.

Besides, this aisle smells sweet, like a rainbow of sugars—brown sugar, molasses and honey, caster sugar, pearl sugar, and sugar cubes as large as gumdrops. I like pearl sugar best. When I pick up the bags, the large crystal chunks crunch and let off a sweet smell that reminds me of lemon and vanilla and sunshine.

Every time I'm in this aisle I feel like I'm standing inside a pastry, and all I have to do is breathe it in and appreciate the scents of sugar, chocolate, custard mix, and hazelnut spreads.

I send my boxcutter along the cardboard box and open the top, revealing the stacks of baking chocolate. The shelf is empty, so I'm right on time. I begin stacking, humming along to the music in my earbuds. It's the Supremes, and even though it hurts to hear them singing that love can't be hurried, I ignore the throb in my chest and keep stacking the chocolate.

A little girl runs past, her red hair flying behind her as she searches the aisle, jumping up and down to see the top shelves. Sometimes customers ask me where something is, but usually, they ignore me. I'm not especially good at telling them where products are. I haven't been here long enough to know everything yet. But if she's looking for sugar . . .

I'm about to ask if she needs help when she runs off, dashing into another aisle.

I shrug and go back to the chocolate.

My head is down, my music is playing, and I'm focused on counting how many packages are left, which is why I don't hear him at first.

"—me?"

I turn and notice a man standing next to me. He has expensive brown leather shoes, dark jeans, and that's as far as I get before taking out my earbuds and saying, "Sorry. What was that?"

"I'm looking for—"

I don't hear what he's looking for.

Because it's him.

It's the voice I've been hearing in my dreams for the past three weeks. It's the voice I hoped to hear every week for the past three years.

It's *Max.*

His deep, rich tenor reaches through the chilly, fluorescent-lit aisle and spills over me like a stream of sugar.

His nearness hits me with the strength of a hurricane, and I'm nearly knocked over. I brace myself and grip the edge of the box, fighting the urge to stand and fling myself into his arms.

I want to so badly. I want to cry and laugh and kiss him and love him.

I may have been able to pretend I didn't miss him. But I've not been able to pretend I don't love him.

And here I am, crouched at his feet, kneeling over a box of chocolate. I know him. I see him. And he doesn't see me.

I'm in my uniform, a gray and navy unisex collared shirt tucked into baggy polyester pants. It's possibly the ugliest outfit I've ever worn. My curly hair is tied into a bun and tucked under a handkerchief I put on when unloading the truck earlier. I don't know if he'll recognize me. He didn't when I spoke.

My hand trembles, and I still my fingers on the cardboard.

I close my eyes and brace myself. *Don't react. Don't smile. Don't . . .*

I don't even have to look at him.

I don't have to look up.

I once said that looking at Max was like looking at something so beautiful it hurt. I think if I looked at him now it would break me. I'm not sure I could look him in the eye without giving away everything I feel.

He's waiting. Standing next to me, waiting for me to respond.

I can feel his gaze on me, moving over me with a peculiar intensity.

I shake my head, taking a shaky breath at the hot, burning feel of his nearness.

"I'm looking for baking chocolate. I'm told it's essential for the perfect cake. May I have—?" He holds out his hand, pointing to the shelf I'm stocking.

He leaves his final sentence as a question.

He has no idea who I am.

None.

He expects me to take one of the packages of chocolate and place it in his hand.

I drop my chin, angling my face away from him. Even though the market is chilly at best, a drop of sweat slides down the back of my neck. My heart races and I fight the urge to turn around, jump in his arms, and kiss him. Or beg him to kiss me.

That would be a disaster.

Slowly, as if I'm in a dream, I reach out and grip the cold paper packaging wrapped around the chocolate square. I take it in my hand, my heart thumping, and reach out to drop it in his open palm.

My earbuds hang free, and from them the magnified sound of Diana Ross's singing crackles in the air.

There's a bright, thrumming feel coalescing around us. It's a stream of sunlight slipping through the ether, a river of stars pouring into a deep indigo lake; it's a chain of broken sapphires reflecting the light of a thousand suns.

I drop the chocolate into his hand. My fingers brush over his skin and I jolt at the awareness that streaks through me. I drag in a sharp breath and yank my hand back as if I've been burned.

But before I can turn away, Max reaches out and grabs my wrist.

His grip is tight, his hand warm and firm.

My heart races, my pulse pounding against his hand.

He's tense, and all his attention is focused on me. I can feel the heat of his gaze raking over me. The spot where his hand captures me throbs with heat until there's a pulse drifting up my arm, through my veins, and into my core, where it settles in a bright white heat.

It burns.

His grip tightens, and I remember the last time he held me like this. Then, his mouth was on me.

He's waiting.

He won't let me go until I look up at him. I know this.

So I gather all my courage and all my defenses, and I look at Max.

35

———————

I used to describe Max as austere, stark, a fortress of a man who only showed his true self to a lucky few. I thought he smiled sparingly, but when he did it was glorious. I thought he was fair-minded, levelheaded, a good man. I made this judgment after knowing him for three years, and then I amended my opinion after my wish.

It doesn't matter if the wish wasn't real—it still tinged my feelings for him and my view of him. After my wish, I thought of him as a man who thought deeply, laughed often, and loved wholeheartedly. A good man.

Right now Max looks like neither of those men. Not the one I knew before, and not the one I thought I knew.

His grip is tight around my wrist and there's a tension emanating from him. The cold, fluorescent lights shine over him, and while they should illuminate him in a bright, golden light, instead the lights highlight the roughness of his features.

In Saint-Tropez he was rested and sun-brown, a

delirious smile constantly lifting at the corners of his mouth. Here in the chill of the market, he's the opposite of that picture.

I look up into his face and study the changes three weeks have wrought. The last time I saw him in real life was in his library. He was angry then, but still Max.

He doesn't look like himself anymore.

He's unshaven, with at least three days' growth. There are dark hollows under his eyes, his skin is pale, and he looks . . .

He looks how I feel.

When he sees my face, he takes in a sharp breath and his hand loosens on my wrist. Even so, a second later I can feel the tension rocketing through the rest of him.

A white-hot flare of emotion sparks between us. It's so overwhelming, so overpowering, that I'm surprised the circuits don't break and plunge the market into darkness.

I stand, my legs unsteady. Only a few seconds have passed. I'm waiting, my stomach rolling, my heart pounding.

What does he want?

What could he possibly want?

It's been three weeks. There was no letter. There was no wish. Yet the way he's dragging his gaze over me strikes a match in every cell of my body, and I'm ready to combust.

But he's not looking at me with love or happiness or relief or even confusion.

No—it's anger. He's angry.

"You." His voice scrapes over me like fingers rubbing over bare skin. "You work here? *Here?*"

His question is accusing. His eyes are dark and his mouth is tight. And I realize this isn't a reunion of love, or even a reunion of former employee and employer. This is a man unexpectedly finding a woman he dislikes in a place he frequents. It's like finding a thumb in a can of beans. It's revolting. You want to throw the can away and never eat beans again.

I yank my arm away and Max lets me go, his expression shifting from anger to surprise.

Then the little girl from earlier runs between us and tugs on Max's arm.

"Max! Mummy says to tell you that if you can't find chocolate, then—"

I don't wait to hear more.

As soon as Max looks down at the little girl I run down the aisle, turn the corner, run down another aisle, and then slam my way into the back room. My supervisor is there, scanning a new shipment of olive oil.

"I have to go," I say, out of breath and trying very, very hard not to cry. "It's an emergency. I'm sorry. I have to—"

I don't say anymore. I grab my purse out of my locker and hurry out the back door.

The door slams behind me as I rush into the back parking lot. The air is warmer than the market, humid and filled with the scent of warm concrete and the exhaust of delivery trucks.

The loading area is empty and the streetlights shine in dim pools over the pavement. I blindly turn to the left, walking toward a concrete retaining wall that runs along the parking lot until hitting the busy street at the front of the store.

I don't have a destination in mind; I just have to escape. I need to get away from the overwhelming need to run back to Max and ask him to love me. I need to get away from the way he was looking at me—not with love, but with anger. I need to get away from how much it hurts.

I round the corner, hurrying toward the narrow alley between the retaining wall and the market. It's dark. The setting sun is near the horizon and its rays can't reach beyond the wall. Instead a long shadow encompasses the alley. I'm about to step out of the light when I hear my name.

"Anna."

I stop, standing still.

I'm afraid to turn around.

"Anna?" Max asks again.

I clutch my hands, pressing my nails into my palms. "Are you here to yell at me?"

"No. That's not what I had in mind," he says, his voice raw.

"Because when you said you never wanted to see me again, you can't have expected I wouldn't work. I have to work, you know. It's not as if I invited you to shop here."

I turn around, fully prepared to shove past him. But then what he said sinks in. He isn't here to yell at me. In fact, he doesn't look angry anymore. Instead he's regarding me with a cautious, careful expression.

Out front, the sound of traffic passing fills the air in a quick, whooshing hum. But here in the back lot, there's only the buzzing of an overhead light and the sound of crickets singing from the tall grasses, and wildflowers in the retaining wall.

I stare at him, unable to walk away, but unable to walk into his arms.

He stares back, and behind the cautious exterior I can feel a million emotions and a million questions swirling.

What does it mean?

I take a deep breath, breathing in the concrete and the subtle hint of grass and wildflower. The sun is almost down, the shadows on the parking lot lengthening, almost swallowing us.

Max takes a step closer to me.

"I have a question," he says, and the way he says it makes my chest clench.

"Yes?"

The edge of his mouth lifts into a small smile. He no longer looks exhausted, haggard, and worn; instead he looks hopeful.

Hopeful like the Eiffel Tower lit up in the depths of night. Hopeful like a bookmark, keeping your place, waiting for you to come back. Hopeful like reaching out in the dark, waiting for someone to take your hand.

"Did you make a wish?" he asks. Then stepping closer, he looks down at me, his eyes searching. "Do you remember making a wish?"

Is he . . .?

Does he . . .?

Slowly, I nod. And when I do, Max closes his eyes and his shoulders sag with relief.

When he opens his eyes, his expression is full of love and need and, yes, *passion*.

"Come to Paris," he says, his voice breaking. "Anna? Will you come to Paris with me?"

He waits for my answer, his breath held, all his focus on me. It's a test. I know it immediately. Max is asking if I experienced my wish too.

I shake my head no. "I've been to Paris recently."

He lets out his held breath and gives me a disbelieving look.

"And Saint-Tropez," I say, and when I do, he understands.

He takes another step forward so the both of us are bathed in the last sliver of sunlight. The sky is deep indigo-blue and we're covered in gold.

"You left me," he growls. "I asked you not to, and you left me. And you didn't come back. Anna, you didn't come back."

The force of his words rolls over me and I take a step toward him. Then another.

"I'm sorry," I say. "I didn't want you trapped in a wish where I made you love me. I wanted to give you a choice."

Max grips my arms, pulls me close, and then says, "That last wish, it wasn't yours. It was mine. I wished on the parure. I wanted to know what it was like to love without reservation. To fling myself off a cliff into open air—"

"You . . ." I stare at him, uncomprehending. "You wished . . . That was your wish?"

When he was desperately in love with me? When his love for me was as wide and as deep as the ocean? That was his wish?

Max smiles at me. "It turns out loving without reservation didn't feel any different than how I already felt. I just made myself forget this other life for a bit."

"I thought you'd hate me," I say, shaking my head. "I thought you forgot me. I thought. . ."

"I've been looking for you since the second I woke up and you weren't there. I called your boss—no answer for weeks now. I sat outside your building for days like some crazed stalker…I've been going out of my mind. You disappeared."

He pulls me against him and I take in his heat. The

air around us shimmers, and I feel warm and delicious. I rest my cheek against his chest and he lets out a shuddering sigh, then he rubs his hands down my back, along my arms, touching me everywhere as if he's reassuring himself I'm real.

"I looked for the letter. It wasn't there. I knocked on your door—"

"After a week of waiting I dug it up. I burned the damn thing myself." He stares down at me, his eyes as dark as a starry night.

I reach up and run my hand over the thick stubble on his jaw.

"I'm glad," I say.

He smiles. "I wish you'd knocked on my door again. It would've saved me three weeks of believing I'd lost my mind, but wishing desperately that you'd come back and try to steal my necklace again—"

"I never—" My words are cut off by Max's grin.

"I know," he says. "That doesn't mean I couldn't wish it."

"But Madame Blinken said you told her to call the police—"

"No." He closes his eyes then opens them, realizing. "That was before. I told her before. I forgot. If I'd known you were knocking on my door, I would've run to answer it. Anna . . . I wished for you."

I shake my head, suddenly worried we're two people who don't know anything about each other at all.

"How much of it was real?" I ask him.

The feeling between us is still there. The rightness, the resonance. But what was real, and what wasn't?

Max reaches out and brushes his hand over my cheek. A warm tingle rushes over my skin.

"We're not married," I say. "We don't have seven years behind us. We don't have a history. We just have . . ."

"Love?" Max asks.

"Remember I told you I fell in love with you at first sight?"

Max nods, his hand brushing over me comfortingly. "And I said I'd give up anything to spend even a single night with you."

"But how do we know it's real?"

"I suppose we could try it and see," Max says, watching me with that happy, hopeful expression. He rubs his thumb over my lips, leaving a shimmery tingling in its wake. "Did that feel real?"

I nod, darting my tongue over my lips.

The evening is shifting to night and the air is cooling. I tuck myself closer into Max's heat, breathing in the soft leather of his jacket.

He smiles. Lifts my chin and sets his mouth to mine.

His lips brush across mine, familiar yet new. His hands cup my jaw and he tilts my face so he can tease my mouth open. Then he slips inside, tasting me and drawing me to him. His hands curl in my hair and he makes a small, thankful noise. He tastes like chocolate and hazelnut, wine and passion. His mouth moves erotically over mine, sparking fires in me everywhere.

I press myself into him, trying to bury myself in him. I touch him everywhere, lifting his shirt so I can run my hands over the heat of his skin. Finally, he tears his mouth from mine.

He's breathing heavily, his chest heaving and his heart rocketing. I'm floaty, my blood throbbing with a needy heat, and all I want to do is wrap my legs around Max's waist and keep kissing.

"That," Max says, taking another taste of my lips, "was real."

"Yes," I say, gripping his shoulders.

He drops his forehead to mine, and I reach around him and hold him close. I can feel every breath, every heartbeat, every place we meet.

"I love you," he says, looking into my eyes. "That feels more real than anything. I want to love you for the rest of my life. You said your love was exponential. I know how you feel. I want to experience every possible variation of love. I want to know what it is to love you in every possible way. When you're happy, when you're not, when you're still young, when you're old, when you've changed from who you are today and are someone new and the only thing I recognize is that I still love you. I want to be there for it all. In quiet love and passionate love and the kind of love that holds on even when everyone else would let go. I love you without reservation." He kisses me again, pressing his love into me. "Do you feel it?"

"Yes," I say, washing on the waves of his love.

I was wrong—there weren't two choices in love, one side a calm turquoise expanse and the other a tumultuous sea. There are infinite choices in love. It's a river of light, sparkling in millions of different variations, and we get to experience each and every one of them.

"I feel it," I tell Max, reaching up and wrapping my arms around his shoulders. "I feel your love."

He smiles—that happy, wicked smile I love. "We should make sure," he says, "that you really feel it. That it's really real. Just to be certain. We should go home and make sure."

I laugh, feeling light and buoyant.

"I love you," I tell him. "I love you so much."

And then he kisses me again. The sliver of sunlight is gone, night is here, but I barely notice, because Max and I are making our own light.

Then he picks me up and carries me to his car, not taking his mouth from mine until he's strapped me in and made sure I'm really, really, really real.

36

I LIE CURLED IN MAX'S ARMS, FLUSHED, SWEATY, AND blissful. His hand roams over my bare skin, featherlight and barely touching, leaving a glowy warmth. We're sprawled on one of the thick, luxurious rugs in the library, my legs tangled with his, my arms around him.

We didn't make it to the bedroom. We barely made it through the front door. We hit the wall, knocked over a marble statue, kissed our way toward the stairs kicking off shoes and stripping clothes, and then lost ourselves when a dark room with a soft rug presented itself.

The lights are off, the library dark. It's cradled by the deep indigo of the sky and the silver glow of moonlight. There's a soft, humming contentment flowing through the open room, vibrating over me.

Max presses a kiss to my neck, his mouth hot. His hands linger at the base of my spine and caress the curve of my hips. We're wrapped in the quiet of the library, books and moonlight, and the awareness that this is where it all began. Even now, the necklace is nearby, hidden behind the oil painting, tucked in its golden case.

I press my cheek to Max's chest, settling into the rise and fall of his breath and luxuriating in the quiet feel of his warmth pressed into mine. He's lean, hard-planed, sharp-lined. It's so easy for my curves and softness to fit against him.

I'm filled with so much contentment, so much love, that I can barely take it all in. I feel as if I might burst from the joy building inside me.

I lift myself off Max's chest, shifting in his arms. The carpet scrapes against my knees as I move over him, lifting myself more so I can look into his eyes. The library is dark, but not so dark that I miss the smile curving on his lips.

"I know I already said this about a thousand times in the past hour, but I'll say it again," he says, his hands dragging over my hips, pulling me closer. "I love you."

I kiss him, luxuriating in the slow, unhurried draw of his mouth over mine. The desperate, need-you-now, please-please-don't-stop, oh-there-there, don't-stop, love-you-love-you lovemaking is done, and now we're settling into a soft, wondering, blissful exploration of each other.

I lift my mouth from his, the taste of him lingering on my lips. The library may be filled with the scent of old books and polished wood, but above that, there's still the essential imprint of Max, and now Max and me together.

"I love you too," I say, and the words still feel magical, still feel as if they're a gift I've been given. I look over toward the desk where I first saw the sapphire necklace. "What do you think would've happened if I'd never made my wish?"

Max shakes his head and drags his hand through my

hair, curling a long strand around his finger. "I imagine we would've arrived here eventually. It just would've taken longer."

I nod. I think he's right. "Where we are seems inevitable. Like a diamond formed millions of years ago. It was always there, hiding in the earth. We just had to uncover it."

"Make a ring from it," Max says, a smile in his eyes. Then he snaps his finger and shifts. "Hold that thought."

I sit up, bemused, as Max strides across the dark library. The moonlight shines over the muscles of his back, his long legs, and then he turns back, catches me staring, and winks.

I laugh and wrap my arms over my chest, keeping myself covered. The air is cool and my skin is prickling now that I don't have the warmth of Max wrapped around me.

Then he's back, kneeling at my side with a gold ring in his hand.

There are six gemstones glinting in the yellow gold, the facets catching and reflecting moon shards back at us.

"I had it made after . . ." Max glances at me, checking my expression. When he sees that I understand, he smiles.

"What does it say?" I ask.

It's an acrostic ring, and every gemstone is a letter. It's a message from Max to me.

"White sapphire, iolite, sapphire, hematite, emerald, diamond," he says pointing to each gemstone.

I take in the letters, and then I say, "Wished."

He smiles, a quick flashing of his teeth. "Wished," he agrees. "You wished that we were married and in love, and I wished the same."

He takes my hand, and I can't look away from the expression on his face when he slides the ring onto my right ring finger.

"Now, whenever you want something," he says, holding onto my hand, "all you have to do is ask."

"And what about you?"

"Same. I just have to ask."

"If you could ask for anything right now, what would it be?" I move toward him, wrapping my arms around him. Suddenly I feel like my goal to become a genie when I grew up came true. The way Max is devouring me with a heated, happy gaze confirms it.

"I'd ask . . . would you like me to carry you upstairs? To bed?" He lifts an eyebrow, a tilted smile on his face.

"Yes," I say, holding out my arms.

He lifts me and I wrap my legs around him. His hands grip my hips and I hold him close. He presses a kiss to the corner of my mouth.

"What else?" I ask, holding on tight as he strides from the room.

"I'd ask . . . would you like to make love all night long—?"

"Yes."

"And then have croissants and coffee in bed—?"

"Yes."

"And I'd ask if you'd like to stay here for the week, and then the month, and then, perhaps, for the rest of your life."

I don't even have to think about it.

"Yes," I say, grinning as he takes the stairs, holding me tight.

"I'd ask if you'd love me for as long as we live."

"Yes," I say as he strides down the long hall.

"I'd ask if you'd marry me. Marry me, Anna?"

He kicks open the door to his bedroom. I laugh at the expression on his face. The love there, the joy, the hope.

"Yes," I say.

I really am able to grant wishes. I feel in this moment that I'm able to do anything.

"Diamonds or sapphires—which do you want? I'll make you a ring that outshines the sun."

"Yes," I say. "Yes to both. Yes to everything."

Max drops down on the bed, laying me on the feather comforter and covering me with his weight. I sink into the mattress and wrap my legs around him. He makes a low noise at the back of his throat, and I stretch up and drag my mouth over his neck, tasting the salt and the heat of him. He presses against me, ready again.

"One last wish," he says, pressing his mouth to my cheeks, my eyes, the corner of my mouth.

I arch into him, running my hands over him, opening myself to him. "What's your wish?"

"Let me love you," he says, his voice rough-edged and loving. "Let me love you."

I smile at him. I'm soaring again, flying into the stars. But this time Max is there with me. We've jumped off the cliff together, and below us is a sparkling turquoise sea, an ocean of love.

"Always," I say. "I'll let you love me always. And I'll love you just as long."

At that Max smiles, and it's glorious.

And then he loves me—in a million shining, different ways.

EPILOGUE

Max

5 years later

I wake up from the strangest dream. For a short time I was back in that place where I was alone, certain I didn't want love or a life full of passion. I reach across the bed and pull Anna close, brushing a kiss over her neck and breathing in the scent of her.

She's sand and saltwater and jasmine, echoing the day we spent at the beach. The curtain nearby flutters, and the sound of the waves crashing over the sand is its own lullaby. Anna stirs, shifting closer, pressing her curves into me.

I wrap my arms around her and she murmurs, "Love you," in her sleepy, husky voice.

"I love you," I whisper, but she's already back asleep. I smile into the pale light.

It's hours before dawn and the stars and moon reflect off the sea, casting that magical, silvery illumination you only find on the Côte d'Azur.

I settle back into the warmth of the bed, the soft breeze drifting over the sheets, and I'm starting to count all the things I'm grateful for—

When a soft cry breaks through the sound of the waves.

Anna sits up, immediately awake. That's what moms do.

"What? Oh," she says, blinking, starting to kick aside the sheets.

"I'll get her," I say, stroking back her hair and pressing a kiss to her mouth.

"You're sure?"

I nod and give her a final kiss. "Get some rest."

Then I'm out of the bedroom and across the hall, lifting Madeleine (named for her mom) out of her crib. She kicks out her feet and waves her arms, letting out another unhappy cry.

A change and a bottle later, we're settled in a rocking chair.

As she wraps a hand around my finger, watching me with wide blue eyes, I'm almost overwhelmed by the expanse of love I have for her. The first time I saw her I almost fell to my knees, that's how hard I was hit. It hasn't lessened—I've just learned to hold it in better. Those first few weeks I was a gushing father of the worst variety.

But I don't have to hold it in here. So I begin. "Before you woke up, I was about to list all the things I'm grateful for."

Madeleine watches me with sleepy eyes, drinking from her bottle.

"Exactly," I say. "There's a lot to be thankful for. You. Your mom. Don't tell her, but tomorrow all our friends and family are coming for a surprise birthday party. Your grandma. Be prepared for spoiling. Dorene, who is a terrible influence. Do *not* listen to her Paris stories. Your Aunt Emme, she tells me she's going to paint a wall for you. What would you like? Boats? A beach?" When Madeleine makes a little noise, I nod. "The beach. Good choice. Let's see. Who else? Fiona, Aaron, all their kids, of course. Daniel and Jillian, their son Beau, who has a penchant for tossing off his clothes and jumping into the sea every chance he gets. You haven't met Serena and Henry, but you'll like them. They have two corgis named Higgs and Boson and three-year-old twins who are already reading Tolkien. It's quite frightening, but I think they'll read to you if you ask."

I smile at Madeleine and she squeezes my fingers, her eyelashes fluttering. At six months she has her mom's eyes, my black hair, and all our love. Her eyes slide closed and her hand loosens, falling away. I pull the bottle from her mouth and set it on the nightstand nearby.

Then I rock her a little longer, making certain she's deep asleep. "I'm grateful," I tell her, "for our home here on the water, where we can be together. I'm grateful for our home in Geneva. It's not cold anymore—your mom made it beautiful. She does that. You've seen her kitchens all over the country? She has a big heart. I'm grateful for that. It was big enough to love me. I'm lucky. Did you know, I made a wish and I was lucky because it came true?"

I look up at a noise from the door. Anna's there, her nightgown whispering against her legs as she steps into the soft glow of the night-light.

"Hi," she says, her eyes sleepy, her hair messy, a pillow crease on her cheek.

A wave of love nearly knocks me over at the sight of her. I don't know how I got so lucky.

"Is she asleep?" Anna whispers, smiling at Madeleine snuggled in my arms.

I nod and lift her back into her crib, settling my hand on her belly as she stretches, kicks, and then falls back to sleep.

Anna moves next to me and brushes her fingers over Madeleine's hair. I know, just like me, her wish is that Madeleine's life is full of as much love as ours has been.

But when I look over at Anna, there's something else in her eyes.

I take in a sharp breath and my body lights up.

"I wanted to ask," Anna says.

I nod, spanning my hands over her hips, the silk of her nightgown whispering under my fingers. "Yes?"

"If you'd like to come back to bed."

I nod.

She takes my hand, links her fingers with mine, and pulls me toward our bedroom.

"Anything else?" I ask.

She folds herself into me, pressing her mouth to mine. "Love me."

"And then?"

"Love me some more."

So I do. I love her until the sun comes up, shining over the water, sending bright light over the sheets of our bed. It reflects over us, bringing in a new day.

And when she settles against me in the soft whisper of morning, before our daughter wakes, before our friends and family arrive, in that quiet moment where it's just us, I hold her close, and I love her.

I love.

Don't miss any of the Ghosted Series:

Ghosted
Switched
Fated
Wished

Find *Ghosted* and more at: www.sarahready.com.

JOIN SARAH READY'S NEWSLETTER

Want more *Wished*? Get an exclusive bonus epilogue! When you join the Sarah Ready Newsletter you get access to sneak peaks, insider updates, exclusive bonus scenes and more.

Join today for an exclusive *Wished* epilogue: www.sarahready.com/newsletter

ABOUT THE AUTHOR

Multi award-winning author Sarah Ready writes women's fiction, contemporary romance, and romantic comedy. Her books have been described as "euphoric," "heartwarming," and "laugh out loud."

Sarah writes stand-alone romances, including *Josh and Gemma Make a Baby*, *Josh and Gemma the Second Time Around*, *French Holiday*, *The Space Between*, and series romcoms including *Ghosted*, *Switched*, *Fated*, *Wished*, and romcoms in the Soul Mates in Romeo series, all of which can be found at her website: www.sarahready.com.

You can learn more and find upcoming titles at: www.sarahready.com.

Stay up to date, get exclusive epilogues and bonus content. Join Sarah's newsletter at www.sarahready.com/newsletter.

ALSO BY SARAH READY

Stand Alone Romances:

The Fall in Love Checklist

Hero Ever After

Once Upon an Island

French Holiday

The Space Between

The Ghosted Series:

Ghosted

Switched

Fated

Wished

Josh and Gemma:

Josh and Gemma Make a Baby

Josh and Gemma the Second Time Around

Soul Mates in Romeo Romance Series:

Chasing Romeo

Love Not at First Sight

Romance by the Book

Love, Artifacts, and You

Married by Sunday

My Better Life

Scrooging Christmas

Dear Christmas

Stand Alone Novella:

Love Letters

Find these books and more by Sarah Ready at:

www.sarahready.com/romance-books

Printed in the USA
CPSIA information can be obtained
at www.ICGtesting.com
CBHW020458150924
14363CB00008B/118

9 781954 007826